Growing Up Wilder

Melissa Newman

Martin Sisters Publishing

Published by

Martin Sisters Publishing, LLC

www. martinsisterspublishing. com

Copyright © 2013 Martin Sisters Publishing, Inc.

All rights reserved. Published in the United States by
Martin Sisters Publishing, Inc.
ISBN: 978-1-62553-003-5
Literary
Printed in the United States of America
Martin Sisters Publishing, LLC

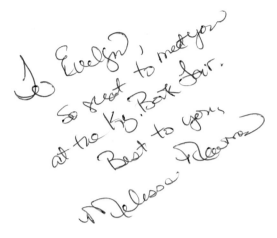

For *my daughters Brittani and Brooke ~*
Momma's Wilder girls.

Acknowledgements

Thank you to Susan Weaver, winner of the Wilder Woman Contest, for introducing Isabella Catelyn Bleufield Maymore Jacobson Claxton Perryworth to the Wilders. I don't know how Everett, Dancy, and Marla ever got along without her.

Special thanks to Kathleen, Agnes and Bob for their undying dedication to my story.

CHAPTER ONE

It's All Greek

My hand hovered over the blanket until my fingers reached my sister's eyes. I rubbed the end of my pinky over the ends of her eyelashes. I'd done it a hundred times before, but it was still funny. She tried to swat my hand away, but her sleepy reflexes didn't allow for much more than a slow-motion wave. She scrunched her nose and moved her lips back and forth like someone trying to budge a squatting fly. Waking Marla was always a dangerous maneuver. Bringing her out of a deep sleep too quickly would usually result in a slap in the face or a kick in the stomach. Tickling my sister's eyelashes was the only way to wake her gradually. My momma had taught me how to do it; one of many valuable and necessary skills for surviving in the Wilder household.

Marla had been buzzing quietly in the darkness with a rhythm that both annoyed and comforted me. Her lips were wrinkled together like one of the old apple-faced dolls at the flea market. Her eyelids twitched.

I could have sworn I heard the yelling again. Loud voices were what woke me in the first place. I had dismissed what I heard as a dream; remnants from the sounds of the earlier argument. Now there was only silence. The fight had started exactly like the final arguments with all the other women who had come and gone from the Wilder house. Frona had asked my father if they would ever be married. Although I had fallen asleep before what I thought was the ending, I was sure I'd never see Frona again.

My father made it no secret to his women friends that he already *had* a wife and didn't need another one. But that never kept some of these women from thinking *they* were special enough to break the bond between Momma and Daddy. Still, if any of Daddy's girlfriends ever had a chance at scooting Momma out of the picture for good, it would have been Frona. If the Greek goddess couldn't manage to shatter the marriage, I was sure no one would. Knowing that fact made me both sad and relieved. I wanted a mother, but I wanted my own mother. I knew now that Daddy felt the same—he wanted a wife but wanted his own wife.

"EVERETT!" I heard bellowing from outside.

"It wasn't a dream," I said, relieved I hadn't just imagined the yelling that woke me up.

Marla's eyes were now open and locked tightly onto mine. We both quickly jumped to our knees, our fingers grasping the headboard.

"It's her again." I looked at Marla for confirmation although I already knew I was right.

"Yeah," Marla said, looking back at me rolling her eyes. "I thought they were done for the night."

"EVERETT!" Frona's scream was raspy and she coughed a little at the end. "I LOVE YOU, I LOVE YOU." Her familiar accent was still thick enough to break through her sobs.

I looked at Marla again for answers but she never turned her head. She was nine and knew much more about love than I did. Seth Jacobson, a boy in her class, even *like, liked* her and wrote her a note once saying that he loved her.

"Why doesn't Frona just go find somebody else?" My breath fogged the window as I spoke. I smiled in amusement when I saw that my nose left a small circular print on the glass.

I looked over at Marla again; her breath was fogging the window, too. I opened my mouth wide and pushed hot air out as hard as I could from my belly. A circle of window fog as big as my head appeared. I outlined Frona's shape in the white moisture with my finger.

Frona was sitting on her knees under the big oak in our front yard. Her hair hung long and unkempt over her shoulders and the rest of her body. The light from the front porch shone on her now patchy, red face. Tears carried her mascara and eyeliner down her cheeks and away from her swollen eyes. She was wearing the shawl Marla and I had loved so much. It was made of painted fabric, sheer and silky. Frona had wrapped me and my sister in it many times to pull us close to her. Inside that shawl she smelled of vanilla and rain. I knew I'd miss the way she smelled, the way she hugged, and her long, shiny hair.

Marla leaned her forehead into the window. "What are you thinking about?" I asked.

My sister pulled her head away from the window. I heard a click as her skin detached from the glass.

"I don't know," Marla said. "I just kind of wanted *her* to stay, I think. Maybe. I don't know. I guess it doesn't matter."

I was startled that Marla was second-guessing herself. She was always so sure—of everything.

"Yesterday you said she was a bitch," I reminded Marla.

"Yeah." Marla contorted her face forcing a bit of recycled anger. "She *is* a bitch."

When Marla and I heard the bottom of the storm door scrape against the concrete, we both sat up a little straighter and craned our necks so we could see better. Daddy was coming out.

"You're going to wake the girls," Daddy said, as he walked over to Frona. "Now, don't act like that. You've got to go. We've been through all this."

Frona put her arms around Daddy's legs and her face into his knees.

"But I love you," Frona sobbed. "Didn't it mean anything? All this?" She lifted her hands like she was presenting our house.

"What do you mean 'all this'"? Daddy's tone grew defensive. "*All this* was here way before *you* got here. Don't even act like *you* had anything to do with *this* ..."

"I don't mean it that WAY," Frona screamed at the end. "WE WERE HAPPY."

"NO," Daddy was yelling now. "*YOU* WERE HAPPY."

Frona was trying to speak through her sobs, but they were so strong she had to keep gasping for air.

"It sounds like she has the hiccups," I said, trying to lighten the mood. I poked Marla in the ribs with my elbow.

"Yeah, it kinda does." Marla made a little humpf and a tiny grin quivered across her face. "It really does."

Daddy had Frona in his arms now and was guiding her toward the car. It was a cute little "foreign jobber" as Daddy had called it when we first met her. We had waited for her at a table just outside the Petra kitchen. She was a "damn fine" chef Daddy had said, "and a pretty one too."

I had never heard of Greek food. Until then, I didn't even know Greeks *had* special food and I certainly couldn't understand why, with all the American food around town, we needed a Greek restaurant. Marla said she had heard about Greek food before. I didn't believe her until she told me she read about the cuisine in one of her world books. Marla was always reading. She was one of the smartest girls at our school. Even the way she explained Greek food and why we needed it made sense.

"Well, what about all the Greeks who come here to live? Think about it like the French," she explained. "If we didn't have French fries then what would they eat?"

"Hmm," I said, nodding my standard reply to my sister's usual deductive reasoning. Still, I had never seen any Greeks in Rayes County but I didn't argue.

I had ordered just about everything on Petra's menu and Marla had too. I'd let my sister try anything new first and then the next night I'd order it.

It was the night I ordered the Monte Cristo and Marla the Falafel, when Frona first emerged from the shiny silver double doors.

"Yes?" she had formed a question to Daddy, tilting her head in his direction as she fluttered her eyes. Her voice coated my eardrums like thick chocolate as she spoke.

"They said you wanted to see me?"

"Yes," Daddy cleared his throat and scrunched his eyebrows together. He narrowed his eyes to no bigger than slits just like he did when he was mad. "I need to talk to you about the food here."

"Yes?" Frona seemed startled as she tilted her head slightly again, her eyes sparkling even under the dim lighting.

"It's wonderful!" Daddy broke into a big toothy smile, laughing as he touched her arm.

"Oh, I'm so glad you like the food." Frona's laugh was as stunning and steady just like her smile.

"These are my girls," he said, presenting me and Marla to his new interest like we were a prize she had just won in a game show.

Marla and I tried to make ourselves more attractive at a moment's notice. We sat up a little straighter, smiled pleasantly but not too eagerly.

"I'm Dancy," my voice squeaked.

"I am Marla," my sister had said, as she stood and firmly shook Frona's hand.

It was then that Frona sat down with us and removed her kitchen hat. Her hair fell like silk over her shoulders as she released it from its twist. Frona had then immediately stuck her finger into one of Marla's dimples. I flinched, expecting my easy-to-agitate sister to smack Frona's hand away, but she didn't. I had felt the urge to giggle as Frona stroked the back of my head and ran her hand down my long hair.

"Your girls are so lovely," Frona had said with her beautiful words.

I could have listened to her talk all night, and even Marla looked interested in what Frona had to say.

I could see our reflections, the four of us, in the shiny silver double doors. We'd been sitting at that table almost every other night for the past two weeks. Daddy was trying to catch a glimpse of the Greek goddess through those round windows. He had practically worn a path to the men's room that took him past those big silver swinging doors.

We looked good together, the four of us, reflected in stainless steel. It didn't matter that Marla and I were tow headed, as Daddy always called us, and Frona could never pass for our real mother. Suddenly I could imagine her taking me shopping, out to lunch, driving me to school ...

Marla snapped her hand back just as I caught her about to touch Frona's hair. It was love at first sight, at least that's how Marla had later explained our first encounter with Frona. Marla had said it happens to people all the time—like being struck by lightning or hit by a car.

In my father's ongoing search to replace or replicate Momma, Frona was close. A little darker than Momma and much softer, but even I could see the main ingredients were similar. Frona was closer to the way Momma *used* to be, not what she had become. I had seen pictures of my mother in skinny-waisted dresses before she and Daddy were married. At least I had been told it was Momma, although it certainly didn't look like her now. If my mother ever was a dress and lipstick-wearing debutante, I couldn't imagine it.

Frona's house was beautiful like her. Antiques from Greece and family heirlooms passed down from generations of grandmothers brought an enticing depth into each room, luring me in to see what other treasures were hidden there. She was the only person from her family to go to college in the United States. She had studied under famous chefs whose names I could never remember or pronounce, even though she said them to me several times.

She had shared with Marla and me a promise she made to herself.

"I said I will open a restaurant in America and build a house just like the one my mother had," Frona had said to me and Marla. She stood tall and confident and then pointed to the

13

patio just behind her house. "And I promised myself I'd put one of every species of flower my garden. Young ladies, I want you to know you can do anything you want when you live in America."

Frona always sounded like she was about to break into song with, *Oh beautiful for spacious skies for amber waves of grain ...,* when she talked about coming to America.

Still, she was rightly proud of her home *and* her restaurant. She had done exactly what she came to do. From her flower garden to her Monte Cristo, everything was handled with a perfectionist's touch.

Flowers were always in bloom around her house somewhere, even in late fall and winter. She could name them all and tried to teach the names to me and Marla. We remembered a few of the formal names but when it was too hard I'd call them by the way they smelled—lemon soap was one of my favorites and green Kool-Aid was the other.

"Hyacinth," Frona had said one day, sniffing the white flower. "Or, as *you* like to call it, lemon soap." She patted the fluffy plume on its little head and then lifted its tiny chin so she could see its face better.

*

"I'll miss her rolls," I blurted out as my memories of how we met Frona floated seamlessly into the present chaos. I could almost taste the melting butter as I continued to watch Daddy and Frona's dramatic break-up taking place in our front yard. She made the best homemade yeast rolls. The dough would sit out and rise. I loved to watch Frona's delicate hands disappear into the mound, then re-emerge as pounding fists as she beat the mass into submission.

"I'll miss her beef tips," Marla spoke quietly to the window as she stuck her forehead to the glass again.

The car door slammed. Daddy stood at Frona's window for a few moments, the bottoms of his pajama pants swaying slightly in the wind as he squatted there. Frona was shaking her head as her lips continued to form the word "no" over and over again.

Daddy stood up, backing away from the foreign jobby. He pointed to the end of the driveway and then flicked his wrist to and fro so Frona would understand that she needed to go.

The gravel Daddy poured at the end of the driveway to keep rainwater from gathering there crunched underneath her tires as her little car drove over them.

"Shew," Marla said, pulling her head away from the glass. "I'm glad that's over."

I wasn't glad it was over, not glad at all. But Marla was my leader.

"Yeah, me too," I hesitated but spoke the words I knew my sister wanted to hear. "But you know Frona was about damn near perfect. No telling who we'll get next."

"Maybe she *was* damn near perfect," Marla turned to me and said. "But no matter how perfect any of them are, he still won't keep 'em. They ain't Momma."

Marla gave a crisp nod, "Now, I need some damn sleep. I've got school in the morning." My sister rolled her eyes and shook her head, ashamed for the grownups and the uncivilized display that had just taken place in our front yard. Marla then plopped herself down in the bed. I snuggled in beside my sister, hugging my front to her back and was happy she didn't tell me to go to my room. We pretended to be asleep when we heard Daddy's footsteps coming down the hall. I watched as the shadow of his feet broke the beaming light shining through the bottom of the doorway. He walked over to the bed, kissed Marla on the head and then me. He smelled of apple pipe tobacco and cinnamon.

"I love you girls," Daddy whispered into the night and then quietly left the room.

"Marla," I whispered. When she didn't answer right away I tried again, "Marla, Marla."

"WHAT!" She snapped at me in a loud whisper as she turned her head back toward me.

"What about love at first sight?"

"Crap, Dancy. There's no such thing. Now go to sleep. We've got school tomorrow."

CHAPTER TWO

The Beatnik

"Danielle Wilder, will you come to the front of the class and show us how to do number seven?" Mr. Montel pointed his chalk at me and then to the board. Butterflies awakened in my stomach as he said my name—Danielle Wilder, "Mmmm," I sighed.

I rose from my seat carefully so the chair legs wouldn't squeak against the tile and floated gracefully to a standing position.

"Yes, I'll be glad to, Mr. Montel." I smiled sweetly and blushed. If I had known what a curtsy was I'd have done that too.

Mr. Montel was super foxy, a term I had learned the day after arriving in his class. He was the new teacher. No one wanted to be in a new teacher's class: last in lunch line, last to the library and first back from recess. I had prayed all summer for just three things: the hippie my father was living with to leave our house, to be put in the Lion's class with the smart kids, and to get Mrs. Turner for a teacher. None of my prayers had been answered, but the outcome was still good in at least two instances. I was in the Tiger's class, the not-so-smart but not-so-dumb class, and my teacher was the foxiest man on Earth.

One look at Mr. Montel had everyone in the Lion's class wishing *they* were Tigers. My seemingly mediocre seat had become a coveted one. Girls from the Lion's class would wait for the Tiger girls in the restroom just so they could talk about Mr. Montel. Did he have a girlfriend? Who would he marry? What was it like to be in room 225, gazing upon his handsomeness all day? The best part: Mr. Montel thought I was smart in math and even said so many times while I was at the board.

Mamaw always said prayers were never answered right away and that patience is a virtue, whatever the hell that meant.

Terry, the Beatnik hippie, which is what Mamaw called my father's newest girlfriend, had not left Daddy—she was still there playing her Rod Stewart albums every day when I got home from school and I was sure that when my school day was done today would be more of the same.

Hitchhiking across the country with nothing more than the shirt on her back was Terry's claim to fame. She bragged about it whenever she got the chance. Terry ended up in Rayes County because "it was meant to be," she had said. When the Beatnik spoke of how she ended up in our little Tennessee town, she would push her fist against the middle of her chest like she was embracing her heart. She always said she was looking for a place where she could be truly free and she was "so close she could smell it in the air."

For the rest of us, the smell Terry spoke of was more like incense mixed with body odor. Marla and I had named it "the Terry smell."

The school day passed quickly. With any other teacher a seemingly shorter school day might have felt more like a perk. But tearing my gaze from Mr. Montel's handsome presence proved difficult. Knowing the Beatnik was waiting for me at home made leaving school even harder, and today Marla wouldn't be there with me. I stepped off the school bus and heard the music even before I got to the front porch. I looked back to make sure the bus was long gone before I pushed our front door open. The Wilder house had become sort of a Pandora's Box. I never knew what might be going on in there, so it was best to enter with a bit of caution.

"HOT DAMN," Terry sang as she whirled her hair around her body and danced, moving her head in a circular motion. I knew the song was *really* called "Hot Legs" and Terry had the words wrong. But when I entered the living room armed with my eight-year-old knowledge of rock and roll and Rod Stewart, and told her she was misquoting the lyrics, she forced me to sit with her and listen to the record over and over again to prove her point. I eventually gave in and agreed that Mr. Stewart really was being worn out by hot damn.

"You're such a little grown up, Dancy." Terry stood after the song was over, her long hair caught in her rose-tinted, wire-rimmed glasses. "And besides, who cares what the lyrics say? Isn't it really about how they make you feel, man?"

"Well, *you* cared what they said a few minutes ago when you thought I was wrong," I hurled what I thought was a blistering comeback.

19

"Right, wrong—there's an overabundance of that negative salt and pepper in this world," Terry said, gently forming her body across the couch and placing her feet on the armrest.

"Daddy doesn't let us put our feet up there like that," I said, wishing my eyes could shoot darts at her.

"Your father is trying to lighten up a little, and I am hoping you and Marla might do the same."

Terry pulled a cigarette from a half-smoked pack of Salem Menthols that had been scooted to the edge of the coffee table.

"Where is Marla anyway? She didn't come home with you, did she?"

Terry looked all around the room like she'd find Marla perched somewhere on the walls or ceiling.

"No, she *didn't* come home with me," I rolled my eyes. "I've told you every day this week and you ask again every day. Marla is at band practice. Daddy is picking her up later."

"Oh yeah," Terry said, slowly rising to a normal seated position. She spent the next minute combing her fingers through her hair blowing out puffs of grayish-blue smoke.

"I remember now—yeah, you told me that." Terry's delayed reaction to my explanation was typical.

Marla had joined band at the beginning of the school year. Fifth graders were the only students at Rayes County Elementary allowed to join. It was supposed to get them ready for middle school band in sixth grade and marching band in high school. Marla was already making plans to be the drum major.

When Daddy would take me and Marla to see the high school boys play football—the RCHS Hornets—my sister and I were more interested in watching the cheerleaders, which is what *I* wanted to be, and the drum major at half-time, which was Marla's dream title.

I never understood why Marla chose an instrument like the flute, it just didn't suit her. To me she looked more like a saxophone player. I would listen to her practice and ask her to play it louder. It didn't sound at all like a trumpet or trombone; it was a quiet, squeaky little instrument, frail and fragile.

"They're having that concert for something aren't they?" Terry's silky voice was sing-songy again today. I knew why, but I didn't dare say it.

"Yes, the Harvest concert at school," I asserted. "I told you yesterday *and* the day before."

I rolled my eyes one last time and turned toward the hallway thinking I could escape to my room.

"Wait a minute," Terry's yell was throaty and hoarse now. "Come back after you put your books away, and we'll go get into something."

I threw my notebook and history book on the bed so hard the center ring in my three-ring binder bent, "Damnit, damnit, damnit!" I looked at it. It was brand new, maroon and shiny with coated plastic. Now it was going to be broken for the rest of the school year. "Bitch," I said to the wall in Terry's general direction. "What the hell does she want? Stupid bitch."

During the spring of 1974 Daddy had turned our 24-acres of rolling hills into a would-be horse farm. Shortly after that, Terry moved in and he bought three horses, Penny, Buck and Trigger. Penny was Terry's horse, a wild mare that she tried to mount often and was thrown back off just as often. The Beatnik wore the scratches, scrapes and sprains the red mare inflicted upon her like tiny badges of honor. Daddy would have referred to Terry's numerous injuries as battle scars but he no longer believed in war since he met the Beatnik.

Terry assigned Buck, the old gray horse, to Daddy, and Trigger to Marla and me. Trigger was an old caramel Stallion with a blond mane. He didn't even trot, he just kind of shuffled. Having only known Trigger for a little more than a summer, I was still skittish around him. Mamaw had told me to make sure I gave Trigger a fair shake. "You'll find no better friend than a friendly old horse," my grandmother had said.

Mamaw was always giving out advice at her restaurant called Mamaw's Place. She had told me that half the teenagers in Rayes County had worked there at one time or another. Mamaw "practically raised half the damn town," she'd often say. I guess that's why everybody listened to my mamaw and took her advice. Daddy often referred to his mother as the *Hee Haw* version of Abigail Van Buren and would say that she should have her own column in the *Gazette* called *Dear Mamaw.*

I had asked for Mamaw's opinion about my problems with Trigger, so I had to at least listen to what she had to say. Over a bowl of gravy with a biscuit crumbled on top, my grandmother convinced me that Trigger and I could still be friends even if I didn't ride him. Daddy had tried to interject his opinion by saying that riding Trigger regularly would calm my fears. Mamaw shushed him right away and smacked her hand on the counter in front of him.

"If we need your opinion we'll ask for it, Everett," Mamaw had scolded my father. When Daddy tried to speak again, Mamaw snapped her fingers in front of his face. I had to bite my lips together to keep from laughing. Daddy blinked and jerked his head back away from her hand. Mamaw was the only person I had ever seen who could treat my father like a five-year old. After a long sigh, my father got up and walked across the restaurant, joining Marla at her usual perch in front of the jukebox. I knew Daddy had seen those same song titles at least a thousand times before, but he studied them intently anyway. I wondered, but never asked, if some of those old songs were in there when he and Momma had worked at Mamaw's Place all those years ago.

I had told Mamaw I'd try her advice and give Trigger a chance. I stayed true to my word and at times felt that Trigger was starting to warm a bit.

Ignoring Daddy's constant pleading, I hardly ever rode Trigger. The old caramel stallion and I were fine as long as I wasn't sitting on his back. I'd "brush him bald" Daddy would say.

"You treat that horse like a dog; a pet." Daddy would pace around watching me brush. "A horse needs to be run, trotted; not just pampered like some foo-foo poodle."

Even if I was terrified of Trigger's enormity, there were times I felt this four-legged monster and I were beginning to connect on a personal level, somehow. I think he was as tired of Terry as Marla and I were. Trigger would watch Terry closely, examining her every move when she would try and mount Penny. Sometimes Trigger would huff and snort at Terry like he wanted to call her a stupid, lazy Beatnik. I could see it in his eyes.

My response to old Trigger was always, "Yes, I know how you feel." Then we'd stand there together and watch Terry tangle with her wild mare, mostly losing the battle.

I wondered if today would be a repeat of me and old Trigger watching as Terry, once again, tried to prove herself to be some kind of horse whisperer.

I looked at myself in the mirror. I had put on lipstick that morning and I could still see traces of the pinkish-orange hue. The Avon lady had left tiny samples in the mailbox for "Mrs. Wilder." I didn't want Terry to get any ideas that Daddy might make *her* a Mrs. Wilder, so I tucked them inside my purse and saved them for myself. After all, my father *was* still a married man.

"You comin' outta there?" Terry spoke through the door; her words were soft but still raked across my eardrums like barbed wire.

"Yeah, be out in a minute," I said, rolling my eyes at my reflection.

Once outside I could see we were headed to the barn.

"I don't want to ride the horses today," I argued.

"No, the horses are resting in the field," Terry said, throwing a limp-wristed wave back toward me. "We're going to get to know each other a little better."

I could see Penny, Buck, and Trigger grazing out in the field. Out there my giant horse looked so small and harmless. I held my hand up to the horizon; Trigger was actually smaller than my palm from that distance.

Even though I didn't want to ride, I found myself wishing to be out there with Trigger instead of with Terry. I watched as the Beatnik walked ahead; the bottoms of her faded and torn jeans getting caught under her dirty bare heels.

"You're going to step on a piece of glass and cut your foot." My sarcastic tone made Terry turn.

"I think you *hope* I step on a piece of glass, Dancy."

Terry stopped and pulled her foot up so she could see the bottom. Her heels were filthy and scummy around the sides. Her toenails were yellow and brittle. The disgust I was feeling must have manifested itself on my face.

"It's natural to be barefoot, Dancy." Terry put her foot down and placed her hands on her hips.

"You're so uptight, Dancy. You need to loosen up. That's what we're going to do, loosen you up."

Daddy would have never let Marla and I go around with dirty feet. I remember one of the times when Momma was in the hospital and we had to leave the house so fast I forgot my shoes. Daddy paid one of the orderlies to go after his shift at the hospital and buy a pair of sandals for me; but not before I stepped on a piece of glass from a broken IV bottle in the emergency room. Daddy spent the rest of that night in the ER waiting room with my foot in his lap. My father took the little pocketknife he carried and dug the glass out of my heel. Daddy always had a knife, nail clippers and a wooden round TUIT in his pocket.

My father was always anxious to use that round TUIT and he'd wait for someone to say something like, "Well, I'll get around to it," so he could snatch the little wooden disc from his pocket and return with, "Here ya go—*a round TUIT*." It was only clever the first twenty times I saw him do it, after that it was just embarrassing.

At least two or three times a week he'd clip mine and Marla's nails and clean out from under them. When he was finished he'd always sing the song, "I love you a bushel and a peck, a bushel and a peck and a hug around the neck; I love you a barrel and a heap, a barrel and heap and a kiss upon your cheek."

Watching Terry's dirty feet hit the ground as she walked made me wonder how on Earth Daddy could be with someone like her—dirty feet, stringy hair and barefoot. It was beyond anything Marla, me, or Mamaw could comprehend.

"Hurry up!" Terry turned and yelled back at me, breaking into my wandering thoughts. She then jumped up and down to mimic excitement. I pretended to run, just a little, to catch up to her.

When we arrived at the barn I followed Terry up the ladder to the loft. She gathered some of the straw carpeting the wooden floor and made a little pile of it to sit on. I did the same.

"Now," she spoke in a sigh and began rocking back and forth in her Indian-style seated position trying to burrow out a more comfortable seat. I did the same.

I watched as she pulled the front of her jeans out with one hand and reached inside them with the other. She revealed a small plastic sandwich baggie that had been rolled up in her pants. It contained what looked like dried weeds.

"I know what that is," I said, jumping at the chance to show her how streetwise I was. "It's pot." I didn't give her a chance to answer.

"Pot has such a negative connotation to it." Terry's silky voice raked across my eardrums again.

"Marijuana is, is, a much more beautiful sound, kind of like the way it makes you feel."

"So pot makes *you* feel beautiful?" My sarcastic tone made Terry laugh out loud.

"You're such a little grown up, Dancy."

"Well, around here these days *somebody* has to be," I said, rolling my eyes at her as I attempted to get up from my straw pile.

Terry wrapped her bony hand around mine. "Oh, come on and stay. It's so peaceful up here, just be quiet for a minute and listen."

I sat there in the barn loft in total silence for at least the minute she had requested of me. The fall breeze brought the smell of horse manure, straw, and wildflowers whipping through the loft windows. I leaned my back against the wall and pulled my knees under my chin, deciding to give in and just enjoy the evening air.

I watched with interest as Terry revealed a pack of rolling papers from her pocket and pulled a tiny, white sheet from the slit. She folded the thin paper almost in half, but not quite, and made a sharp crease, then sprinkled the marijuana over it.

She gathered all her fingers in a row, palms facing toward her and began rolling the paper upwards with her thumbs. One quick lick across the paper and it was done. I sat silent in amazement.

All my instincts were telling me to leave but I stayed put, watching her every move. When she was done licking the paper, she rolled the joint again between her thumbs and all eight of her fingers, evening out the weed to make it not so fat in the middle.

"Now that's just about perfect," Terry said, holding her fine creation up to the sun in a vertical position to inspect it further.

She put the joint between her lips, winked at me, then and clicked her tongue as she strained to reach in her pocket, pulling out a lighter.

The small flame shot out and danced around in the wind. She tried to shield it with her free hand as the butane blurred a bit of space between us.

"I like that smell," I said, taking one more sniff before the fumes escaped into the sky. "Is that weird?"

She nodded but didn't speak, too consumed with protecting the tiny fire in her hand.

The paper burned quickly just before the fatty began to pop and spark.

The Beatnik inhaled deeply and then tried to speak. "That's the seeds making it pop like that," she spoke a throaty sentence trying to hold the smoke in her lungs. "Here," Terry held the joint between her fingers, her arm moving it toward me.

"I don't want any," I said, shaking my head vigorously and crinkling my face.

"Why not," Terry asked, still trying to hold her breath.

"I don't think Daddy would want me to smoke pot."

Terry held the smoke in her lungs as long as she could and then erupted with laughter the moment I finished my sentence. A blue-gray cloud burst out of her mouth.

"Your father does this all the time," the Beatnik half yelled, turning her red face toward me as she blasted out a laugh.

"MY FATHER DOES NOT!" I argued.

I knew Terry was lying. Everett Wilder would *never* do drugs. There were only three respectable jobs a Rayes County grown up could have: teaching school, working for the railroad, or for the Tennessee Valley Authority. Daddy had been electrical foreman at the nuclear power plant for as far back as I could remember. One thing I knew for sure. There was no way TVA would let a pothead through those steel doors, and my father was no pothead.

"Oh, oh yes he does," Terry said, smiling as she took another hit from the joint. "And he likes it—A LOT." The nasty hippie lunged her face toward mine to emphasize her point. Her breath stank like rotting eggs.

Terry responded with, "Go on, and try some." Her arm came toward me with the joint once more.

Again, I shook my head.

"Suit yourself, Dancy," Terry said, turning her head from me. "You're always going to be a prude, and you'll grow up to be a prudie old lady who never tried anything new. Hell, you won't even ride your own horse."

"Give me the damn joint," I demanded, taking the doobie from Terry's hand and pressing the end of it to my lips. I justified the reaction to Terry's pressure by telling myself I was only taking a toke to prove a point. I *was* a modern woman of the 70s; even more so than the dumb ass pothead with the red face who was sitting there mocking me.

I took one hit and held it for as long as I could until my lungs gave out. A short coughing fit complete with a phlegm and saliva sling quickly ensued. Terry laughed and pointed at me as I tried to catch my breath. That seemed to satisfy her— the Beatnik didn't offer a second hit and promptly plucked her recent gift from my fingers.

Terry burned the joint all the way down to a roach the size of a pinky nail. She sat there quietly for a few moments and then popped the little thing into her mouth like an Easter jelly bean. She winked a bloodshot eye at me as she swallowed it hard.

The sun was big and orange. It looked like I could walk over to the opposite loft window and have my hand scorched as I reached to touch it. But the fiery ball moved as I did, and when I got there it was too far away. I looked at my hand against the orange glow and found myself wondering how I got there—to the top of the barn loft. Where was Daddy? Where was Marla? A wave of panic took my breath.

I turned and saw Terry on the other side of the loft, silhouetted against a darkening sky. Time was no longer relevant. The events of last week and even last year began to ooze together. I wondered if Momma was inside the house waiting for me, and then remembered she was gone. I forced myself to recall the events of the day, hoping to arrive grounded in the present, even if the present placed me in the top of the barn loft with Terry Hardwick, my father's latest love interest who just happened to be a stinking hippie.

Just as my recent history began to rearrange itself chronologically, giving me some indication of how I managed to find myself in the barn loft with Terry, believing I could reach out and touch the evening sun, a familiar but unpleasant vibration hit my eardrums.

"I know what!" Terry said, breaking the connection between me and the big ball of sun. "Let's ride, man, let's ride."

The now stoned hippie got up from her mound of straw, and before I could say anything she was at the bottom of the ladder and out in front of the barn. I tried to follow her, but my legs weren't moving fast enough. I felt like I was sprinting but looked down to see my feet taking only baby steps in quick succession.

When I finally made it to the front of the barn, I could see Terry running across the field toward red Penny. I looked at the driveway; it was almost time for Daddy and Marla to get home, and I was worried about what might happen; what they might think, would Daddy know, would Marla be mad at me for spending so much time with the bitch? I shouldn't have gone to the barn with Terry. Why did I go?

I looked back over toward the field and saw Terry battling with Penny once again. Her fingers were wrapped tightly around strands of Penny's mane; large tufts of red hair sprang out of Terry's fists and between her fingers. Terry had done it. Somehow she had managed to mount that mare and was now riding through the field. I could hear Terry screaming delights, echoing over the rolling hills, her wavy hair dancing behind her.

I walked out onto the field, my feet struggling over the divots Penny, Buck, and Trigger had left there. I was moving slowly in the direction Penny and Terry had gone; not following them but wandering aimlessly, having nowhere else to go. I could hear loud breathing behind me and as I turned, Trigger nudged my arm. I was tempted to mount him bareback and ride just like Terry had, off into the sunset. Buck came to join Trigger there at my side and Penny came a few moments later.

"Penny?! What are you doing here?!" I shouted, realizing that Terry's horse had once again thrown her off. Then I heard a faint scream just over the hill.

The horses turned their heads, as I did, in the direction of the scream, Terry's scream. Trigger huffed and snorted, the other two sauntered to the barn. Another scream came over the hill, this one pierced fear deep into my stomach.

"TERRY?!" I yelled weakly but heard nothing in return.

I hesitated for a moment, thinking, *the longer I wait* ... Then I half-heartedly jogged over the divots. My breath was heavy, and I was still a bit slower than usual. Finally, over the top of the hill I saw her. She held her hand up and reached for me as I walked toward her.

"Dancy," she said, but I could barely hear her even though I was getting closer. "Dancy, it hurts." I continued to walk toward her slowly.

When I was at arm's length I reached for Terry's hand and began pulling her toward me. She screamed in pain and vomited a bunch of white stuff with what looked like blood in it. As the blood-laced vomit ran down Terry's face I wondered if she was going to die. What would I tell people? What would Daddy say? Would I go to prison?

Terry choked and then pulled her hand away from mine. "Call an ambulance," she coughed the words at me.

Our house looked so far away and it was almost dark now. I turned to look at Terry, lying there in the field brush, her eyes full of fear.

"I'll be right back," I said, locking my eyes on Terry's for a just a moment to let her know that I truly *would* be right back. She nodded slightly.

As I ran toward the house, the welcome sound of gravels popping out from under the tires on Daddy's Gran Torino both soothed my fears and heightened them. Suddenly I was able to run faster than I had ever run before. I had to get to Daddy.

The long, yellow door flew open, and my father emerged. Taking quick note of the terror in my face, he took long steps toward me.

"She's over there, over the hill, over there. Penny threw her."

Daddy listened intently to what I had just said, hesitated for a moment and then ran over the hill in great strides until I saw his head disappear from the horizon.

"What in the hell happened," Marla asked, struggling to balance her book bag and flute case as she got out of the car.

My sister's pissed off tone would have normally set me off but in that moment I found it comforting. I looked over my shoulder to make sure Daddy was long gone and then muttered, "Penny threw Terry again." I spoke quietly, afraid Marla would hear the guilt I carried in my words.

"Oh God!" Marla rolled her eyes and then threw her book bag on the hood of car, placing her flute case on top. She stood tip toed to get a better view over the hill where Daddy had gone to save Terry. Once Marla realized Daddy and Terry were not within her sites, she turned to me and began to inspect my face. I turned my torso this way and that, trying to avoid my sister's inquisitive motives. With each turn Marla followed me, dancing around my still feet.

"Have you—have you—been crying?" Marla scrunched her forehead and crinkled her nose. "Hah! You've been crying over that bitch!"

"NO, NO I HAVE NOT!" I screamed into Marla's face.

My sister stepped back as I yelled, barely parting her lips as the next sound came out of her, "Ewwwwwww, your breath stinks—you smell like pot!" Marla stood perfectly still and waited for my response. I had none.

"Well?" Again Marla waited for an answer. "Well?" She crossed her arms and patted her foot firmly against the gravels several times. When I still didn't respond my sister firmly grabbed both my shoulders and shook me.

"WELL?"

"Leave me alone," I said, jerking away from Marla's hold. With nothing else to say I turned and began walking toward the house.

"DANCY WILDER IS A BEATNIK POTHEAD!" Marla yelled as I reached the front porch.

The last words I heard her say about the matter were muffled through an already-closed storm door, "I'M TELLING DADDY! YOU KNOW I'M GOING TO TELL DADDY!"

For some reason I just didn't care.

*

Marla and I sat on our knees, chins resting on our folded arms across the back of the couch. I strained my eyes to see in the dark as Daddy carried Terry over the hill toward the flashing ambulance lights in our driveway.

"Humph!" Marla raised her head and turned toward me. "Must not have been much of an emergency, they didn't even turn the siren on."

"Yeah," I found a sarcastic tone then turned to my sister. "When Momma was sick they always turned the siren on."

I waited for Marla's response. Thinking she didn't hear me, I spoke again, "Yeah, when Mom—."

"Yeah, Yeah, Dancy, I heard you the first time," Marla snapped at me.

I could feel my eyes getting hot and wet so I turned away, sopping up the moisture with my shirt sleeve before my sister saw me crying. As I turned back toward Marla with what I thought was a clean face, she had already locked onto my eyes.

"Sorry," Marla said, taking her thumb and wiping a rogue tear from my face. "I didn't mean it."

"I know," I said, as we both turned back toward the window.

Expecting Daddy to go with Terry the way he used to with Momma, Marla and I were surprised to see him walking toward the porch as the ambulance pulled away.

"You all right, Dancy?" Daddy's voice boomed in the quiet room.

"Yeah, I'm fine," I said quietly, my tone squeaking a bit at the end. Marla and I turned from the window and she pinched me on the arm. "Tell him," my sister mouthed the words to me.

I pinched Marla's leg mouthing back to her, "No."

"You girls hungry?" Daddy asked, as he stood with the refrigerator door open.

"Yes," Marla was the first to answer. I simply nodded.

"Well," Daddy said, diving deeper into the fridge. "As usual, there's nothing in here but this soy crap."

Marla chuckled and I smiled for the first time since before going to the barn with Terry.

"Let's go to the Root Beer Stand!"

Daddy had no more than gotten the words out when Marla and I were on our feet. We hadn't been to the Root Beer Stand since the Beatnik had moved into our house. There had been no burgers, no fries, no hot dogs, no onion rings—no anything good for so long, that Marla and I had started turning the color of granola. Or, at least that's what Mamaw had said last time we went to the restaurant. Our grandmother had told Daddy she needed mine and Marla's help with something in her kitchen and then sneaked a burger for us. Marla and I laughed quietly when we heard the Beatnik order two plates of steamed broccoli for each of us. Memories of that last burger had long dissipated as I pined day after day for anything that wasn't a vegetable or grain. Just the words, "The Root Beer Stand" made my mouth water.

"Are you two coming or not?" Daddy held the front door open as Marla and I were still dancing around the living room. My sister and I raced to the car and didn't even argue about who was going to sit in the front seat. Marla and I both jumped in the back at the same time.

"Well, this is different," Daddy said, looking in his rearview mirror at us.

It *was* different; a good different. Terry had been sitting next to him in our Gran Torino for over a year; Daddy looked good up there by himself. Just as the thought of the three of us alone again entered my mind, the words escaped my lips, "What about Terry? Are we going to the hospital?"

Marla kicked my foot.

"No, EMTs said she just got the wind knocked out of her," Daddy said, casually draping his long arm over the back of the seat as he began to pull out of the driveway. "We'll go and pick her up after we eat."

I looked at Marla. She rolled her eyes. "Should've left the bitch out there," my sister said under her breath, looking over into the field.

CHAPTER THREE

The Book of Truvy

"You girls be good now, you hear?" Daddy placed his arm over the back of the seat, with a fist full of dollars that Marla readily snatched.

"We will," Marla and I answered in unison.

"C'mon, Dancy, let's go," Marla said, as she got out of the car. I followed my sister, hanging onto the back of her jacket.

We had missed the first night's showing of *Star Wars* at the Mansion Theater, but it was Saturday night and *that* was even better. Most of Marla's friends were there waiting with Janie's mom—that's who *I* really wanted to see. Marla and I stood near the curb as Ms. Jameson stuck her head in the window and spoke to Daddy.

"Don't worry," she said. "I'll take good care of them."

"I know you will, Bev," Daddy said, winking at us through a backseat window.

I loved Janie's mom and loved it even more when we got to go places with her. Bev was a pretty name, not beautiful but pretty. The name Bev fit her. It sounded cool. Bev was cool. She didn't look like a mom, but she smelled like one; fresh and clean like Ivory Soap. Her smile was contagious; or at least it was for me. Her laughter would dance around in my head and always make me smile.

It wasn't often that we got to be with Bev—mostly at the movies and only when Janie invited Marla. I just tagged along. Marla said she liked that I went with them but had to act like she didn't in front of Janie because I was still in elementary school. I didn't mind being the younger one when we were with Janie and her mom. I liked sitting next to Bev, eating her popcorn—just being with her. Janie was so mean to her mom, rolling her eyes and flipping Bev the bird when her back was turned. I would never flip Bev the bird. She was too nice.

*

The Resistance had won its battle. Han Solo was alive and Darth Vader had been given a swift kick in the ass by young Skywalker. Marla and I left the movie theater with the memory of Luke, Han Solo, and the sounds of booming instrumental excitement burgeoning forth from the movie screen. Good had triumphed over evil, and I was sure there was hope for the Universe once more, and *I* could keep it safe for all mankind if only I had a light saber.

Once outside, I stopped when Bev did, so she could rifle through her purse and look for her keys.

"Yes! There they are," she said, shaking her head and then looking down at me. "I need to clean out my purse."

I smiled and began walking with her again.

"Oh, look," Bev said, pointing to the road. "There's your father and …"

Bev slowly put her arm down and with a puzzled look on her face asked, "Do you know who that is?"

"Who?" I asked, more interested in looking cool than searching for Daddy's car.

"That woman – in the car with your father?"

I looked up from my moment of pre-teen normalcy and out into the parking lot, scanning the cars for any sight of the Gran Torino. The long, yellow chariot stood out among the blues, browns and reds. I couldn't see Daddy; he was blocked from my view by a woman in the passenger's seat. I could see the back of her head. Platinum blonde was the only clue. It could have been anyone.

I left Bev's side and walked over to Marla and Janie, who were standing several feet behind Bev and me with their backs to us. The two of them were trying to act like they were unsupervised. Marla and Janie were talking to another group of girls whose parents were standing somewhere in the crowd as well.

"Hey," I said, pulling at Marla's shoulder. She was busy talking and didn't respond. "Hey," I repeated, raising my voice.

"What?!" Marla snapped, whirling around with a frustrated look. I said nothing, only pointed to the Gran Torino and the blonde.

Marla's eyes slowly moved to meet mine. Like me, she was confused.

"See you guys later," Marla yelled to her friends as she turned to walk toward the parking lot.

"Hey, wait up," I yelled after her and then waved to my surrogate movie mom. "Bye, Bev."

"Bye, girls," Bev yelled after us.

Marla and I walked quickly, weaving in and out of the parked cars, looking for the shortest route and the quickest answer to who this new woman might be.

As soon as Marla touched the back door handle, the blonde lady turned around. I was less than a foot behind my sister, so I crashed into her when all motion left her body. Marla and I stood frozen in our tracks. Time had slowed so that milliseconds passed like minutes. I recognized the woman immediately and from the look on her face, I knew that Marla did also.

The familiar blonde twisted around, turning her head toward us and then smiled through the glass, mouthing the word, "Hi." She waved her little hand at us and then turned back around so she could greet us again as we slid into the back seat.

"You girls know Truvy," Daddy stated, not turning around. Marla and I were too stunned to speak.

"Yes, we all know each other," Truvy spoke for us, noting our discomfort. "These girls and I go way back, don't we girls?"

Marla and I nodded slowly in unison. This seemed to satisfy Truvy enough to make her turn around and face the dashboard once again.

"Ice cream?" Daddy asked and exclaimed at the same time.

"Oh, that sounds wonderful, doesn't it girls?" Truvy leaned over and kissed Daddy on the cheek, whispering, "You're such a good father."

"Why don't we go to Mamaw's?" Marla asked. "She's got milkshakes."

I knew my sister was thinking the same thing I was, that Mamaw just simply had to see this to believe it. The look on my father's face was familiar. I had worn it many times myself when I was trying to hide something. Like the week I spent smoking a pack of cigarettes out in the barn while I pretended to be grooming Trigger. It was obvious my father didn't want his mother to know the identity of his latest love interest. Although I couldn't blame him, I was sorry we were going to miss watching Daddy turning red-faced when Mamaw would surely say, "What the hell have you done now, Everett?" My grandmother was always skeptical of any woman Daddy brought around. Mamaw would always find ways to work Momma into the conversation.

"Probably not tonight girls," Daddy said, wheeling the car out of the lot.

"Oh, I just love that lady who runs it. I think her name is Beulah," Truvy said, looking at the side of my father's head as he drove. "Do you guys go there a lot?"

I wasn't surprised that Truvy didn't know Mamaw was our real grandmother. But I was a little disappointed that my father had opted not to tell Truvy when the perfect opportunity had just presented itself. I had heard few people ever use my mamaw's real name. Most just called her what we called her— Mamaw. When someone did call her Beulah it just sounded weird.

"More than you know," Daddy answered Truvy's question and then pulled the car out onto the road. "More than you know," he repeated. I could see his mischievous smile in the rearview mirror.

"That Beulah is a real character," Truvy looked back at us and smiled.

"Sure is," Marla said right away, letting Daddy know his secret was safe for now.

As Truvy turned back to face the front of the car, I looked at Marla, her mouth was gaped open just like mine. My sister turned to me and mouthed the words, "Oh my God!"

I mouthed back, bulging my eyes at Marla, "I know."

We sat silent all the way to Kay's Ice Cream Café where Daddy's peanut butter milkshake, my hot fudge sundae, and Marla's strawberry sundae awaited. Other than looking at one another every so often to make sure we were still in agreement that Truvy and Daddy being together was still awkward as hell, we never said a word.

"Your father tells me his favorite is a peanut butter milkshake," Truvy said, stepping behind me and Marla, stroking the back of both our heads as we walked across the parking lot. Marla and I turned together, looked up and nodded at Truvy. My sister and I had suddenly turned into mimes. Had it not been for Marla's sudden stroke of genius, we might have stayed silent forever.

"Daddy," Marla finally spoke. "Me and Dancy gotta go to the bathroom. Get us the usual."

Marla grabbed my arm, both of us taking long strides toward the one-toilet bathroom. Marla was first to arrive at the door. She opened it quickly; looking around like she thought someone might be following us then shoved me inside. Taking one last look toward Truvy and Daddy, she shut the door and locked it, keeping us safe in case someone tried to break in.

"Oh my God," Marla said.

"Oh my God," I replied.

"Oh my God, Oh my God," Marla said, cupping her hands over her cheeks and pressing in hard.

"I KNOW!" I yelled and then fastened my hand over my mouth for a moment. For dramatic effect I moved my hand for one second to blurt out the final blasphemy, "The preacher's wife!"

Marla and I did very little business in the bathroom, opting instead for more, "Oh my God" comments and "Holy crap" exclamations.

"You girls in there?" Truvy spoke through the door. "Your daddy wanted me to check on you."

Marla and I looked at one another and then at the door, answering, "Yeah, we'll be right out."

When we finally emerged from the bathroom, we found Daddy and Truvy sitting together on one side of the booth. A hot fudge sundae sat across the table from Truvy and a Strawberry sundae was across the table from Daddy.

Daddy and Truvy hadn't realized we came out of the bathroom. They were busy making goo-goo eyes at each another. Truvy was blushing, and Daddy was showing his most toothy grin with his fist placed firmly under his elbow as he gazed at her.

It was at that moment I knew Daddy was going to keep her—at least for a while.

*

Truvy had been our Sunday school teacher at Redlawn Baptist Church back when Daddy and Momma were still together. Truvy and Momma had made all the costumes for the Christmas play one year—a story Mamaw had told me, although I was too little to remember it myself. Truvy was in charge of everything except the Three Wise Men; it was up to Momma to craft those costumes—the most tedious and elaborate.

Redlawn Baptist was a special place for Marla and me, not just because it was God's house and we were supposed to feel good about going there, but because the church's structure was so unique. The building sat out in the middle of nowhere with a railroad running just next to it. At one time Redlawn had been one of the most ornate hotels in the state, that is, until the highway, twelve miles north, had re-routed its patrons. The grounds were made up of four buildings all covered in regional quarry stone. The main building greeted hotel guests, now turned congregation, with rounded doorways and stained glass windows. The church had three floors, a grand staircase, a ballroom, a large dining area and three bars, complete with fully stocked scotch, highball, wine and shot glasses. Two of the buildings ran off each side of the main building and contained twelve former hotel rooms each. This was now where various Sunday School classes and Wednesday night youth meetings took place. The fourth building was for the groundskeeper back in the hotel's heyday, Daddy had told us. It was full of large iron tools and some old metal wagon wheels. Now, it was where the church bus was kept and where Rubin, the bus driver, spent most of his time.

Our pastor, Don Silvers, resembled Jesus himself, I always thought, and Mom did, too. Sometimes I'd look at the large portrait of the likeness of Jesus and then look at Brother Silvers and wonder if the two were the same. If you took away his suit and tie, he'd be a dead ringer, right down to the beard and long, thinning hair.

Marla and I learned to find the books of the Bible quickly at Redlawn. The Baptist Convention had tournaments for youth in which points were gained for how quickly one could find verse and chapter as it was called out to them. Redlawn was always among the top ten in any contest its youth entered and also placed top among all churches, not just Baptist, in the softball league championships each summer. Only the boys got to play softball, but Marla and I could certainly place a finger on John 3:16 in less than two seconds.

Truvy was in charge of events at Redlawn. We had visiting magicians, pop singers, religious comedians, and movie nights. Marla and I loved going to church there and were sad when one Sunday morning, Daddy got up and said we'd go to the park for a picnic instead. Had I known the Sunday before was going to be my last, I would have had a better time and explored the room on the top floor, opening the door that was always locked. Maybe Marla and I would have made one more memory playing Miss Kitty's Saloon at one of the bars.

Now, as I watched Daddy and Truvy together, I wondered about poor Brother Silvers and what might have happened to him. How would Redlawn Baptist Church go on without Truvy, the visiting comedians, magicians, singers, and Bible contests?

"There you are," Truvy said, smiling as we walked toward the table. I scooted in first and Marla slid in next to me, bumping my hip as she did.

"Your ice cream is probably melted by now," Daddy said, finally turning around and looking at us.

Marla and I both smiled back and immediately began slurping ice cream from our spoons. Daddy and Truvy both turned to watch us. It was like Marla and I had become fish in a tank. As my hand moved my spoon from the bowl to my mouth, their eyes moved with me. As Marla picked out strawberries from her ice cream, they watched with amazement like she had found gold nuggets in there or something.

The two of them looked at one another, and then Daddy spoke.

"Girls, I know you must have a lot of questions about me and Truvy."

The two of them looked at one another again. Marla and I both made sure our mouths were full at all times so we wouldn't have to speak.

"Truvy and I have been talking for a while," Daddy continued, pushing his eyebrows together to show his more serious side.

Marla shrugged her shoulders and I did the same. "No, not really," my sister responded. I simply shook my head. We really didn't care. Other than the exciting scandal it would cause in the community and the fact that we couldn't wait to tell Mamaw, we didn't give two shits about who temporarily sat across from our ice cream table. Once Daddy realized we had become aloof regarding his love life and who was in it, he moved onto topics that *did* interest us.

"I was hoping that this weekend we could go to the park and ride our bikes on the trails," Daddy said, looking at Truvy. She smiled back at him.

"You know Truvy is quite a bicyclist. She's been all over the Appalachian Trail and back again, isn't that right?" he asked her.

"Yes, yes I have," Truvy nodded.

"And we got you both new bikes," Daddy's voice boomed. He couldn't wait to get to the details. "While you two were watching Star Trek ..."

"Star Wars," I corrected him.

"Well, *anyway*," he continued, pretending to be frustrated that I had interrupted his good news.

"Me and Truvy bought you guys some new trail bikes. They're waiting for you at home."

Marla and I looked at one another and smiled.

"What color are they?" My sister's constant concern over style was always amusing.

"Your bike is purple and Dancy's is pink," Daddy said, pointing to each of us as he named the colors of our bikes.

Whatever happened between Brother Silver and Truvy was no fault of mine and somewhere between the words "new, trail, and bike" I had stopped feeling sorry for the good reverend all together.

The smell of Bev's Ivory Soap had followed me into the car and even all the way to our favorite Kay's Ice Cream booth. Or, at least that's what I thought at first. Then, I realized it was Truvy—the soap smell was Truvy. A pleasant smile ran across Truvy's face once more when she caught me staring at her. She gave me a quick wink.

I was suddenly reminded of Mamaw's constant explanation for anything I couldn't understand, "The Lord works in mysterious ways, Dancy."

CHAPTER FOUR

Aliens

When I first saw the three of them coming toward us, I thought they looked like various sized figures of Davy Jones. As they got closer I felt even more like I was watching a Saturday morning episode of *The Monkees*. One wore glasses; he was the oldest. He was taller than the other two and his bike a bit bigger. Their pasty faces were visible now, egg-shapes forcibly protruding through what looked like brown helmets made of hair. The oldest had very dark brown hair. The middle one had more of a chestnut brown and the youngest was a bit blond.

Marla and I stood straddling our bikes as we watched them approach. I began to quietly sing the intro to *The Monkees* TV show.

"Hey, hey we're the Monkees, and people say we monkey around ..."

"Shut up, Dancy," Marla barked as she fisted me in the shoulder.

"Ow, you jerk," I said, hitting her back but not quite as hard.

I knew better than to really hit Marla hard. I never let her know it, but I always knew if she ever tore into me, she could give me quite a bashing. We argued all the time but rarely fought. In the few instances when we did end up in a shoving match, somehow we'd always make sure Daddy was close by to break us up. Deep down we knew better than to throw more than a few licks at each other, and we wanted to make sure our father was there to stop us before things got out of hand.

"Daddy wants us to help these kids get used to it here," Marla scolded me for making fun of them.

"Okay," I said, throwing my hand up near her face to make my point. Then I began singing again right where I had left off, "... but we're too busy singin'."

Marla hit me again.

"Ow," I said. "Stop that." I smacked her thigh then sang louder, "... we're just tryin' to be friendly."

Marla shot me a look and kicked my front tire just as the boys simultaneously skidded to a stop in front of us.

"I love that show," the youngest one said, looking at me like I was some sort of an oasis in the middle of the desert.

From the awkward silence that took hold of the moment he might as well have said, "My balls are on fire."

"Yeah, Nathan," his oldest brother said, glaring directly at me as he spoke. "Everybody watches that show, *even* people down here in the South," he continued, making sure to speak more slowly and clearly as he put emphasis on the word "even." His insult was subtle but effective.

I could see Marla out of the corner of my eye. She was taking a deep breath. It was one of those "I told you so" breaths, the kind she puffed out often in response to something I'd said or done.

My face began to get hot, and I could feel the tips of my ears begin to sting. I looked away from the boys and stared up into the mountains. I focused intensely on the evergreens like there was something very important to examine up there. Marla continued the conversation in my mental absence.

"I'm Marla and this is my sister Dancy," she said as she pulled at my arm.

"Oh, yeah. Hi," I said, wishing I was somewhere up in those mountains not having to face those kids after they had just caught me making fun of them.

The oldest one spoke for the rest. "I'm John, this is Brian, and that's Nathan, the one who likes *The Monkees.*"

Marla gave a full, slow nod twice and then smiled but didn't speak. It was like Marla thought they were aliens from another planet and could only understand universal gestures. Just as I expected one of them to say, "Please take us to your leader," the little one peddled up next to me.

"Wanna race?" he asked, as he slung his head back, his golden hair whooshing around his face then landing perfectly back into its helmet shape.

I looked back at Marla and did my best to ask with only a facial expression, "Do I really have to do this?" My sister winced and shrugged a silent answer, "I don't know."

Neither Marla nor I knew what to say to these alien creatures. Not only were they boys, they were Yankees who had invaded our private countryside, and now we were expected to make them feel at home.

For as long as we had lived on Chestnut Lane, there had only been four houses—the Andersons', the Hyders', the Apgars' and of course, the Wilders'. The Andersons, Apgars, and Hyders were old people, and they belonged to us. We had stayed with each of them at least once or twice when Daddy was out of town. At the Hyders' we played Yhatzee and stayed up late, ate Cheetos, and drank Coke. At the Andersons' we played Rook and ate cornbread and milk, and at the Apgars' we mostly just lounged in front of the TV. These old people were *our* old people.

"No, I don't race," I finally answered the little one. He backed his bike up to its original position just next to his brothers.

"What do you mean you don't race," the middle one, who I had suspected of being mute until this very moment, spoke.

"I just don't race," I answered, rolling my eyes and then looking off into the mountains again. I didn't even care if Marla thought I should or shouldn't. I wasn't going to race this little kid.

The aliens, who had up to this point, been careful in their approach and communication with us, had begun to banter back and forth with one another.

"Girls can't ride fast," the youngest one said to his brothers.

"...bikes are too slow," the middle one said.

"It's pink," the oldest one exclaimed pointing at my bike.

I had finished my gaze into the mountains and was focused on the graveled roadway when I felt a pinch on the back of my arm.

"Ouch," I hissed at Marla. "What the hell?"

When I looked at my sister for an answer as to why she had just tried to tear a chunk out of the fleshy part of my arm, I saw it; she was done being nice. The boys continued to buzz among themselves about how girls wouldn't race because there was no way they could win while Marla and I telepathically agreed that, yes, there would be a race today and, yes, we *were* going to win.

"She said she *didn't* race, not that she *couldn't* race," Marla yelled over the alien banter.

The two younger boys looked at the older one like he was a bike-racing prophet of some sort.

John was silent for a moment as he looked up into my mountains then answered, "Sure. Why not?"

"Where do we start from?" Nathan, the chatty one, asked.

"Let's race around the loop," Marla answered quickly.

"Let's go," Brian, the quiet one, spoke for only the second time.

They turned their bikes in the direction of the loop. As I started to follow, Marla pulled at my arm. "Wait a minute," she said quietly. "Let them go on."

"Why?" I demanded. "I want to get up to the loop and get ready."

"I think we can beat them," Marla said, as she slowly pedaled her bike in the direction of the loop.

"Really?" I asked, as I pedaled up beside her to hear her diabolical plan.

"Yeah, I do," she said with a confident grin. "They're city boys—used to riding on pavement."

I looked down the gravel roadway and up toward the loop. As usual, Marla was right. The county trucks had just come the week before and dumped several fresh loads of those awful walnut-sized gravels all over Chestnut Lane and her loop. It always took several weeks of wear before the sharp gravel became manageable for bicycle tires. Ounces of lost flesh and blood out on the lane had taught Marla and me how to carefully navigate new gravel. The aliens didn't stand much of a chance. We didn't have to beat them. We only had to let the gravel take its toll on those milky-white, tender legs. I could see them struggling up ahead of us already.

As we reached the mouth of the loop, Marla shared one last bit of wisdom.

"Go fast, and just let the rocks fly," Marla said, burying a shoe into the gravel just next to her pedal. "Our bikes are new, and our tires are new."

I knew this was good advice. I had followed it before, but it never hurt to be reminded. Strong focus was essential. One stray gravel to the shin could make even the most experienced biker take her eyes off the road, slow to a crawl and lose balance, along with a lot of skin.

Marla and I looked at the boys. The oldest was next to Marla and the other two were next to me, side by side. We collectively made a decision to let John fire the starter pistol, so to speak, since he was the oldest.

"READY, SET, GO!" he yelled.

John was already six or so feet ahead of us while the other two boys were behind. Since John was the obvious contender we stayed focused on him. I watched with pride as my sister passed him, leaving only a breeze that blew his mop top bangs away from his forehead. The pressure was off. I knew Marla was going to beat John.

I could hear wailing in the distance behind me but I dared not take my eyes off the road. Marla was well ahead of John when he kicked the brakes, his bike skidding in the gravel and then crashing. I passed him just as he was picking himself up off the ground and looking at the cuts on his legs.

Marla was already at the finish, holding a hand up over her eyebrows to block the sun as she looked to see how the rest of the race was going. I took one hand off the bars for a moment to wave at her, wobbled a bit, and then grasped them firmly again. I was going to come in second. I didn't even mind. The Wilder girls had triumphed over the aliens. Again, I heard wailing in the distance, and again I stayed focused. Just next to Marla on her bike, I skidded to a stop, gravel flying in every direction.

"...one small step for girls, and one large leap for girl kind." I managed to get the words out as I was panting for breath.

"Hey, we won! We won," I said to Marla, who wasn't listening to me, but looking out over the lane.

As I turned to see what was so interesting, I saw John carrying Nathan, and Brian holding his little brother's shoe.

"Oh my God! What happened?"

"He wrecked his bike," Marla said as she watched the boys carefully trekking across the big gravels. She looked concerned so I followed her lead, placing my hand up over my brow to block the sun for a better view.

"Where are they going?"

"Home, it looks like," Marla said, turning to me.

"Home?" I questioned. "It looks like they're going to the Andersons'."

"Yeah, that's their grandma," Marla said. "Don't you ever listen to anything?"

"Grandma?" I questioned again.

"Remember? Daddy said they were the Andersons' grandchildren?" Marla questioned me in a sarcastic tone.

"No," I responded, shaking my head.

"You're hopeless, Dancy," Marla said as she began walking toward the Andersons' house. "Come on," She called over her shoulder as she followed our victims.

I walked next to Marla trying to remember any conversation about these new boys being the Andersons' grandchildren. I could think of nothing. Maybe Marla was right, I hadn't been listening.

We watched as the boys reached the house and a middle-aged man emerged from the front door. The man took Nathan from John and sat him down in the porch swing. As we got closer I could see that Nathan's foot was swollen and blue.

"Go get my wallet," the man said to Brian in a loud voice.

John ran inside the house. When he came out, a lady was with him.

"Oh my good graciousness," she said as she looked at Nathan's foot. Then she began to cry.

"I told you we shouldn't have come here!" she yelled at the man.

"Now is not the time!" the man shouted back at her. "John, take your mother into the house. I'm taking Nathan to the hospital."

By now, Marla and I were on the porch watching with Brian as Nathan was being lifted out of the porch swing and taken to an awaiting car. John, who was followed closely by his mother, got into the back seat. As the car sped out of the driveway, Brian raised a hand toward his family and started to speak, but then in slow motion lowered his arm and said nothing.

"You want to come in?" Brian asked.

It seemed weird that *he* would be inviting *us* into Mrs. Anderson's house.

"Okay," Marla said as we followed him through the front door.

The familiar smell of musty quilts and pinto beans on the stove made me relax. I could hear Mrs. Anderson humming to the radio in the kitchen, her soprano way off key as usual.

"Well, hello young ladies," Mrs. Anderson said when she saw Marla and me. "My how you've grown," she said, absurdly emphasizing the last word.

"Yeah, we haven't seen you in a while," Marla said as Mrs. Anderson hugged us up together.

"I see you met my grand young'uns," she said, smiling at Brian and patting his head.

Almost instantly, Marla and I found ourselves seated around the kitchen table with Brian's grandmother pouring three glasses of milk. She then placed a dinner plate covered with dry, cracked shortbread in front of us. Mrs. Anderson smiled and nodded her head toward the plate. "Go on," she said.

We each took a cookie, and as I carefully guided mine across the table, most of it crumbled onto the surface. I looked over at Brian; his cookie had crumbled as well. Marla seemed to be having better luck by using two hands, one to hold the cookie and the other to catch the crumbs.

"My son and his family are building a house out back here," Mrs. Anderson pulled back a flowery set of kitchen curtains to reveal the beginnings of a foundation and stack of trusses.

I looked over at Marla. She was eating her cookie bit by bit. "Yeah, Daddy told us they were moving here," Marla said between bites.

I furrowed my brow and looked at Marla like she had suddenly grown two heads.

"Daddy told us," she whispered loudly at me.

"My sister never listens," Marla said to the old woman.

"Oh, never mind that," Mrs. Anderson said, tapping Marla on the arm. "We all know *now*, don't we?"

Mrs. Anderson was talented at mediation. She had exercised this gift at least a couple of times before on me and Marla. She knew how to extinguish a spark that, if given some fuel, could turn into a raging fire. Then, she would change the subject quickly so even the instigators never knew what hit them.

"Is Nathan going to be okay?" I asked, suddenly caring for the small alien who had been injured during the bike race.

"Oh laws, yeah, he'll be fine," Mrs. Anderson threw up a hand and gave a quick wave in front of her face. "These boys, I'll tell you what, these boys get into more—shew, I'll tell you what," she went on.

I noticed that Brian's face was getting red as his grandmother glared at him each time she'd say, "these boys." Since Brian was the only boy in the room, Mrs. Anderson was shoveling heaps of blame onto the boy I had deemed the quiet one.

"This is the third trip to the hospital since they've been here."

"How long have they been here?" I asked, wondering at this point if I had been stricken with amnesia. How could I have missed the presence of these aliens along with the building of a new house on Chestnut Lane?

"Been here about three weeks now haven't you, Brian?" his grandmother asked. He nodded, accepting her recollection.

"Who else had to go to the hospital?" Marla asked.

"Well John, the oldest one, decided he was going to make a slide out of those trusses and ended up with a splinter in his behind about the size of a led pencil. Doctor couldn't get it out. It's still there but doc said it'd work its way out."

The quiet one was obviously amused by his older brother's mishap. "I told him not to do it," Brian defended. "I told him he'd get splinters. He did it anyway and he got a splinter, just like I said; a big one, too."

Everyone around the table erupted with laughter, Brian cackled the loudest.

"What was the other hospital trip for?" I asked, still laughing a bit as I imagined John with a huge splinter still stuck in his ass.

"Bees," Mrs. Anderson said. "John found an old hornet's nest in a tree near the edge of the clearing." She motioned out to the back yard and over to the fence line.

I knew the nest she was talking about. It *was* a big one.

"He thought he'd hit it with a stick and watch the bees fly out," Mrs. Anderson said. "Problem was they all flew all over him. He was lucky; only had about a dozen stings."

Marla looked at me; her milk was almost finished. Again, the quiet one spoke, "I told him not to do it, and he wouldn't listen. He told me to go back home, so I did. Next thing I knew he was screaming and running toward the house yelling 'get Mom, get Mom'!"

We laughed again. This seemed to please Brian so much so that he grabbed for another crumbly cookie without even being told by his grandmother to take one.

"How's your mother, girls?" Mrs. Anderson asked, without warning.

My stomach flipped as she said the word, "mother." Immediately, visions of my mom came into focus. I missed her, at times ached for her. As much as I got to see Momma it still was never enough. And even though I loved hearing her voice on the phone when she would call, it made me sad when I heard the dial tone after we hung up.

I looked over at Marla to see if she would answer Mrs. Anderson's question but my sister had stuffed her mouth full of cookie. I was on my own.

"She's fine," I answered. "Calls every Sunday and visits a lot, too. She's fine."

59

"Well that's good," Mrs. Anderson said. "Glad to hear it. Your mother is a fine woman. I've known her for years. We used to do some canning together when we had the garden out in the clearing. Yes, your mother is a fine woman," the old woman repeated herself.

"Girls, are you in there?" Truvy's voice came through the kitchen as soft as a winter blanket. My muscles immediately began to loosen.

"Here," I shouted a little too loudly, but I wanted to make sure she heard me.

"Come on in here," Mrs. Anderson said to Truvy.

"Hello, I'm Truvy, a friend of the girls' father," she said as she extended her hand to Mrs. Anderson.

"Yes, I know who you are," Mrs. Anderson shook Truvy's hand. "The girls came in after there was a bit of an accident out there on those infernal bicycles."

"Oh, are you two okay?" Truvy looked at Marla and then me, scanning us for injuries.

"The girls are fine," Mrs. Anderson answered before we could. "Those grandboys of mine—I don't think they've ever been allowed to play outside before," she quipped. "They're gonna have to toughen up a bit if they're going to make it here in Tennessee country," Mrs. Anderson said as she pinched Brian on the arm.

He flinched and grunted.

"See what I mean—soft as a marshmallow," his grandmother said.

"I'm sure they'll be fine. Everett's girls seem to do okay out here," Truvy smiled, as she stepped behind my chair. She squeezed my shoulders a bit and kissed the top of my head. I could smell her scent, clean and fresh.

"Are you girls ready to go?" Truvy asked. "Your father sent me over to check on you and bring you back home."

"Yeah, we're ready," Marla answered for us both.

"Let me walk you out," Mrs. Anderson said. "I want to show you how the house is going up."

"Everett said it was going to be a nice one," Truvy said as she followed Mrs. Anderson out the door.

Truvy was always polite. She never had an ill word to say about anyone, at least that's what Mamaw said about her after she had gotten over the shock of her son stealing the local preacher's wife.

"That boy of mine. I swear," Mamaw had said, shaking her head.

Marla and I were all too anxious to tell Mamaw all about Daddy's new interest. I then felt a little sorry for my father after I heard the lecture he got about treating women like toilet paper.

"You just think you can wipe your ass all over them and then flush 'em away," Mamaw had said. "This one's different," Mamaw said, referring to Truvy. "She's got a family, Everett."

I watched Truvy and Mrs. Anderson walk ahead of Marla and me and smiled as I imagined my father trying to literally wipe his ass on Truvy. Mrs. Anderson's head was bobbing quickly as she rambled on about the new house, her grandboys, and their shenanigans.

Truvy listened politely as she and Mrs. Anderson continued walking over to where the new foundation had been poured. Mrs. Anderson told Truvy about how Roy, her oldest son, had lost his factory job in Hobso, Indiana. Roy and his wife had to sell their home and move to Rayes County, so he could work at the railroad.

61

Mrs. Anderson said her grandboys would be starting school at the Rayes County School District in the fall.

"They'll be going to go to our school?" I asked as Marla and I ran up in front of Truvy and Mrs. Anderson.

"Yes, that's right," Mrs. Anderson said. "We were hoping you and Marla would take care of showing them around when school starts back next fall."

I thought about *The Monkees* going to our school with their mop tops, paisley shirts, tight pants and thick Yankee talk. *They're going to be pulverized.*

I felt Truvy squeeze my arm. I looked up at her. She was smiling at me, and I suddenly felt the urge to say the right thing.

"Sure we'll show them around," I said before consulting with Marla. She looked at me behind Truvy's back. I winced and shrugged at her.

"I don't think me and Dancy ever knew you had grandsons," Marla said to Mrs. Anderson.

"Well I was sure you did, Marla," Mrs. Anderson said. "I could swear I've shown you their pictures."

"You did, Mrs. Anderson, but I guess that's where Dancy and I got confused. We thought those pictures were of your granddaughters," Marla smiled big and then punched me in the arm to make sure I got the joke.

"No. You and Dancy are about the closest thing I have to granddaughters," Mrs. Anderson said, either not understanding Marla's insult or just plain ignoring it.

"Girls," Truvy reprimanded us in a whisper. She squeezed the backs of our arms tightly to gain some control over our mouths and then skillfully managed to change the subject.

"This is such a beautiful place to build a home," Truvy said, as she walked across the newly-formed foundation.

I saw the wooded edge of the clearing, and our house was nowhere in sight, obscured by the tall Star of Bethlehem trees that grew there.

"You can't see this from our house," I blurted out, realizing that's why I never knew it was there.

I looked over at Marla, who was rolling her eyes at my sudden epiphany.

Mrs. Anderson gave us the grand tour of the would-be home, room by room.

"This is my room," Brian said as he jumped up and down on a clump of grass. "Come on in here and see my room."

Truvy pointed us in the direction of Brian's soon-to-be room. She and Mrs. Anderson followed close behind us.

"Why are they building around all these old trees?" Truvy asked. "If it were me I'd have picked that spot over there where there aren't any trees; then you could plant some dogwoods, Bradford pear trees, and redbuds—blooming trees, trees with flowers. Here, there's too much shade to grow much of anything."

I was much more interested in what Truvy had to say than I was in Brian's yet-to-be room. Besides, it was too small, much smaller in comparison to the oldest boy's room. Maybe the quiet one didn't need much square footage.

Mrs. Anderson looked around the lot at the landscape and up at the tall trees that Truvy was referring to. We all followed the old woman's eyes as she inspected the vegetation next to the foundation.

"Well, I guess you *could* build somewhere sparse and put in all new trees; they'd be pretty in blooms all year round and in the spring for sure," Mrs. Anderson said. "But you know there's just something about a tall oak tree, a sturdy sassafras, and a loyal maple," she continued as she pulled at a purple leaf she had picked off one of the branches. "These trees have put in a lot of time in this earth. They have a history of sorts with this family. It's like they know us. Roy got his first sprained ankle when he jumped off of that lowest branch," she said, pointing to the sassafras. "There's more beauty in that memory than there is in a bunch of spring blooms. And, heck, if it's blooms you want, plant some flowers, dear."

Truvy looked up into the tree as Mrs. Anderson spoke. It was like she could see Brian's dad up there sitting in the crook of the branches.

"I guess there *is* beauty in that," Truvy finally spoke. "C'mon girls, your dad's expecting you home."

Truvy was quiet as we gathered our bikes. We walked with her and rolled them alongside all the way home.

"I don't like those boys," I said, trying to break the silence.

"Me neither," Marla said.

"They're stupid," I added.

Truvy emerged from her deep thoughts with a chuckle.

"Girls, now girls," she shamed us. "Boys are just different. They only care about right now, not what's going to happen. That's probably why they get hurt so often—no thoughts about the consequences of their actions. That's why they need good mothers to tell them what's going to happen even before it does."

I had unintentionally reminded Truvy of her boys. I was sure they missed her as much as I missed Momma. Marla thought I never listened to anything, but I had heard Daddy and Truvy talk about her family. Truvy's boys were mad at her for leaving, and they had told their father that they didn't want to see their mother any longer. I couldn't imagine what kind of children wouldn't want to see their mother, especially Truvy— sweet Ivory Soap Truvy.

"We won, Dancy," Marla shouted like it had just occurred to her.

"Yeah, I know. It was great," I said as I led my bike a little faster. "That'll teach them to make fun of us again."

"Yeah," Marla said. "Especially now that we know about John's ass splinter."

"Marla!" Truvy snapped at her.

"Oops, sorry. I meant butt splinter," Marla apologized but then got my attention and pointed at her own butt and laughed.

"I must have missed that story," Truvy said. "You girls need to be careful playing around with those boys. They sound pretty rough. You might get hurt."

"Hah! That's freakin' hilarious," Marla said. "Those boys are as soft as marshmallows. Even their grandmother said so."

I laughed. "It's true, Truvy," I defended my sister's insult. "Those boys are really, really girly."

"Hmm," Truvy thought for a moment and said, "Maybe when my boys come over next week the Anderson boys can play with them and give you girls a break."

"What?" I asked in surprise. "Your boys are coming over?"

I looked at Marla for answers. She had none. She shrugged her shoulders. Truvy looked straight ahead.

"Yes, Joseph and Joshua are coming to visit us next week. I'm very excited to see them," Truvy said, looking at Marla and then me. "I hope you girls will treat them nice. They've been through a lot lately."

Great, more aliens.

CHAPTER FIVE

Hot Thing Wilder

"Breaker, breaker, one nine, this is Hot Ginger looking for the Pony Express. You out there tonight, Pony?"

Marla and I looked at each other and rolled our eyes at the same time. The voice coming through the CB speakers was as soft as Georgia cotton and just as southern. She spoke in breathy tones like someone who had just been awakened. She reminded me of the receptionist at the doctor's office. Heck, maybe it *was* the receptionist at the doctor's office. But I had seen *her* wedding band. It was hard to miss, at least an inch wide with a scatter of diamonds the size of a penny perched right on top. Hopefully, it had caught Daddy's eye, too.

We were sure he'd learned his lesson about messin' around with married women after what happened with Truvy. I remembered the day her husband came to move her out of our house. Daddy tried to act like it was some mutually agreed upon decision. Marla and I knew better and so did Mamaw. Our grandmother had asked Daddy right in front of us how it felt to have a woman wipe her ass on him and then flush him away.

It was the same night we had steak on the grill. Daddy pulled *Hot Thing Wilder* out of the storage building even as Truvy, her husband, and boys were backing out of the driveway with the last of her things. I remembered touching the pink triangle-shaped scar on my leg as I always did when the black monster's flame was torched.

Hot Thing's wheels screeched under its heavy weight as Daddy scooted the grill across the patio. He was determined to get it as close to the house as possible, directly under the eaves. He said it might rain and he didn't want the bad weather to spoil our cookout.

I had looked up into the sky for any sign of a cloud more than cumulus. There were none.

Finally, it came to rest just beside the back door wedged perfectly against the back of the house. *Hot Thing Wilder* was born in our barn during the summer when Daddy taught me and Marla how to weld.

It had been two years since our father torched the original steel drum open with an even cut all the way around. Marla and I had used files to wear down the jagged edges afterward while Daddy fashioned the hinges.

We put on our dark goggles and watched as Daddy laid down the first row of beads. Watching the rod melt into the steel reminded me of the piping on the display wedding cakes at Teaster's Bakery downtown.

"Girls, try not to look directly at the flame, it'll burn your retinas," Daddy's voice was muffled through the cylindrical-shaped helmet. "You can see what I'm doing by using your peripheral vision. Just don't look directly at the flame."

Telling me not to look directly at the flame was like telling our dog, Cricket, not to chase the chickens at the Apgar farm next door. He'd act like he was looking away while you were scolding him but the least sign that you were turning to walk away and his neck would snap in the direction of the cackling every time.

The more I tried not to look directly at the flame, the more my eyes were drawn toward it.

"Are you girls using your peripheral vision to watch?" he had asked.

"Yes, Daddy," I had answered. I didn't want him to make me go inside. I wanted to weld.

I kept glancing at Marla to see if she was looking directly at the flame. Her goggles were too dark and I couldn't even see her eyes but, like me, I knew she was practically salivating at the thoughts of getting her hands on that torch.

"You're probably going to get to go first," I yelled at Marla over the sound of the welder's motor. She looked at me and mouthed the word, "What?"

"You're older. You're going to get to go first," I yelled again, and again she couldn't hear me.

"Girls, pay attention if you want to learn something," Daddy yelled at both of us.

One again, Marla focused on the rod as it melted seamlessly into the metal.

"Now," Daddy said as he released the torch trigger and rose from his crouch near the ground. "The first leg is almost done and only three more to go," he announced proudly as he raised the hinged helmet from his face.

"What should we call it?" he asked, with a furrowed brow. I knew he wanted to get the name just right. There would be no stupid pet names for this creation. This was serious.

I looked at Marla, her goggles were now perched on her forehead, her bangs tangled through the nosepiece. I threw my hand up over my mouth to stop a burst of laughter but then noticed she was about to do the same. We looked equally ridiculous in those things.

Daddy had wiped his face with the back of his hand so as not to get the black metal residue on him. He had failed miserably several times from the looks of the streaks along his cheeks, black marks over his eye, one on his forehead, and one on his neck.

Marla and I both wore our own fingerprints on our pants and various parts of our skin.

"I know!" Marla blurted out her idea. "Let's name it Wilder Grill."

I waited for Daddy to respond before giving or withholding my personal stamp of approval.

"Well, that's a good one," Daddy said, rubbing his chin and marking his face with black soot even more. "But I don't know. We'll take half that idea and call it Wilder something, but Wilder what?" He looked up into the barn loft as he thought, like an idea was laying up there just out of his grasp.

Still, I said nothing. I looked to Marla to see if she had any more suggestions. She shrugged her shoulders.

"I know what," the words exploded from my mouth even before I knew what I was going to say. Suddenly, I had Daddy and Marla's undivided attention. "The Wilder Warmer," I hesitated and then said with the utmost confidence. Daddy and Marla both nodded slowly, trying to convince themselves it was the greatest grill name they'd ever heard.

"Maybe, we're on the right track. Wilder, warmer, hotter . YES," Daddy said, smacking the steel drum with the palm of his hand. "Wilder Hotter," he exclaimed.

Marla and I cackled wildly.

"What? What?" It's a good name," Daddy defended.

"It just sounds funny," I said.

"Yeah," Marla agreed. "Sounds funny; the two words don't really go together."

The three of us agreed in disappointing nods.

"Something will come to us," Daddy said, accepting the setback.

Marla and I gulped while taking turns drinking water from the thermos.

"Who's next?" Daddy's asked as he took the thermos from my hand and started to drink. "What about you, Dancy?"

"Me?" I questioned, looking over at Marla, who was not only puzzled, but pissed off at the same time.

I smiled sweetly at her, "Sure, I'm ready."

Daddy had wasted no time placing the helmet on my head. It was wet with sweat and smelled of burnt metal. He flipped the hinged safety glass out so I could see and then knocked on the helmet, "You all right in there?"

"Yeah," I answered with nervous laughter.

"All right then," Daddy flipped the dark glass back down and directed me over the first leg of the grill where he'd been working. "Goggles, Marla," I heard him say. Although I could not see him, I was sure he made the motion for my sister to take the goggles off her head and put them on her eyes.

I had been playing with the starter all day even though Daddy had told me not to, but now with it in my hand and the gas ready to light, I couldn't make it strike. *Scrape, scrape*, the flinted metal sounded but my grip was too loose and my striking action too slow to make a spark.

"I don't think so," Daddy said, taking the torch and striker from my hands. "I'll light it and hand it to you. Then I'll hold the rod, and you maneuver the torch."

That made me a lot less nervous, knowing I'd be able to grasp the torch with both hands.

The hissing sound of the torch and the fact that I could now see through the dark glass meant it was lit, and I needed to be ready.

I could hear myself breathing in loud, whispery throngs like Darth Vader. I formed my mouth into an oval shape and made the sound even more pronounced.

"You ready?" I heard my father's muffled voice through the helmet.

I tried to nod my head but the weight of the helmet forced my whole body to move back and forth.

"Okay, here you go," Daddy said as I watched the flaming torch enter my hands. "Hold it tight."

I knew exactly what to do as he laid the rod in the center of the two pieces that would soon become one once my "light saber" melted them together.

"Okay now, hold the rod with your left hand and keep the torch with your right hand," Daddy said sliding the rod into the oversized leather glove on my left hand. I grasped it firmly, placing it in the seam where Daddy had left off. Before I knew it, the rod was completely gone and the first leg was securely attached. My father placed his large gloved hand over my hand and the torch trigger. "Let go now," he said.

As the flame disappeared I threw off the helmet to inspect my work further. I blew on the row of beads I had set down just as I had seen Daddy do before.

"Looks pretty good," I said, turning to Marla who was still a little pissed off that she did not go first. Still, she was curious enough to show some interest in my work.

"I guess," she said, folding her arms.

Daddy towered over her to inspect my work.

"Not too bad, Dancy," he said.

I gave Marla a sour look.

"Now, for the second leg of the Wilder creation," Daddy said, as he readied Marla to lay down the next set of beads.

I laughed when I saw her doddle under the weight of the helmet.

"Dancy, goggles," Daddy voice boomed at me.

I put my goggles down over my eyes and watched as Marla placed the next row of beads along the second leg. I inched closer and closer to her, as the flame drew me in.

"SON OF A FUCKING BITCH!"

A red, hot piece of shrapnel had penetrated my jeans and my thigh was on fire. Daddy smacked at the shard. I could see my blackened and bloody skin under the new hole in my pants. It burned like a thousand needles sticking in my bones.

"Hold on there, Dancy," Daddy said as I swayed dizzily and then vomited onto the slab of plywood beneath us. I didn't remember much after that.

When I finally opened my eyes again, I could see an orange sun setting just behind the big oak. I lifted the blanket, pulling it aside to look at my leg, now bandaged. I flexed my thigh muscle,

"Ouch," I squished the word through my teeth. Yes, it had actually happened. A red-hot piece of metal had burned a hole in my leg.

"Son of a bitch," I said as I swung my legs around and touched my feet to the floor. I turned on the lamp and looked at my reflection in the TV glass. I could barely hear Marla laughing in the distance. As I opened the screened door, Daddy and Marla were in full view.

"There she is," Daddy said as I limped down the three steps to the patio. "Feeling better?"

"Yeah, what happened?" I asked, still half asleep.

"Hot Thing Wilder shot you in the leg," Daddy pointed in the direction of the barn where the one-legged black monster still lay.

I looked toward the barn and then back at Daddy. "I know that," I said rolling my eyes at him. "I mean after that?"

"You fainted," Marla offered between slurps of her watermelon. "Cold out," she said, slurping again.

"How long have you guys been out here?" I asked, looking at Marla's lap full of spat out seeds.

"We came out a while ago," Daddy said. "Didn't want to wake you."

Marla continued slurping. Daddy patted the seat on the lawn chair next to him, then gulped his beer.

"Care for a swig?"

"No," I furrowed my brow and wrinkled my nose in disgust. I hated beer, the smell of it, the color of the can.

"You sure?" my father asked again and then grinned. "I figured anyone who could cuss like you would be able to handle a can of PBR," Daddy said, taking another gulp.

I instantly remembered the string of profanity that came from my mouth the moment the shard had penetrated my blue jeans and then my skin. I instinctively touched the bandage on my leg.

"Oh, I know," Daddy said, looking at the bandage. "I'm going to let this one slide, Dancy. But my God, girl, what makes you think it's okay to talk like that?"

"I dunno," I squeaked my answer. "I'm sorry."

Daddy's blue eyes locked onto mine. "I hope you *are* sorry," he said. "If your grandmother ever heard that, I'd be in a shit load of trouble. See you watch your mouth from now on, Dancy."

"I will, Daddy," I said, my face getting hot and my eyes filling with warm tears.

"Oh now, come on," Daddy said. "Get you a piece of watermelon." My father got up to cut a slice for me.

"We named the grill," Marla said. She had knocked the seeds in her lap off into the grass and took her rind to the garden. "While you were passed out Daddy said, 'that thing was hot' and I started laughing. That's when Daddy decided to call it *Hot Thing Wilder*."

Hot Thing Wilder had been retired since Truvy moved in because the smell of charcoal had triggered her migraines. That meant that there had been no outside barbecues while she at stayed at our house. That was all about to change.

After coating the bricks with starter fluid Daddy struck the match on the side of the grill and threw it in the fire. The explosion of heat and flames that soon overtook the smell of Ivory soap that Truvy had left lingering around everything she touched left no doubt in my mind that her departure was not temporary. Even inside the house, the smell of charcoal and steaks consumed the last of her presence.

Surely after all that, we were done with married women, and if the woman on the other end of that squawk box actually *was* the receptionist at the doctor's office I was certain Daddy would quickly move onto his next conquest.

"Pony, this is Hot Ginger, you out there?" the voice came across again.

Daddy seemed to be counting in his head, nodding swiftly in short movements.

"I don't want it to look like I'm just waiting for her out here," he said, as he turned to explain himself to us. Again, Marla and I looked at each other and rolled our eyes.

We had been sitting in the back seat of the Gran Torino almost every night since Daddy had come home with that box.

"You know what this is?" our father had asked us as he cleared the kitchen table with one swipe of an arm. "A Citizen's Band radio," he answered before we could even respond, placing the box on the table. There we could view it more clearly under the dining room light.

I recalled taking one step back and wrinkling my forehead while Marla began helping him unpack the components of what would become one of the most necessary pieces of equipment inside or outside the Wilder home, even more so than our new riding mower, or our beloved toaster oven that Marla and I used mostly for frozen pot pies and pizza after school.

Night after night Daddy would mosey out to the car under the pretense that he was checking something under the hood, the oil, the transmission fluid, or the hoses. Marla and I were never far behind. Once our homework was done we'd head out to the driveway and see him through the front windshield, holding the mic close to his mouth. When Daddy would see us and then realize we were close enough to hear the static and feedback, he would motion for us to come on in and sit with him.

"There's the Little Princess and my Golden Girl," he'd say.

Those were our handles. I was the Little Princess and Marla was the Golden Girl. Even in a world that only existed on the airwaves, a world where anyone could become anyone else just by renaming themselves and talking to strangers, I was perceived as a child. Yes, choosing just the right handle was crucial in the remaking of oneself on the CB radio and even I knew the Little Princess was just not very cool. The Pony Express had purpose and meaning and the Golden Girl had a nice ring to it. But when Daddy asked us to think of a handle we wanted, I drew a blank. I got stage fright. I couldn't think of anything at all, especially not anything clever. So a handle was chosen for me.

"Breaker one nine, this is the Pony Express out here," Daddy said. "I've got my two best gals on the air, and one of them needs a handle."

"Put her on there, Pony. This is Cabin Fever."

Daddy handed the mic to me. "Now, squeeze this button when you're ready to talk," he held the mic out so I could see the button clearly. "Now, go on. Don't be afraid."

"Hello," I said squeaked. "This is the Pony Express's daughter."

"Well you sound just like a Little Princess," Cabin Fever said. "Come on back now, Pony Express. You hear?"

Daddy and Marla excitedly accepted my new persona although I was a bit reluctant at first. "It just sounds like such a baby name," was my argument. But my stage fright continued, and I wasn't able to think of anything better, so I became the Little Princess among Daddy's new CB radio friends.

Hot Ginger continued to call for Daddy over the box. Marla and I watched as he looked at himself in the rearview mirror, adjusting some of the loose strands just over his newly receding hairline.

"This is your Pony coming back at ya, Hot Ginger," Daddy finally squeezed the trigger on the mic.

CHAPTER SIX

Hot Ginger and Other Spicy Things

I couldn't help but laugh when I saw Marla standing there shrouded in fur.

"Shut up, Dancy," she scolded. "Come over here and look." She pointed to the mirror.

I bumped Marla's shoulder as I nudged her out of my way. She smirked as she gave me her trademark "see, I told you so" look. The three-way mirror caught every angle. From collar bone to knee bone, we were covered in fur, gray, white, tan, brown...

"It's rabbit, girls." Hot Ginger had fallen in behind us. She closed her eyes in ecstasy and we watched as her hands disappeared into the lapels of her jacket. "It's luxurious, isn't it?" she asked.

Marla and I nodded at the same time.

"We'll take three of these, Dahling" Hot Ginger said to no one, because no one else was there. She batted her eyelashes and rubbed the back of her hand back and forth over the coat.

"Doesn't it just make you feel like Eva Gabor?" she asked, looking over our heads.

I thought of Lisa on *Green Acres* and imagined if I wore these things back to our house, I'd look as much misplaced as she did entering Sam Drucker's store wearing Princess Lace and pink fur. It wasn't like we were in Bloomingdale's in the Big Apple. We were simply at the mall inside Nickelson's Department Store. Still, it was a far cry from the Big K where a shopping cart filled with soap powder and toilet paper could also include a fancy new coat, albeit not rabbit fur.

Marla grinned, and I saw the muscles in her neck moving as she tried to stifle a laugh.

"I think they're neat," I finally said.

"Really?" Hot Ginger asked. "You don't think they're too much?" she said as she twisted from side to side admiring the fur again.

"No, I like them too," Marla finally spoke.

"Oh, you girls. I just don't know what I ever did without you," Hot Ginger said, hugging us up from behind. We looked like three heads poking out of the same large mound of fur— like we were being birthed from a giant hare having triplets.

As much as we liked to make fun of Hot Ginger, we did like the things she bought for us. They were never things we could wear to school, or even to the skating rink, but they sure were glamorous and fabulous. Never before had Marla and I been exposed to so much sequins, satin, and gold-threaded polyester.

Linda, who was known across the main CB channels as Hot Ginger, had most recently set about filling mine and Marla's closets with the remnants of tiny woodland creatures. We had fur coats, fur purses, fur boots, fur hats, and even fur stoles, but no evening gowns, well, not yet.

Even before we met her for the first time over the CB as Hot Ginger, we knew her. She worked at Dr. Chaney's office. My first memory of her was the day of my tetanus shot. I had stepped on a rusty piece of metal from an old can when we were cleaning out the chicken coops. Mean Ass Marla, as I began to call her after that day, told me the doctor was going to give me fifty shots in my belly. I was so scared that my knees were knocking together as I was trying to walk in the door. I saw Hot Ginger there – her long, thick, red hair moving around her white jacket. When she called me back, I started to sob.

"Dancy Wilder," she said as she opened the waiting room door, looking straight at me. Immediately I didn't like her very much. As usual, Marla had lied to me. There were no shots in my belly, only one in my ass but still, it hurt like a mother.

After that day, I finally took my father's advice and started taking the time to put on my shoes. I also tried my best never to believe any more of Marla's lies. I knew this pact that I was making with my own psyche was one that I could never keep. Marla was too good at making up believable stories; in fact, she could be incredibly convincing. I never understood why she did it unless it was just for fun. My sister's stories were never lies that did anybody any good, not even her. They just kept me in constant emotional turmoil and sometimes got her a good slap on the ass if Daddy caught her in one, or if I decided to tell on her.

When I first discovered that Hot Ginger from the CB was also Linda at Dr. Chaney's office, I wasn't too happy about my father's new love interest. But the newly-divorced Ginger's genius contribution to the Wilder CB family persona, specifically my handle, made me like her a little more.

"Little Princess?" Ginger had questioned my CB handle with both shock and displeasure, which beat the hell out of my reaction of total complacency on the night I was dubbed a princess with no crown as I sat in the back seat of the Gran Torino. "Well that just doesn't suit you at all," Ginger had contemplated while wrinkling her nose like something stank rotten. "Let me think, let me think.," she poked a long, red fingernail into her chin. "I've got it," her eyes twinkled. "How would you like to be called Peppermint Pattie?"

I liked it. I really, really liked it. It wasn't as grown up as Marla's Golden Girl but it was a hell of a lot more admirable than The Little Princess. Grateful to Hot Ginger for my new CB handle, I made a cautious deal with myself that I'd let her get a little closer to the young Wilder approval committee of two. Marla had agreed with a pinch to my thigh and a quick nod of the head.

A couple of months and a few furry items later, Marla and I were once again at Ginger's favorite place, doing her favorite thing—shopping.

"Now you girls go on out to that bench right there and wait for me."

Ginger pointed out to the mall corridor.

"I'll get these things and meet you out there," she said, taking our new fur coats.

"How about some money for a pretzel?" Marla asked.

"Yeah, here you go," Ginger said, handing my sister a five-dollar bill. Marla could always get money out of anyone. She would just ask, like she just expected that the person would comply. I, on the other hand, was a little more subtle. We had passed those pretzels at least four times. With each pass I'd make sure that Ginger was within earshot and then I'd throw out, "Boy, those pretzels sure do smell good," or "Wonder if that cheese is hot?" None of these passive observations had gotten me anywhere, or they at least hadn't gotten me a pretzel.

I knew Marla wanted one too but she had remained silent, letting me do all the heavy lifting for her as usual. That is until she blurted out her pretzel demand. My sister gave no credence to all the work I had done, wearing Ginger down enough so that Marla's demand was a seamless transition to getting money for the pretzels. Marla pranced around in front of me, her chest out and chin high. The five-dollar bill curled with the wind from her quick steps. I knew I had been an instrumental force in getting that five dollar bill. Daddy would have called it laying the groundwork. I'm sure my sister did not, and never would, see it that way.

"I'm glad we don't have to wait in line," I said, looking back into the department store. "Look at it; she'll be in there for at least half an hour."

"Yeah, sure will," Marla said. She was now not more than fifty feet from the pretzel stand.

I looked inside my shopping bag for at least the one hundredth time since leaving Nickelson's. Every time I looked inside that bag I got butterflies. When I thought of all the times I had almost mustered up the courage to get my ears pierced and then backed out, it made me roll my eyes. How stupid I was. It really didn't even hurt all that much. And Ginger pinched my hand at just the moment it happened, which at first really pissed me off until I realized the piercing was over. The first ear was already done and all I felt was Ginger's pinch on the top of my hand. Then, the second one was even easier. I told Ginger to pinch me even harder than before, as hard as she could, so that I wouldn't even feel a tingle in my earlobe. It worked. Ginger was a type of fashion genius, I had decided

It had been a good day; new stuff and now heading for the pretzel stand. It just didn't get any better than this.

Marla's arm hit me in the chest with a thud, stopping my casual stride as we headed to Teeny's Pretzels.

"Wait," she said.

I finally tore my eyes from the treasures in my shopping bag to see what was going on. Whatever Marla wanted, it had better be good. In my bag were more pairs of earrings than I had ever seen all together in one place, other than on the jewelry rack at Nickelson's. Now, they were mine. My ears burned a little just like the girl at the piercing counter said they would, but I didn't care. I had a bag full of sparkling jewels to stick in those burning holes, and I was certain that would make the discomfort all better.

"What the hell, Marla?" I pushed her arm off of my chest and shot her a dirty look.

Before I could take another step her arm flew into my ribs.

"Dammit, Marla," I belted out after I caught my breath.

"Wait," Marla half-yelled through gritted teeth. "Look over there," my sister immediately grabbed my face, holding it firmly in her hand so I wouldn't fling my head around to see what she was talking about. "But not right now," she whispered and then nodded in the direction of the adjacent corridor.

"Ginger," I said her name and then started to run toward her.

Marla grabbed me by my jacket collar and jerked me back.

"Don't you dare go over there, Dancy. I swear to God if you do I'll leave your ass here by yourself."

I stopped when I heard the fear in my sister's voice.

"Don't look over there again and I mean it, Dancy. Don't do it."

"Okay," my voice was low and my lips quivered as I spoke. "What do we do?"

"We have to go the other way," Marla said, pulling me toward the opposite hall. "We'll go get something to eat at the food court and wait."

"Wait to see what happens?" I had finally realized that something big was going on.

Marla nodded. "What's going to happen is they're going to take her."

"Oh," I said, trying not to look back to where I had last seen Ginger.

We walked slowly at first. "We don't want to draw any attention to ourselves," Marla said.

As the smell of the food court got closer I could barely keep up with Marla. With her more than ten steps ahead of me now I couldn't help myself, I had to look back.

Ginger's fur coat was on the floor and her purse was lying next to it, with the contents spilled out on the tile. She sat on a nearby bench with her head in her cuffed hands. One of the officers pulled items from her shopping bags one at a time, while the other wrote on a notepad. Ginger looked down the corridor right into my eyes. Her face spoke to me. It was like she was trying to say, "Go on, Dancy. I'll be fine."

Only moments before, I, we had been on top of the world; all my new treasures, my shiny jewelry, the new holes in my ears. The girls at school would be so jealous.

I could feel Marla's hot breath on the back of my head now.

"What the hell are you doing?" She grabbed my shoulder and turned me around.

"I should turn these in," I said, holding my bag out to her.

"Dammit, Dancy. No, no, no." Marla took my bag, wadded it up and put it in her own bag. "Get your ass to the food court."

I saw Marla's eyes lock onto Ginger's but only for a second. My sister immediately and purposefully looked away, grabbed my arm and didn't let go until we had our burgers and fries and were seated so we could watch the action but not be seen.

"I think they're leaving now," Marla said. "God, that took long enough. I thought they were going to set up camp there."

I stuffed my mouth with French fries, knowing that Marla would have a lot to say about the arrest.

"You know, I knew something was wrong with that woman," Marla said and then sucked on her straw. "Nobody shops like that. I mean nobody. Mamaw said it seemed like she was crazy over spending money or something. She said that's all Ginger talked about, all the time."

I waited for Marla to get her mouth full before I spoke.

"What did Ginger steal? They took *all* her bags. She didn't steal *everything* did she?"

The mustard on the corners of Marla's mouth didn't seem to discredit my perception of my sister as an expert at law enforcement and all matters criminal.

"Well, that's what it looked like to me," Marla said, looking down at the empty corridor. "Daddy's gonna be so pissed."

"Why will he be mad?" I was confused.

"Not at us, dumbass, at Ginger," Marla said and then finished the last bite of her burger. "What a crazy bitch."

It occurred to me that Daddy wasn't off work for another four hours. We had no ride home and had just spent the only five dollars we had on burgers and fries.

I could see Marla's eyes darting around the food court. I knew she was looking for an answer to the question that I had just asked myself. I followed her eyes so I could see what she saw, if she happened to see anything at all, which she evidently didn't.

We had never been alone inside the mall alone before. I had always wished that Daddy would drop us off there like some of the other parents did, so that Marla and I could shop without having him follow us around. It always made me feel like such a little baby, seeing him outside the store, sitting on the bench, his eagle eyes locked on us through the store windows. Empty benches split the corridors from one end of the mall to the other. God, right now I would've given anything to have seen him sitting out there waiting for us.

I looked at Marla, she started to speak, but nothing came out so I offered my advice.

"Well, if we have to, we can just sit here until Daddy gets off work and then call him to come get us."

"Yeah," Marla agreed, biting her bottom lip contemplating my plan, which was the obvious thing to do.

"Or we could walk home," Marla finished the sentence abruptly.

"What the hell? Walk home? It's a long way from here," I half yelled. My confidence in Marla's decision-making was fading quickly. "What's wrong with you? Daddy would kill us."

"What other choice do we have, Dancy? Your idea doesn't sound so hot to me." Marla was trying her best to be a smartass, but her fear was showing. This was my chance to talk her down.

"We could call Mamaw," I carefully offered.

"Dancy, she has to run the restaurant. And besides, Daddy would kill us if we called her. I think they had a fight."

She was right, and I knew it. Daddy *would* kill us if we called Mamaw. She wasn't happy about Daddy's new relationship with Ginger, and this would just make things worse, especially if she ever found out that Ginger had been shoplifting. Mamaw was always saying how she could stand anything but a liar and a thief, "... a drug addict, an alcoholic, a smartass, anything but a thief and a liar," Mamaw would say.

"Well, instead of calling Daddy right now, we could wait here and then call him when he gets home from work," I pleaded with my sister to change her mind.

"Dancy, it's like this, I don't want Daddy to know that we were out shoplifting all day, do you?"

I touched my earlobes with the new pegs sticking out of them. They were hot and swollen now and stung as I squeezed them. We hadn't shoplifted anything, and I knew it. But Marla was carrying the evidence of an entire morning worth of loot. It was like everyone knew what we had done. I felt dozens of eyes on us as shoppers walked by our table. Our guilt-ridden faces were nothing compared to my bulging, throbbing earlobes beckoning to anyone who would listen, *Come and see our new ear bobs; they're in the bag; we stole them.* I quickly put my hands over my ears and my eyes were hot with tears.

"What the hell is wrong with you?"

"My ears hurt, dammit!"

"Great, just fucking great," Marla rolled her eyes at me and sighed.

"Can't we just call Momma?" It was my last card, but I had to play it.

Marla stopped sighing, rolling her eyes, moving and even breathing. She glared at me and her chin began to quiver. She looked like someone had just thrown an invisible hot blanket over her head. Her cheeks grew red as she moved her face closer to mine.

"No, Dancy. We cannot call Momma," Marla's voice was low, hollow. Her words carried a sarcastic tone. "What do you want, World War III on your hands?"

My sister was right. Calling Momma *would* cause a war. Momma always said to let her know if we got into trouble and if she wasn't there that Chick would take care of it. This sure seemed like trouble to me and definitely something she or Chick could handle. Chick was my momma's friend and she had been staying at his place for the past year or so. I remembered when I first met him. I thought he and Momma had some sort of a romantic thing going on. Marla and I were appalled at the thought of our mother being interested in a large chunk of ugly flesh like Chick. But once we realized Chick and Momma were just friends, he grew on us quickly. I suspected many of Chick's friendships started in much the same way. My first impression of him was fear, and I remember thinking to myself that I wouldn't want to run into someone like Chick on a dark, foggy night. Then later, after I had gotten to know him, I remember thinking if I were out on a dark and foggy night and I could pick only one person to be my protector, it would definitely be Chick.

"Fine, then you go on. I'm staying right here." I was sure Marla would never leave me there alone. I had hoped my defiance would cause her to see that the only answer was to call Momma or Chick.

"Fine. Suit yourself, dumbass." My sister was calling my bluff.

Just as Marla was getting out of her chair, the cops showed up.

"Hello, girls. I'm officer Jones."

Marla looked at me and quickly sat back down at the table. We both nodded, but neither of us spoke.

"You two wouldn't happen to know a Miss Linda Loomis?"

"No," Marla was quick with an answer.

"Oh, I see," the cop nodded slowly, clicking his tongue. "And what about you," he turned to me and asked. "Do *you* know a Miss Linda Loomis?"

Stricken mute, I said nothing but shook my head slowly, left to right.

He mimicked my motions. "Soooo, that's a no then, young lady?" Officer Jones asked.

Still mute, I nodded. This time, my head went slowly up and down.

"Okay then girls, I'll leave you to it. But if either of you see two young ladies about your age here wandering around aimlessly, let them know that Officer Jones will kindly take them home if they need a ride. It seems there was an incident here a little while ago that left these two girls without transportation."

He rapped his knuckles on the table twice, looked at each of us separately and waited for a confession. When he got none, he clicked his tongue twice just as he did before. "Good day, girls," Officer Jones said as he walked away.

My mouth was as dry as a new sponge. I watched as Marla studied Officer Jones as he disappeared into the vastness of the mall corridor.

Momma always said it was good to have a healthy fear of bees, stray dogs, and cops. I guess she said it so many times that it finally stuck. I wouldn't have taken a ride home in a police car for all the new earrings at Nickelson's, and I could tell by the pissed-off look on my sister's face that she felt the same.

I stood up, slinging my sequined purse over my shoulder. The high-pitched screech of the metal chair legs on the tile floor got Marla's attention.

"You ready?" I asked.

Marla sat there smirking for a moment. "Say I was right," she demanded. "Then we can go."

"Kiss my ass, Marla," I pushed the chair under the table hard and began walking away.

"Hey, you can't leave without me," I heard Marla's voice right behind me. "Hey, wait up, shit head."

*

"How much farther is it?" I asked even though we'd only been walking about fifteen minutes.

"I've been thinking about it, and it takes Daddy about ten minutes to drive it, and he's usually going about 35 miles per hour, so I guess about five miles," Marla's forehead was crinkled. She was deep in thought. My sister was so damn smart and most times I hated her for it. The only time I was ever any good at math was in Mr. Montel's class. I was never sure if it was because he was an easy teacher or just easy to look at. Whatever the phenomenon, I never got good grades in math before or after I was in his class.

"So, as I see it," Marla continued her mathematical rant on how long it would take us to get home, "we should be there in about two and half hours?" She was starting to question herself now.

"Don't ask me," I said, shooting her a dirty look, complete with eye roll.

The sun beat down on the pavement, making it a full ten degrees hotter than it really was. It was too hot for my jacket, but the cool air made my arms cold as the cars passed us.

"So, what do you think they'll do to Ginger?" I asked.

"I guess put her in jail, Dancy."

"Do you think Daddy will go get her out?"

"Eh, hard to say," Marla's ingenious math skills had gone to her head and now she was becoming an armchair psychologist. "I never really got a good, clear sense of how he feels about her, you know, whether he thinks she's worth the trouble or not."

"Yeah, I don't know either," I added, hoping to get Marla talking about it some more. "What do you think? Will he take her back?"

"Hard to say, Dancy. You know how he surprises us sometimes."

"Yeah," I agreed, because my sister was right. Our father had a way of holding to his values: don't lie, don't cheat, don't steal, don't drink, don't do drugs ... but those rules seemed to only apply to me and Marla. His lady friends were held to quite a lower standard. Still, I felt for Ginger. I was even worried about her. I touched my swollen earlobes.

Thinking about Ginger was making me feel guilty. "I wonder if she had shoplifted just to buy *us* these things?" I asked my sister.

"I doubt it, Dancy. Remember the other day when were at Hill's?"

"Yeah, what about it?" I asked, anxious to hear what Marla had to say and hoping that it would make me feel better.

"The sales lady asked Ginger not to take her purse into the dressing room. I thought that was weird. Didn't you think that was weird?" Marla asked me.

"Yeah, I guess so. But it didn't seem to bother Ginger," I said, looking into my sister's face for a clue as to what she was getting at.

"Well, if you remember, we didn't *buy* anything that day. And, don't you think it's weird how she always has new stuff? I mean, how much can she make answering the phone at the doctor's office?"

"Yeah, Mamaw said that too." I kicked the gravels as I walked, thinking about all the things Mamaw had said about Ginger. *Her skirts were too short. She wore makeup like war paint. She was too affectionate with Daddy in public. Someone needed to watch her when she was with me and Marla.*

"Ginger is trouble, just plain trouble with a capital T," I mocked what I had heard my Mamaw say.

Just as I was in the middle of my impression of Mamaw talking about Daddy's women, Marla grabbed my arm.

"Dancy," she said through her clenched teeth, not looking at me but straight ahead. "Don't look over there but just walk fast. There's a man standing with his door open," she said as gravel popped from the back of her sneakers. She pulled me along with her as she quickened her pace.

Almost the instant she told me not to look, I did. From that moment, everything moved in slow motion. We had just passed the Obed Creek Bridge and were in unfamiliar territory, a shortcut through a sparsely populated subdivision, Turner Loop. He was fat, his skin the color of a pig, pink and fleshy. He was wearing glasses, the Roy Orbison kind, and his thinning hair was greasy and long. Sparse strands of it hung around his shoulders, and he was balding. I looked at him smiling at me, holding his penis and swinging it around and then rubbing it on the glass of the storm door. He was so close, only about twenty feet away. Though I was only entranced for a moment, my head wouldn't move. My knees were buckling and my mouth gaped open. The pig man broke my horrified stare when he began knocking on the glass. I screamed.

Marla grabbed me and ran. I saw her throw everything she was carrying, even my precious earbobs that Ginger had gotten for me, but my sister hung onto me.

The man knocked even harder on the glass. It rattled and he yelled, "Come here, little girls."

Marla and I were already at a full sprint when we heard the screech of the door opening. We ran faster and faster.

Gravel flew from under our feet. I was panting for breath and my ribs felt like they might cave into my lungs. I knew that Marla was feeling the same pain but in spite of it, we ran and ran until we couldn't run any more.

"Stop! It's okay now," Marla pulled me behind a sticker bush next to Mrs. Tollet's house.

"Oh my God, Marla! Oh my God! I can't breathe," I panted so hard that dry noises were coming from my throat like a whooping cough as I pushed air in and out of my lungs.

"Put your head down here, Dancy." Marla sat up Indian style and had me lay my head in her lap.

"It's okay, Dancy. He can't see us, and Mrs. Tollet is on the back porch. I can see her from here."

I turned my head and I saw Mrs. Tollet's house, then I saw her outside sweeping. With one last rush of adrenalin I popped up and ran toward her.

"Dancy Wilder?!" Mrs. Tollet was surprised to see me coming out of her sticker bush. "Marla?!"

My sister must have been right behind me but I didn't look back. "Are you girls okay? Why, Dancy, you're as pale as a sheet. What on earth are you two doing all the way over here?"

Marla started to speak but before she could get a word out, I half-yelled, "I need to use your phone, Mrs. Tollet."

I looked at Marla not to ask her permission for what I was about to do, or to get her validation that I should do it, but to let her know that I was going to make that call no matter what she said.

A sense of relief washed over me the minute the cool air from the kitchen hit my face.

"Can we get some water, please," I heard Marla's voice crack. She sat down at the kitchen table.

Mrs. Tollet brought Marla's water and then got a glass for me. I was already next to the phone in the foyer. Marla never looked up.

"Go ahead, dear and make your call," Mrs. Tollet said kindly.

My fingers were weak. Even turning the dial seemed difficult. I knew the number by heart. I had called it many times.

"Hello." A familiar voice comforted me. It was Chick.

"Is Momma there?" My voice was shaky but determined. "This is Dancy."

The gravelly voice softened. "Dancy? Little Dancy?"

"Yes," I hesitated and then responded with an obvious question. "Is that you Chick?"

"Yep, it's me," Chick said, trying his best to sound jovial.

"Can you get Momma?" I asked Chick.

"Sure, honey," Chick said, sounding serious now. He then laid the phone down with a thud. I could hear voices in the background. It almost sounded like the school cafeteria on a Friday when the teachers would say, "The natives are restless." I couldn't make out a single word. They all ran together with no certain rhythm or tone. Then I heard Chick again.

"Lou, hey Lou get over here," his voice was gravelly again. "You've got a phone call." I pictured him there in the kitchen, yelling out over the bar for Momma to come to the phone. I'm sure he could tell by the shaky tone of my voice and the fact that I didn't kid around with him for a while on the phone like usual that something was wrong. I could certainly hear the urgency in Chick's voice as he yelled for my mother. Normally, we'd talk for at least a few minutes if given the chance. I hoped I hadn't hurt his feelings.

Chick was the last in a long line of Harvard-educated lawyers, Momma had told me and Marla. His great grandfather was a lawyer, his grandfather, and his father. Chick stood to be the fourth to inherit the Rawlings Law Firm's wealth and power in Rayes County. On his way to becoming the rightful heir, Chick's father had him work in the office as an associate. I had heard Momma tell Daddy once about a case that Chick handled that got national media attention. It was a case in which a young child had been molested by his school teacher. Chick was part of the legal team that defended the school teacher, and eventually the firm won the case. After that, Momma had said that Chick became so well known for his defense work on that case that pedophiles were coming out of the wood work to secure his legal services. Momma said he made a fortune defending pedophiles and setting them free. Then, his drinking got so bad his father threw him out of Rawlings Law Firm and told him not to come back until he was clean. Momma said Chick had told her that he would never feel clean even if he did quit drinking because of all those bad people who were still walking the streets because of him. Momma told Daddy that's why Chick opened his home to those who wanted to get clean. She said Chick had hoped that he could make up for all the bad by helping other people do something good with their lives. That, Momma had said, was how Chick's Place was born. She was always going around saying, "Thank God for Chick's Place."

The butterflies in my stomach awakened as I waited for my momma to come to the phone, as I stood there at my second-grade teacher's phone table. Now that I had the phone in my hand and my mother was about to be on the other end I had no idea how I would explain to her what had just happened.

The pictures on Mrs. Tollet's walls were familiar to me. David and Dana, her twins, covered almost every spare surface. The pictures showed the twins at different ages, just like the photos at my house of me and Marla. David and Dana weren't the only twins at my school, we even had a set of triplets; but Mrs. Tollet's twins were the only set that was a boy and a girl. That made them unique in a lot of ways, but they also had red hair. And *that* really set them apart.

It was weird being in a teacher's house. Seeing her outside of school like at the grocery store or the gas station was weird too, but this was different. We were in her house, her world. It was quiet and solemn, not at all like her classroom.

Mrs. Tollet was known for many things, but quiet and solemn were not the words anyone would use to describe her. She was always talking, laughing, and cutting up with the students and the other teachers. She was a bit of a jokester, but you wouldn't know it by walking into her house. It was clean, too clean, really. Nothing was out of place. A lot of the pictures I saw on the walls were ones I had seen before.

Every school year before Christmas, the school pictures came back and the unofficial annual winter break picture exchange took place. The more wallet-size photos you collected, the cooler you were. It meant that you had a lot of friends and were popular. Marla always came home with a stack at least an inch high. David and Dana were always in that stack. They were in her grade, most times in the same class with her.

I looked over at my sister as I began to consider how weird this must be for her, too. There Marla was, sitting at the kitchen table having a conversation with Mrs. Tollet. I pulled the receiver away from my ear slightly so I could hear what my sister and Mrs. Tollet were saying.

"They go every weekend, and really, I've kind of gotten used to it," Mrs. Tollet said. "I wouldn't want them to feel bad for leaving me here. You know what I mean don't you, Marla?"

My sister nodded, letting Mrs. Tollet know she understood. I read the disappointment on Marla's face as she looked over at me. Marla and I looked at the pictures of David and Dana and then back at one another, our movements almost synchronized. Mrs. Tollet turned her back to us and gazed out the kitchen window.

I jerked the phone flush against my ear as I heard the clattering of acrylic on the other end of the line.

"Hello." As much as I tried to fight it, the sound of my mother's voice always made me cry. I had created a world where she didn't exist until I heard her or saw her. I never really missed Momma that much, more than Marla, but still not horribly. But for some reason when I'd see my mother or hear her on the phone, it was like all those days that had passed without her were suddenly filled with her memory, or at least the memory of me missing her.

"Momma, it's me, Dancy."

CHAPTER SEVEN

Momma Knows Best

Once, my momma had stomped the tile floor in our dining room so hard that it left her heel print there permanently. I'd stick my foot in it every now and then just to see if it would fit. It always set snug down inside the indention carved out by her riding boot. I wondered if she'd make another one tonight.

Momma had been fighting with Daddy since me and Marla went to bed. I guess they figured if we were in bed we wouldn't hear them. But we weren't trying to sleep. We were listening.

When they first started, we were lying with our heads near the crack at the bottom of the door but as the fighting got louder, we ended up just sitting in the bed. It was much more comfortable there and we could hear everything they said. They might as well have had megaphones pointed at Marla's bedroom. My sister didn't ask me to go back to my room like she normally did when I had shown up with my pillow and blanket. "Stay if you want," she had said, rolling her eyes.

Marla and I laid there in her bed with our feet up in the air and made monster shadows against the wall with our legs and the light from Marla's lamp.

"Is it weird that I miss her yelling?" I asked as I watched Marla dance her leg shadow across the wall.

"Yeah, Dancy. It's weird. That's one of the reasons you're such a little weirdo."

"Do you miss anything about her being here?" My sister seemed tired and defeated, the perfect time to talk about Momma.

"No," Marla's answer was short.

"Nothing? Really?" I pressed for more.

"Nope," Marla said, as she twisted her legs together, making what looked like a big, dead tree shadow. "I don't care what they do. When I grow up I'm gettin' the hell out of here and then they can do whatever they want."

I put my legs down and turned to my sister. With an arm inquisitively propped under my chin, I asked simply, "And where do you think you're going?"

"College." Marla never looked at me while she spoke. She just kept spreading her toes and waving her feet in the air, making what looked like tree branches blowing in the breeze.

"Where?" I wasn't finished quizzing Marla yet.

"I don't know, but somewhere," she said, finally taking her legs down and turning to look at me. "I decided the other day when I was watching the five o'clock news."

"Where was I?" I asked, wondering why I had not been informed of Marla's sudden plans to leave home.

"You were there. Remember that night that Margie Ison was talking about things she did when she went to college at the University of Tennessee?"

"Yeah," I said slowly, not understanding what the channel 6 weather girl and my sister leaving home had to do with one another.

"She said she studied meteorology at UT, you know, the clouds and stuff," Marla's eyes grew wider. "I'm going to be a weather girl on channel 6."

The screaming from the dining room seemed muffled as I lay there and pondered the possibility of Marla leaving. It was a long way off, but the fact that she'd been thinking about going away made me wonder what I would do without her.

"I'm going with you," I announced as I rolled onto my back and began making shadow giants with my legs just like Marla had been doing before she confessed her plans to me. "I guess I'll be a weather girl, too."

"Dancy," my sister said with her signature aggravated sigh. "You can't always do everything I do."

"I'm not doing what you do," I said in a smartass tone that was usually characteristic of Marla. "I just decided I'm going to be a weather girl, and there's nothing you can do about it."

I watched Marla from my peripheral vision as she rolled her eyes. "Do whatever suits you," she said, and then rolled over on her back, joining me once again in the creation of shadow monsters.

"Oh I *will* do whatever suits me," I said, not letting go of the argument I had tried to start. I kicked hard at her legs, pushing them away.

"Hey," Marla snapped at me and then kicked at my legs. As the battle of the shadow monsters ensued, the fight in the dining room had escalated into what sounded like an all-out war. Marla and I froze as we heard the shattering of glass.

"I told you, goddammit, that I don't sleep with any of them," my mother screamed. "They are my family. It's not like what you think, you sick son-of-a-bitch." Another glass sounded like it hit the rock wall next to the stove. Momma must have been standing near the dish rack and Daddy by the oven.

"I hope he's covering his eyes," I whispered to Marla then realized they could never hear my shrinking voice over the verbal artillery that was being fired at random four rooms away.

"I'm sure he's fine," Marla said, casually discounting that either of them were in any real danger. "They used to do this shit all the time. It'll be okay—always is."

My mother and father had developed a language all their own after they had been fighting for a while. Regular cuss words like shit, damn, hell, bitch, bastard, and fuck, were no longer deemed effective after a couple of hours in the heat of a Wilder battle. So much like the way me and Marla would tie fireworks together with rubber bands and twine to get a bigger explosion on the Fourth of July, my parents did the same, only with cuss words. What was once a simple insult like "you dumb son-of-a-bitch," would be strung together with a few other expletives to make even more of an impact: "you dumb, fuckin' son-of-a HELL bitchin' mother fuckin' bastard!"

It was comforting to hear my father's voice. I hadn't heard him yell for at least a minute or so and was wondering if my mother had finally killed him.

"You sorry bitch of a mother! You make me sick!" my father screamed. Marla and I were raised at attention until the moment we heard his words and then both of us relaxed and laid back down.

"I was beginning to wonder if he was still in there," Marla said wincing as she spoke to me.

"Yeah, me too," I said, propping my head up with a fist under my ear. "I hope she doesn't tell him."

*

Before Daddy got home from work, Momma, Marla and I had all made a pact not to tell Daddy what had happened. Sure, he knew about the shoplifting and that Hot Ginger was in the Big House downtown but not about the other thing. It was too embarrassing. I didn't want my father to know I had seen a man's penis. I couldn't get the image out of my head. I didn't want him to feel the same way I did, dirty and sick for having seen what I had seen.

Marla wouldn't even name the body part. She just kept saying it was over and we shouldn't talk about it anymore. We had made Momma promise not to tell Daddy either. He would already be upset enough that we had tried to walk home by ourselves and then called Momma instead of him when we got to Mrs. Tollet's house. It was Mrs. Tollet that drove us home, and within a couple of hours Momma met us here.

I ran to the door when I heard the growl of her bike. Her light hair hung in waves out of the bandana she wore on her head to tame her locks.

As I walked out to the driveway I could see myself growing larger and larger in her mirrored-lens glasses. No matter how much weight my mother lost, her boobs were always the same size. She had tried to trap them in the leather bustier with lots of string and a couple of chains. Still, as usual, they were trying to escape.

One side of her mouth was smiling while the other clenched a freshly lit cigarette. She booted at the kick stand and took a long draw off the fag, burning it about a third of the way down then flicked the rest over into the field. She flung her long leg over the back of the bike and held her lanky arms out for me.

"Dancy, are you okay?" The familiar smell of hot leather, cigarettes, and stale Sweet Honesty held me in her arms for far longer than was necessary.

"I miss you, Momma," I said, my voice muffled against her skin. I didn't even mind that she was sweaty and I could taste the salt as I kissed her neck. As I broke my hug to look at her face, I could see Marla's reflection in my mother's sunglasses.

"Momma's here," I said instinctively to Marla.

"Yeah, dumbass, I can see that," Marla said, rolling her eyes.

"Now, Marla is that anyway to talk to your sister?" my mother asked, reaching out to hug my Marla. My sister evaded her by walking around to the other side of the bike.

"Nice ride," she said. "Is it new?"

"You could say that," Momma said, as she rose from her squatted position next to me. "It's new to me. Bought it off an old biker over in Sweetwater."

"Cool," Marla said, continuing to stare at the bike, making sure that she did not make eye contact with me or Momma.

In the span of a few minutes I had inspected my mother from head to toe and yes, I was correct and knew the answer even before I asked the question.

"Is that a new tattoo?"

"Yes, baby it is," my mother craned her neck to look at the new tat that was impossible for her to see just below her right shoulder; then she looked back at me and smiled. "Do you like it?"

There really wasn't much to like, a triangle with a circle inside it. It looked like some sort of homework question from geometry class. My mother seemed pleased with it though, so I gave the response she needed. I was sure it was symbolic of something that was special to her. Every time she came home there was always something new with a profound and symbolic meaning. Last time, it was the amethyst stone that she had pierced into her belly button. It was still there.

"Yeah, it's cool," I lied. "What does it mean?"

My mother pulled her glasses from her face and looked down at me. Laugh lines pointed into her eyes like half starbursts as the sun beat down on her head.

"It means I'm better, Dancy," my mother said in a solemn tone. "It means I'm better."

Marla's head popped over from the other side of the bike as the hum of my mother's friends approaching got louder. I could see them coming over the hill on Chestnut Lane riding in bird-formation. The vibration of their engines rattled the inside of my stomach. Momma shielded her eyes from the sun as she watched her friends ride toward us.

"I wondered where the hell you guys were," she said to them even though they were too far away to hear.

"I thought they got lost," she turned and said to me and Marla.

The group of them broke formation as they rolled into the driveway two by two. Momma's friends looked like hornets and even sounded like a swarm of bees as they revved their engines just before shutting them down.

My mother turned to face her friends as Marla came up behind me, grabbing hold of my shirt and ready to drag me into the house at the slightest sign of trouble. The silence after the last bike was turned off left a sort of stillness in the air that I neither felt nor heard. It just hung there waiting for something to crash into it again.

Their leathers creaked and crunched as they got off their bikes. Some of Momma's friends took off their sunglasses, some didn't. There were twelve of them, including my mother, five women and the rest men. I was glad to see Chick was among them, but I didn't recognize the others.

"I was beginning to wonder about you guys," my mother said to Chick.

"Girls, you remember Chick?" Momma asked and then presented him like a trophy.

Marla and I both nodded. I instinctively gave him a hug as he crouched down in front of us.

"You girls okay?" Chick asked, pulling me and Marla into a hug. Marla's attempts to remain aloof were finally thwarted by Chick's massive arms.

Momma set about introducing the rest of the crew. There were always new people in my mother's circle of friends. One time when I asked Momma why so many people came and went over at Chick's Place, she said all the coming and going wasn't always a bad thing. It just meant some who came there weren't ready to commit or they were better and ready to move on. Either way, she said, it was all a part of their recovery.

"This is Janie and her man, Duke," Momma pointed to a woman who was about her same age. A very short man was revealed as he leapt off his bike and onto terra firma next to his woman.

"This is Benny and Jasmine." Benny nodded to me and Marla while Jasmine gave us the peace sign.

"This is Johnson, Scout, and Billings," my mother continued. I half expected a law firm to come forward but instead it was three younger men all wearing the same type of bandannas, sunglasses, and leather jackets. Each of them saluted to us as their name was announced.

"Here are Loretta and Yvette," my mother said as she continued to move through the crowd introducing her friends. "And this," my mother said as she walked over to a man who looked more like the janitor at our school than a biker dude, "is Jock. He's just came to us last week."

Obviously, he was new. His jacket was gray canvas and his boots were snakeskin, not leather. This guy wouldn't be cool even among the rednecks in Rayes County.

"You about ready to roll?" Chick yelled out over the small crowd of people to Momma.

"Where are you going?" I blurted out as Momma came walking over.

"Girls, we've got some business to attend to," my mother said as she mounted her bike. "Come on. You girls can go with me. It's not that far."

She scooted back on her seat as far as she could go, making room for me and Marla.

"Um, you want us both to get on there?" Marla finally spoke and made eye contact with Momma for the first time since she got there.

"Why not?" Momma answered.

"I just don't think it's safe," Marla's sarcastic tone caught Chick's ear. He had pulled his bike up next to Momma's.

"Safe! Safe? Safe!" Chick kept commenting and asking all at the same time, obviously trying to think of something clever to say. "Why your momma is the best rider in this group. She's never once flipped her bike, and I'm sure she'll be extra careful with such precious cargo aboard." Chick's attempt to smile sweetly failed as usual. He could only manage to look creepy even though Marla and I both knew he wasn't.

As Marla was turning to look back toward the house I jumped on the front of Momma's seat.

"Hey, Dancy, get off there!" my sister demanded. I shook my head. She folded her arms and scowled at me and Momma.

"Come on," my mother said as she chuckled at her oldest daughter. "We'll be right back, this won't take fifteen minutes."

"Where are we going?" I finally asked.

"To take care of a little problem," my mother smiled at me and motioned for Marla to get on the bike.

"This is probably a bad idea," my sister mumbled as she climbed onto the seat in front of me.

"Stop worrying Marla," Momma said, squeezing us both from behind. "Like I said, it won't take more than fifteen minutes."

"Well, it better not," Marla snapped at her. "Daddy will be home in just a little bit."

"We'll be back before your father gets home," Momma said as she popped up the kickstand and revved up the bike.

Momma drove in front of the formation this time. I could hear the others close behind us. The warm air did little to cool me as I was sandwiched between Marla and Momma. But it felt good that they were both near me at the same time. The wind was causing Marla's hair to hit my face, but I didn't care. I felt like I could scream at the top of my lungs and no one would hear me.

"WHOOOO," I couldn't help myself as I threw my hands up in the air. Marla laughed and then put hers up too. I could hear the light sound of my mother's laugh in the wind. Up and over every hill, Marla and I squealed and screamed. All the while, I could hear Momma laughing.

We slowed to a stop at the Turner Loop sign. Marla grabbed my leg and pinched it hard in her grip. My mother did a cut-throat motion back to the others and they cut their engines.

"Oh shit," Marla said.

"Oh shit," I repeated my sister's words.

"It looks like no one's here," Marla said to Momma as she shut off the bike once we reached the pervert's driveway.

"Oh, he's here, he's here," Momma said, as she popped the kickstand with her boot. "You girls stay right here. I'll be back."

Marla and I were like mannequins, completely stiff. Even when the bike shifted to lean on the kickstand we never moved. Marla and I watched our mother walk in what seemed like slow motion toward the front porch of the house that me and my sister vowed to never go near again for as long as we lived.

"She's gonna break that glass," Marla finally spoke what both of us were thinking.

Momma had pulled a knife out of her boot and began hitting the glass door with the butt end of it.

I felt Marla's muscles release as my mother placed her weapon back inside her boot and walked off the porch.

"I guess no one's home," I said, as I let out the breath I had been holding.

Marla and I both jumped as Momma picked up a rock from a nearby flowerbed and threw it into the door.

Glass danced like hail from a storm across the pervert's porch and even down the steps and spilled onto the sidewalk in a million little pieces.

Momma stood on the bottom step and waited. Finally, the door opened.

"What the fuck are you doing, bitch?" the pervert yelled at Momma.

"Oooohhh those are big words for such a little man," my mother said as the pervert walked out onto the porch looking around at the carnage.

"Louise? Louise Gardner?"

"She knows him," I spoke quietly into Marla's ear. She shushed me quickly. "Listen," she scolded me in a whisper.

"Yeah, dumbass, it's me," she towered over him by at least a foot.

"What the ..." the pervert tried to speak but my mother kneed him in the nuts and jerked his head back, holding him by his greasy hair. With her free hand, she pulled her knife from her boot once again, this time holding it to his throat.

Marla and I gasped almost simultaneously.

"Do you recognize these girls?" Momma pushed his face out into the sun toward us as we sat there in the driveway.

I held Marla tighter but neither of us moved.

"You're not answering me you sick little pervert," Momma held the knife even closer to his throat. "Feel like you're in high school again, Jerry?"

"WHAT DO YOU WANT?" he spat out in desperation. Momma ignored him.

"Girls is this the man who did that awful thing today?" Momma shoved his face toward us. My insides were shaking like jumping beans.

I could see Marla's head nodding slightly, so I nodded as well.

"Well, as it turns out you're still just a slimy, sick pervert," Momma said.

"I DIDN'T KNOW!" he yelled.

"Didn't know what?" my mother's sarcastic tone hit a high pitch. "Didn't know you'd get caught? You'd better be glad I came instead of their father. I come with a warning, he'd have come with a gun."

"I DIDN'T KNOW!" The man's voice was choppy and the terrified look on his face made me almost feel sorry for him.

I could hear the buzz of nearly a dozen motorcycles coming up the road. I knew who it was and I was glad they were coming. Maybe they would stop my mother from cutting this guy's throat.

As the distant buzzing transformed into a deafening roar, I felt a breeze as the bikers flew past either side of us and surrounded the pervert's porch. As the engines revved, I could see him crying out but could no longer hear him. Momma spat on the man and then let him go as Chick turned off his bike and came up onto the porch.

As Momma headed back to the bike where we were waiting, the little man tried to run into his house. Chick grabbed him by the back of the shirt and pulled him down onto the concrete porch among the shattered glass. Chick then pulled the aluminum storm door from its hinges and threw it like a paper wad into the front yard.

"I guess he won't be able to hide behind that anymore," Momma half-yelled as she climbed onto the back of the bike behind me. As she started the engine and backed the motorcycle to the end of the driveway, her friends drove around in circles in the pervert's front yard, and then one by one flew past us and took off down the road.

As they left, my mother held her hand out so they could each slap her five before heading out.

Chick was the last to leave. He slowed his bike and then stopped just next to us.

"I told him I'd be coming by here pretty often, and if I ever saw another glass door up there, I'd tear it off again," Chick winked at my mother and laughed, sounding a little like Santa. As Chick raised his hand to give me and Marla a high-five, we both slapped him one.

"Not bad," Chick said and then nodded as he pulled away to follow the other bikers. I took one last look at the pervert lying there on the porch.

He'd been kicked pretty hard by Chick and Momma. He was covering his penis with both hands, the very same one he had been so proud of earlier in the day.

"Go ahead, you know you want to," my mother yelled at us over the blubbing motor as she flipped him the bird. Marla and I did the same as Momma pulled the bike out into the road. We never put our middle fingers down until the pervert's house was well out of sight. I held onto Marla tightly until she put her arms out into the wind. When I saw that Momma wasn't going to scold her I held my arms out too and we flew like birds all the way home.

We got back just a few minutes before Daddy came home. Momma managed to throw some food together and get it on the table. We could hear him hollering for us even before he got to the porch. I watched him as he half-trotted, squalling the whole way into the house with his usual kid call. "Marla? Dancy?" He paused no more than two seconds. "Dancy? Marla?" I wondered if he thought switching the order of our names would somehow result in a quicker response.

Normally, I'd have let him yell a few more times, but the panicked look on his face prompted me to react with a few pecks on the window. "In here, Daddy." He looked at me and half smiled as I pressed my face into the window. The bottom of the storm door screeched against the concrete as I bounced off the couch. A few steps later I was in front of my father as he entered the door.

"Momma's here," I announced, wanting to be the first to tell him. He didn't look at me. His eyes were locked onto the swivel doors in the kitchen entryway.

"I see that," he said, still not looking in my direction. He gave the swinging door such a harsh shove that I heard it hit the wall on the other side.

"What the hell are you doing here?" I heard him say to Momma in a low gravelly voice.

"Well, nice to see you too," Momma said, just as I came through the doors after Daddy.

His jaw was clenched but he managed a tight smile when he saw me standing next to him. Momma looked funny in his apron. She was so skinny, the strings wrapped around her twice. She had gathered them in a teeny bow at the front.

She had taken the scarf from her head. There was a stark contrast in skin coloring where Momma's face had tanned and her forehead had been covered. My mother's attempt at pushing her long bangs over to cover her pale skin above her eyes only drew more attention to her awareness of it.

"Supper?" Momma asked my father, pointing her cigarette downward to a plate of diagonally cut sandwiches. My father stood solid as a statue, staring straight at her.

"Well?" Momma asked him again, this time pushing the plate toward him.

"Dancy, where is your sister?" my father asked, still not acknowledging the plate of tiny sandwiches.

"Her room," I replied and then reached to grab a triangle of bread. As I bit into it, my mother winked at me, and my father broke his silence again.

"Go tell her we're going to eat," Daddy pointed me toward the hallway.

"You mean out?" I was excited but tried not to let on too much.

"Yes," his reply was solemn as he continued glaring at Momma. He took the plate, walked over to the back door and went into the mudroom. Momma and I watched as he slid the sandwiches off the plate and into Cricket's bowl. Daddy screeched out his signature two whistles, and in seconds Cricket appeared and immediately devoured more than half of what Daddy had given him. Cricket then licked my father's hand and quickly ate the rest. "Good boy," Daddy said, patting Cricket on the head.

I turned to look at Momma to see if she was mad. This was the kind of thing that in the past would've caused an all-out Wilder war, but she didn't seem upset. She wasn't smiling in the sense that the corners of her mouth were turned up or anything, but her face had softened. She watched my father as he continued to pet the dog.

"I guess we *can* do better than that," she said, referring to the tiny sandwiches Cricket had just ingested. She put her hands on my shoulders. "These girls have had a rough day."

Daddy rose from his squatted position like a shot and came back into the house.

"Go get your sister, Dancy," he said, taking long strides through the kitchen. "I'll be in the car," he said, looking straight ahead.

"Where are we going?" I followed after him into the living room.

"We'll figure it out on the way," he said as he went out the front door.

Momma had taken Daddy's apron off and was attempting to straighten her hair in the hallway mirror.

Before I could get to Marla's room, my sister came out. "I heard already, Dancy," she said as she walked past me and Momma.

"Your father seems a little upset, girls," Momma said, as she walked down the hallway. "Let me handle this one. It'll all be okay."

"I'm not sayin' a word," Marla's response was certain. She had already decided that her position would be one of silence even before Momma suggested it.

"Me neither," I added and then fell in behind Marla.

It was weird to see Daddy sitting in the car that way. He was staring straight forward, not looking toward us at all. I didn't call for the front seat this time, and neither did Marla. There would be no bickering over that today. We were happy to turn it over to Momma, and it seemed she was happy to take it. Marla and I watched as Momma slid into the seat in front of us. Daddy adjusted the rear-view mirror so we could see him.

"Where do you girls want to eat?" For the first time since he got home, he sounded like our father.

"Burger Queen," my sister and I answered in unison and then looked at each other and started laughing at the unity of our speech.

Daddy turned back to us and smiled as he backed out of the driveway. "Burger Queen it is, then."

*

Dinner at Burger Queen was uneventful. Momma didn't say much, even though she smiled at me and Marla—a lot. Daddy didn't say anything, not one word. He let us put in our own order and he just paid for our food, even Momma's.

Like the calm before the storm, Marla and I both knew the shit would hit the fan when we got home. That's why we went straight to bed, without even being told.

Momma had kissed us both goodnight. Then we heard the slight squeak of the swinging door. Daddy must have been waiting for Momma in the kitchen.

We were at attention again when we heard the dining room table legs screech across the tile. It sounded like a train whistle and made my teeth tingle, like biting down on a Popsicle stick and pulling on it. This had come just after Momma said, "Fuck you, Everett. "This is why no one will ever stay with you, you dumb son-of-a-bitch."

To scoot that table even an inch would have been a formidable task and require an immense amount of strength. It was solid oak, with legs as thick as tree trunks. It had been in the same spot for as long as I could remember. It was immovable. I wondered if it had left a dent in the tile.

"Damn," Marla said, sitting up. "The table."

"Yeah, I know," I responded quietly as we both waited for the next string of expletives to explode from the kitchen.

"Don't you break my Goddamn table," Daddy yelled. I shook my head in disbelief as Marla let out the puff of air she'd been holding in her lungs.

"That's all you worry about," Momma yelled. "Your stupid stuff. If you'd worry half as much about your daughters as you do about your sissy yellow car and your nice furniture."

"She's the one who moved the table," I said to Marla, looking for confirmation that my mother had just scooted the heavy structure.

Marla cocked an eyebrow at me and then glanced toward our closed door.

"You have no right to talk about worrying about the girls," Daddy said. "You're never around here. I'm the one taking care."

"Oh, bullshit," Momma mocked him. "Why do you think they called *me* today? You call that taking care of them?"

"Horseshit," Daddy recycled her words and threw them back at her. "Because I was at work, not because they wanted their mommy, 'cause you're not a mommy. I don't know what the hell you are anymore, but you sure as hell ain't no mommy. Look at you in that getup."

"Maybe I'm not," my mother's voice was shaky and low now. I could tell she was either crying or about to cry.

I looked at Marla, who had, at some point since I last looked away, placed her pillow over her face. I slowly lifted one corner and peeked underneath. At least that way if my sister was crying and didn't want me to see then she could have time to clutch the pillow tighter to her face. If there was one thing I had learned about my sister it was not to look at her when she was crying. I had seen tigers on Mutual of Omaha's Wild Kingdom go at their prey with less fierceness than Marla if you looked her in the eye when she was crying. Once, Marla put her entire hand over my face and clutched it so tightly that I had her fingerprints in my skin for a couple of days. When those prints finally turned to charcoal-colored bruises I was reminded of what my sister was capable of.

When I saw it was safe and there was no reaction to lifting one side of the pillow, I quickly removed it all together, squinting my eyes and recoiling in case Marla came at me with those muscular claws that on most occasions we referred to simply as fingers.

Holding that pose for a few seconds, I realized Marla was sleeping, or at least faking it. I put my ear close to her face. Sure enough, she was asleep. Marla could fake many things: hiccups, sneezing attacks, but not the buzzing; the buzzing was a one-of-kind indisputable noise that could only be made when my sister was actually asleep.

I rolled my eyes and sighed hard, hoping she'd at least open one eye. When she didn't I laid down next to her and put my pillow over my face, thinking that if that had gotten Marla to sleep then maybe it'd put me to sleep, too. I could still hear Daddy yelling, although the volume had been toned down considerably. Even so, there was no way I could drift off as usual. I was envious that my sister found tranquility so easily. All I was finding under that pillow was an overheated head and itchy skin from something that smelled like leftover Downy fabric softener after a low water rinse cycle.

I put my right foot next to Marla's and began moving it back and forth. She fidgeted a little but still didn't wake up. I had to be careful if I woke my sister. I had to make her think she just woke up on her own, otherwise I'd be sent to my room, and there'd I'd be, alone for the rest of the night. Even if Marla *was* asleep, at least she was still there. The sounds from the kitchen were beginning to disappear.

I got up from the bed and slid with my sock feet over to the bedroom door, breaking the light coming through the bottom of the doorway. Momma and Daddy were still talking in elevated voices, just not so loud as to wake the dead.

"I just don't understand how you can live like that," my father's words were still harsh, just not as loud. His disgust for my mother's friends, or family, as she had called them today, was not only evident, but oozed from the tone of the words he spoke to her.

"It's a place I can go and not be judged, Everett."

My mother's explanation was weak. Even I recognized that and welcomed my father's frustration as he sought a better answer.

"Horseshit, again," my father's words were louder now. "It's all a bunch of horseshit! You need to stay here and be a mother to these girls. They deserve more than a phone call every week."

I could hear my mother's muffled sobbing.

I imagined them sitting somewhere within the gates of Tara in *Gone With the Wind*, explosions going off all around them, my father in a white Colonel Sanders suit and my mother donning a lacy, off the shoulder, wide hoop dress. Momma sits there crying as my father presents a pristine white handkerchief that serves two purposes: one to wipe her tears and the other to muffle her sobs. They embrace as the night sky lights up around them and the war rages. They profess their undying love to one another among the rubble they used to call home, on what might be their last days on earth.

I sat quietly by the door, clasping both my hands around my make-believe handkerchief and holding it to my lips, silently sobbing into it, my shoulders quaking and my made up tears soaking my gentleman's token for my grief.

Brought out of my movie-screen romance by the sound of my sister turning over on her side and ripping out a small but powerfully potent fart, I was reminded that there was no pristine white handkerchief behind that door. My mother was most likely sobbing into a now-wet paper towel as she sat there in her leathers.

The chain attached to her black cowhide bracelet jingled a bit, and I imagined that she was wiping the snot from her nose, although I was too far away to see it. My father, still dressed in his uniform, not the military sort but one issued to the electricians who worked at Tennessee Valley Authority's Nuclear Power Plant, was probably sitting on the other side of the table with his head in his hands, trying not to watch as an equal mix of mascara and tears streaked my mother's face.

"I think I'll stay on for a while if that's okay with you," my mother's words brought me out of the scene playing in my head.

"You know you're always welcome here, Louise," my father said in such a way that I half expected the next words out of his mouth to be, "and I'll always love you," as I envisioned him again in his Colonel Sanders uniform standing amidst the wreckage of the war-torn south.

"I think we do need to talk about what happened today," my mother's voice grew stronger.

"Something else happened?" Daddy's tone was confused. Momma had told him about Ginger's arrest and me and Marla walking home but not about the other thing.

"Oh, shit," I half yelled the whisper and then found the nearest item fit for throwing and hurled it in Marla's direction.

"Shit," I whispered loudly into the air. The tennis shoe had missed by a mile and skiffed the end of the footboard.

Flip-flop, I thought to myself. This time I gave myself a moment to aim, not just flinging in Marla's general vicinity. It missed her by mere inches and hit the wall with a thud. Again, she never moved.

"What else happened today?" My father's tone was inquisitive and sarcastic, indicating that not much else could surprise him.

Surely, Momma wouldn't tell him—not about the penis, the pervert.

"Marla," I whispered my loudest yell. "Marla," I tried again. "Shit, shit, shit," I said, as I banged the side of my fist into my head.

"Well, today when the girls were walking home," my mother started to speak again.

I jumped to my feet pivoting first toward Marla and then toward the kitchen. There was no time to explain to Marla what was going on. By the time I got her good and awake and then told her that Momma was about to spill the beans, it'd be too late. I was on my own.

I flung the bedroom door open. It hit the hallway wall behind it and came fighting back at me with a force. I didn't care. I instinctively held my elbow up to catch the ricochet, and just kept on moving. I had to get there before my mother could tell him. The light from the kitchen blinded me for a moment, but I didn't wait to get my sight back. I just blurted it out, knowing that it would change our lives forever. But it was all I had, and I hoped Marla would somehow forgive me.

"You know Marla's leaving!"

My mother and father looked at me and didn't say a word. As my eyes got used to the light and I could see the puzzled looks on their faces, I realized they hadn't understood me so I repeated myself.

"Marla's leaving, I said." I stood there waiting for a reaction I wasn't getting, but at least I'd stopped the impending conversation about the penis, the pervert, and the motorcycle gang fight.

"What do you mean Marla's leaving?" Finally, someone cared about the news I'd just broken even though my father looked more amused than concerned.

"She said she's gettin' the hell outta here," I quoted my sister word for word.

"What?" From the look on Momma's face I could tell she was obviously taking this more seriously than my father.

"And I'm going with her when she goes," I announced.

"You mean like run away?" My mother scooted her chair out from under the table and got up. "That's very dangerous."

"No. She's going to college," I interrupted Momma's would-be lecture.

My mother smiled at me as she sat back down in her chair. She then looked at Daddy, shrugged her shoulders and winced. Had they not heard what I'd just said? I held my hands out and non-verbally asked again for a reaction.

"Well, of course she's going to college," Daddy said, through a gulpy laugh. "But when she's older. Not now, Dancy."

"Well I know that," I said in my most smartass tone. "I'm not stupid. But still, she's leaving. She told me tonight."

The two of them didn't even care. "Figures," I said, rolling my eyes.

"What figures?" Daddy asked.

"That the two of you don't even give a shit that it's so bad around here Marla wants to leave," I blurted out the words and immediately wished I'd used *crap* instead of *shit*.

"Danielle Lynn Wilder, watch your language," my mother said. I rolled my eyes at her. My mother quickly retreated out of her sudden Momma-knows-best role and back into her leathers when she took note of her chains rattling as she pointed an accusing finger at me.

I wanted to say, "Yes. Great. A lecture about the word *shit* from a woman who just earlier today held a group flip-off for the pervert just after kicking his ass. But I had to remind myself that the whole reason I busted into the kitchen and opened Marla's secret in front of my parents was to keep what happened earlier today out of the Wilder Kitchen Battle of 1974.

"Dancy," Daddy's tone was more serious now. "Yes, Marla's going to college and so are you—but not with Marla."

I moved closer to the table and then sat down in one of the empty chairs. I found myself wishing that Marla would wake up and tell them herself. Maybe it would have a bigger impact coming straight from the horse's mouth. I crossed my arms and gave my father a surly look as he continued to educate me on the world of college.

"When Marla graduates from high school, then she'll go to college. Then two years later when you graduate from high school, you will go to college," Daddy said, giving me a satisfied smile and patting me on the arm. I rolled my eyes at him again and then looked at Momma and did the same, handing her a duplicated smartass smirk that I'd just given to Daddy.

"Yes, honey," my mother was now chiming in. "We hope you both go to college when you're old enough."

"She probably won't come back," I said in a certain tone. "I'm sure she won't."

"Well, then that's okay," Daddy said. "That will mean that she's doing fine and is stable enough to live on her own."

"Yes, it'll be sad and we'll miss her," Momma said, reaching over to me. "But that'll just mean that we did what we were supposed to do."

"Who?" I asked.

"Me and your father," my mother responded, trying to look sweetly at Daddy across the table. He gave her a quick wink and smile then turned his attention back to me.

"Aren't you tired, sweetie?"

"Yes, I am tired, but who the hell can sleep when there's World War Three going on in here?" I blurted out, too pissed off and sleep deprived to care what they thought anymore. "Yes, I'm tired," I repeated myself for dramatic effect.

"I'm sorry," Daddy said. "I guess we were kind of loud in here."

I looked at my mother as she mouthed the word *sorry* to me.

"Do you want something to eat?" my mother asked getting up from the table.

"No. Not hungry," I kept my statement brief and my arms crossed. Although I was relieved that I had kept Momma from blurting out the one thing that we had promised to keep secret, I had managed to reveal Marla's secret, only to find out that no one really cared.

"Going to bed," I said as I got up from the table. My arms were still folded as I pushed the chair back into its place with my hip.

The light faded behind me as I walked back to Marla's room. The house was so quiet now that I could hear Marla's buzzing well before I got to the doorway. It still stood open just where I'd flung it. The dim light shone on my sister's face from the hallway. I yawned and stretched in front of the doorway, my shadow large and looming on the wall just next to Marla's bed. It hovered over Marla like a dark monster. I instinctively walked over to lie down beside my sister and then looked at the covers all tangled around her legs and feet. There was no way to get those covers untangled without waking her and having to face the evil she always hurled at anyone who interrupted her slumber.

"Bitch," I said to a sleeping Marla as I walked over to her bed. "Go ahead and leave."

I pulled at my pillow, which seemed heavier than usual, even for a feather stuffed poof, and tucked it under my arm. As I trekked back down the hall and into my own room, I could barely even hear Momma and Daddy talking now. Maybe, I thought, we could all finally get some sleep.

As I lay there in my bed I began to make my own plans for escape. If I couldn't go with Marla to UT then I'd go somewhere better. I imagined myself as Angie Dickenson on a show like *Police Woman,* signing autographs in between kicking the bad guys in the guts just like Momma did with the pervert. Only on *Police Woman* there was no slobbering and spitting. When Police Woman kicks, the bad guy just falls, no mess in between. Just as I was planning my Hollywood debut, I heard voices in the hallway. My head was so heavy I couldn't lift it off the pillow so I lay there as I heard my mother coming through my bedroom door.

"Oh, Everett," she said. "Look at her in here, sleeping in her own room. Has she been doing that more now?"

"No, this is the first time I've seen her in her own bed in, well, I don't know when," Daddy said. I wanted to roll my eyes, but they were closed, and in the dark no one but me would know what I was doing anyway.

"I was going to sleep in here," Momma whispered. "I guess I can just crawl in next to Dancy, but if this is the first time she's slept by herself..."

"You can just camp out in my room," Daddy whispered back to her.

By the time I turned to see what Momma and Daddy were talking about they were walking out, and he had his arm around her.

CHAPTER EIGHT

Chick's Place

Chick had tried to cram cotton in my ears just before he handed me the little gun.

"It's a .38 Special," Chick had said.

It looked like a toy in his hand. I watched as he laid it carefully on the counter.

"Don't touch that," Chick said as he went behind the bar. He ducked behind the counter, and I could hear him rattling things around. "Here we go," he said, presenting an aspirin bottle.

"Got a headache?" I smiled.

"No, but you will if you don't cover your eardrums out there," Chick said as he struggled to open the child-proof cap. His fingers looked like thick sausages as they fumbled around the tiny plastic disc. "There we go," he said, as he pinched at the cotton inside the bottle and then finally nabbed enough of it to get the whole thing out.

He pulled two pieces off and promptly stuck them in my ears at the same time. It hung loosely in in my ear canal. With those fat fingers of his, it would have been impossible to stick anything in even his own clown-sized ears, so he clearly couldn't have stuck anything properly in mine. I pulled the cotton out, balled it up to a normal size and stuck it back in as Chick walked back around the bar.

He looked in my ears one at a time to see what I had done, and let out a small growl, "Eh, I guess that's better'n what I done." He picked up the gun again, and then took an identical one from his pocket.

"Your momma spared no expense on these," he said, holding one in each hand as he inspected them both. His brown eyes looked like acorns rolling around in his head as they darted from one gun and then to the other. "Yeah, they're exactly the same," he said, bringing the guns closer to his face.

Marla and Momma had finally come out of the bathroom. It had been a long ride. Momma had said normally she could do it in about an hour and forty-five minutes, but it would take a little longer today because she was carrying her most precious cargo. We had stopped at Big K to get me and Marla bandanas for the trip. Mine was black, and Marla's was red.

I was still wearing mine, but Marla must have taken hers off in the bathroom.

"Look, Marla," I said pulling Chick's hands down so she could see. "These are ours."

"Guns?" Marla questioned and then gave Momma a cock-eyebrow look. "Momma, why do you have guns?"

My mother looked like she was bracing herself for an impact. "These are for you," Momma said, taking the two guns from Chick and giving one to each of us.

I was excited to finally get my hands around mine, but Marla looked a little like she was holding a half-rotten apple, still trying to determine its edibility.

"It's not loaded," Momma said. "They're brand new. This will be the only time it's okay to play with them."

I jumped off the bar stool and immediately pointed my pistol at the front door. I posed just like Pepper Anderson, then turned to my mother and mouthed, "Police Woman."

Marla rolled her eyes at me. "You're such a little weirdo," my sister said.

"Oh, come on, Marla, you know you love these," I said, urging my sister to join in my role play.

"Well," Marla looked at Momma. "I guess they are kind of cool. But you know Daddy isn't going to like this."

Momma nudged at Marla's arm to go and join me. "Your father will get over it," my mother said.

We pointed our guns at the ceiling where snipers were hiding; at the floor where we'd just cuffed an armed robber; and out the windows, where gangs were trying to infiltrate the bar, but never at each other. Momma said not pointing weapons at each other was rule number one whether the guns were loaded or not.

This wasn't the first time we'd been in Chick's Place. But no matter how many times Momma took us there it continued to look different. Maybe it was because there were always new people there or because the building was always under construction. Momma had told us on our first visit that Chick's Place was a bar for people who didn't drink. But unlike a normal bar, everyone at Chick's had their own room and their own bathroom. Even if Chick's Place had been a real bar I couldn't imagine anyone wanting to travel the four-mile dirt road to get there.

Momma said Chick had built the place for people just like her, a place where judgment was left at the end of that long driveway. The land, she said, was left to him by his grandfather, the richest attorney in Rayes County at one time. Chick never used the land until he hit rock bottom himself and had nowhere else to go. Momma said he had camped there for months trying to get sober, and then one day decided to build Chick's Place. She said lots of people had lived there over the years, and each of them helped him continue to build onto the original structure.

To call his place rustic would have been a heck of a compliment. It had everything it needed: lights, water, a kitchen, lots of bedrooms and bathrooms, but it looked a little like Miss Kitty's Place from *Gunsmoke*. I half expected dancing girls to come down the stairs at any moment with their ruffled pantaloons showing under their frilly skirts.

When one of the upstairs doors *did* open, I recognized the woman immediately, and she wasn't one of Miss Kitty's girls. Marla and I watched as she walked down the stairs. She looked different, cleaner at least. Her hair was combed, her face was washed and her clothes were pressed. She looked like someone who would work at the bank where Daddy kept his paychecks.

"Well, hello you two," she said with a raspy voice. "Remember me?"

"Umm, I think so?" Marla questioned herself.

"I remember you from yesterday," I said with confidence. "You're Janie."

"Yes," Janie said. "That's right."

She then looked at Marla. "It's okay that you don't recognize me. I look a little different, I know."

Marla nodded her head but said nothing.

"I have to look the part when I go to work," Janie said, and then took note of Marla's gun. "Oohh, these are nice," she said winking at us.

"Where do you work?" Marla's question was less of an inquisition and more like disbelief.

"At The Paper Place over in Stig," Janie said, with an air of dignity. "They sell office supplies, and I do their bookkeeping."

"Really?" Marla was not convinced.

"Yes, dear," Janie's voice was higher pitched now. "We all have to work here; else we'd starve to death." Janie laughed at us and shook her head, then walked over to the bar where Momma and Chick were sitting.

I tried to picture Janie in a professional setting with an office, a phone on her desk, and possibly even a secretary. I simply couldn't. Marla must have been having the same thoughts because I noticed she was inspecting every inch of Janie just like I was.

"See you girls later," Janie grabbed a soda from the fridge next to the bar and breezed by us with her leather jacket draped over her shoulder.

"Hey, where's your cotton?" My attention was caught by the sight of Marla's empty ears.

"Cotton?" Marla questioned.

"Chick's gotta put cotton in your ears so the noise doesn't bust your eardrums," I said, now thoroughly educated on the subject of eardrum safety. Bored with our role play we moseyed over to the bar.

"Are we really gonna shoot these things?" Marla asked Momma.

"We're going to have a few lessons on how to shoot and when to shoot," Momma said, taking a sip from a clear glass of water filled with ice cubes. I watched as the muscles in her throat protruded as they gripped the cold liquid. I could see lines on her neck that either weren't there before or somehow I never noticed. Her wavy hair still hung long, framing her face just like it always had, but now I noticed that a few grey strands were mixed in among the gold.

I had always loved my mother's shiny hair. It was almost mirror-like, catching the reflection of the sun and projecting its own light. It was the same now but somehow different too as it possessed more of a matte texture.

"What do you think, Marla?" During this visit, I had noticed that my mother was seeking Marla's approval more than usual. I wondered if it was because Marla had stopped racing to the phone for Momma's weekly calls and was sometimes even too busy to talk at all. Maybe the constant search for approval was because my mother was no longer quite so confident about what she was doing.

"Sure, it sounds like fun to me," Marla said, jumping up on the bar stool next to Momma.

"Dancy said I need some cotton in my ears," Marla looked at me and then at my mother.

I actually believed that I was now an authority on eardrum safety, because my suggestion to Marla had paid off. It made me feel good that my sister finally took advice from me without first questioning the hell out of it.

"Oh, I got you covered," Chick said to Marla, as he pulled out a long strand of cotton. Just like he had done for me, he ripped two small pieces from the strip of cotton and made an attempt at stabbing each piece into Marla's ear canals.

Like me, she pulled the almost-dangling pieces of cotton from her ears and fashioned them into a pair of usable earplugs. Chick furrowed his brow as he watched her redo his handy work, shook his head and then appeared to accept his defeat, having been bested twice now at his eardrum safety lesson.

"You girls ready?" Chick patted his holstered gun. "I got you all set up out there," he jerked his head toward the back door to show us the way.

As we passed through the kitchen just behind the bar, I saw the familiar once-white wall phone with a chair sitting just beneath it. The casing was tan and orange tinted with layers of nicotine and bacon grease. It didn't match the black receiver, but it was still functional. Just next to the chair was a table fashioned from an industrial-sized spool that someone had sawed in half. On top of it there were old phone books, scrap papers, a stack of mail, and some ink pens that had been gnawed almost in two. Next to those sat a blue, glass ashtray full of butts, most of which had been smoked all the way to the end then crushed like bugs.

As we neared the back door, I saw Chick's apron hanging by the kitchen sink. It made me smile. Like the phone, it was once white. Hand-stitched, misshapen cut letters spelled out C-H-I-C-K-S K-I-T-C-H-E-N in faded denim and were affixed to the dingy fabric haphazardly. I guess it was better to scatter the letters about aimlessly than to try and mimic anything resembling symmetry.

"One of you needs to go with Chick and one of you with me," Momma said, as I closed the back door behind me.

"I'll go with Chick," I yelled. Marla didn't seem to mind that I was willing to hang out with the old biker.

As Chick and I walked to our side of the make-shift firing range, I felt the need to break the silence between us.

"So, how big is this place anyway?" I asked Chick, taking note of a tiny fence way off in the distance. I began wondering why Marla and I had never spent any time outside the bar during our visits with Momma.

"Big, pretty big," Chick said, trudging along in the dry dirt. "Used to be bigger. I sold a lot of it off." He looked out over the field. "And I rent some of it for farming. But there's still plenty left for us small folk," he pointed to the land and waved his arm back and forth to show the vastness.

We stopped just in front of three bales of hay stacked on top of one another. I turned to look for Momma and Marla. They too had stopped at three identical bales of hay. I waved to them, but only Momma waved back. It looked like Marla was busy aiming her gun at a row of glass bottles and aluminum cans.

"We'll start with these." Chick directed my attention to my first targets. He had lined up a row of glass bottles and cans on hay bales stacked two high. It looked exactly the same as Marla's but some of my bottles were different sizes.

"She's going to be better than me," I said to Chick.

"It's not a contest, Dancy." Chick took the gun from me, held it in front of him, and pointed at the one of the bottles. "Your Momma wants you to know how to protect yourself, and it ain't nothin' more'n that."

He pointed the gun at the targets, one at a time, as he spoke. He was mentally measuring the distance between each one.

"At first I thought your momma was crazy, but then after what I saw yesterday," Chick started but didn't finish his sentence. He was still focused on measuring the targets by looking over the gun's barrel. "She should've let me kill the son of a bitch."

I was glad Chick didn't finish the sentence. The penis and the pervert were the last things I ever wanted to talk about with Chick.

"So, if Momma stays with us at home then we won't have to worry about it," I said. "She'll be with us."

Chick put the gun down on the bale and removed some bullets from the paper box he carried in his pocket.

"Your Momma isn't ready to come home yet, but she will be," Chick said, popping open the cylinder. "Now, I want you to see how I've done this because I'm going to have you do it after a while."

I watched as Chick pulled the hammer back and popped open the cylinder again and again to show me exactly how it worked.

"What do you mean she's not ready?" I took the gun from Chick and opened the cylinder a few times in front of him so he could see that I knew how.

"Well, she will be soon and until then she can just stay here," Chick said, taking the gun back and opening the cylinder one last time to show me how to place the bullets.

"She told us she was going to stay on for a while," I said, my voice cracking a bit. "I mean that's what she told Daddy."

"Yeah, she's going to visit for a while and spend time with you girls, but she's coming back here to finish out her plan," Chick stopped fiddling with the gun and placed it down on the bale of hay. "Now listen, Chickpea, your Momma *is* coming home. Don't you worry about that," Chick said, as his massive hands grasped both my upper arms to stress his point. I opened my eyes wider so the tiny bit of tears that had glazed them would dry more quickly.

"So, like when she gets a job like Janie then she'll be home?" I asked, not knowing what kind of a plan Chick was talking about.

"Oh, God no," Chick said, chuckling a bit. "I wouldn't want Lou to get a job. She's got her, well, her writing."

"Oh yeah, her writing," I said nodding, pretending to know what he was talking about.

"Yeah, she's just finished her second book. We consider her to be a pretty big deal around here."

Books? I questioned in my head what I had just heard and quickly tried to process it.

"I've never seen any of her books anywhere," I said, wondering if Chick had lost his mind since the last time I saw him. My mother never wrote anything more than a grocery list. I looked over toward Momma, trying to picture her as one of those literary types. I just couldn't see it.

"Maybe you're not looking under the right name," Chick continued talking about my mother's so-called writing career. "She writes under that pen name, U-N-N-A, Unna."

To my own detriment I interrupted Chick before he could finish.

"You mean my mother, my mother," I repeated for dramatic effect, "writes books?!" I blurted out rather loudly.

"Well, how else do you think she is able to send you guys a check every month?"

"Momma sends us a check every month?"

Chick looked like he was standing on the other end of the gun barrel. He knew and I knew that he had revealed something he probably shouldn't have.

"What is Unna's last name?" I wanted to hurriedly press him for more answers before he decided to clam up.

"Oh no you don't, Chickpea," he said, shaking his head at me. "I've already overstepped. You and me need to stick to the task at hand. If you want to know about anything other than how to shoot a bullet into those targets, you'll have to ask your ma. Fact, here she comes now."

I watched as Momma, also known evidently as Unna in literary circles, and Marla walked over to us. I strained my eyes to see Marla's targets. They had been obliterated. Momma must have shot them, I figured. I couldn't believe what I'd just heard. Daddy never mentioned that Momma was sending money. I never thought she had any for herself, much less any to spare for us.

"We square, Chickpea?" I knew what Chick was asking: for me not to tell anyone what he'd just said. "Your Momma will come home in good time and she'll tell you what she needs to tell you in good time. For now, let's just let her be," Chick nodded his head until I began to nod, too. I let him know I understood and that my mother's secrets would be safe until she came home for good, whenever that might be.

"Oh my God, Dancy!" Marla came running up to me and almost jumped in my arms. "You're not going to believe it. I shot every jar, every can, every jug one by one. BOOM, BOOM, BOOM! I shot them all." Marla held up her forefinger and thumb in the shape of a gun and pointed at my targets. Momma was holding Marla's gun or she'd have probably just shot all my targets down right there.

"Momma, can I shoot some more?" Marla was jumping all around her. I couldn't remember the last time I had seen her so excited and especially about anything that had to do with our mother. Momma saw the sour look on my face. I could tell she was disappointed that I wasn't happy for Marla and her newfound talent.

It really pissed me off that Marla was better at everything, and before I had even taken the first shot, I knew she was going to better at this, too.

"Momma, Momma, please let me shoot those," Marla pawed at the gun in my mother's hand.

"Don't worry, Chickpea, I got plenty of targets and all day with nothin' to do," Chick leaned down and whispered to me when he saw the disappointment on my face. "'sides, I want to see what this gal can do," he spoke louder so that Marla and Momma could hear him.

"Well it's really up to your sister. It *is* her turn," Momma said as she looked over at me for permission to let Marla shoot my targets.

"Whatever," I said, rolling my eyes and crossing my arms. It was a half-ass approval, but that's all Momma was getting from me.

"Chick, you ain't gonna believe this," my mother said as she handed the gun over to Marla. "Just, well, watch. You ain't gonna believe it," she said again, this time with a throaty laugh.

My sister stepped up to the stacked hay bales, placed both arms across the width of them and began popping off targets. BOOM, BOOM, BOOM, BOOM, BOOM, BOOM! Cans flew up in the air, glass shattered and the one jug in the lineup seemed to float for just a second before it gave up and collapsed onto the ground. Marla looked over at me almost the minute she finished shooting and said, like she had read my mind, "I know. I can't believe it either."

"That's crazy, Marla," I almost demanded an explanation. "Where did you learn to do that?"

"I didn't," my sister said. "I've never shot a gun, never even held one."

"I'll be damned, girl." Chick looked at Marla, his brows furrowed. "D'she do this down there too?" he asked Momma, pointing to the target he had set up for Marla.

"Sure did. I couldn't believe it either. That's why I wanted you to see it."

"I'll be right back. Don't you go anywhere," Chick said to Marla.

The three of us watched as Chick trotted the fifty feet to my now-obliterated target line up. The old biker tossed the top hay bale onto the ground and then picked it back up and shook the shards of glass off it. He then placed bale back on top. He reached into the metal cylinder next to the bales and presented an orange juice jar, then a few cans and some empty soda bottles. He lined them all up, equally spaced.

"Don't you dare pick up that gun until he gets back here, Marla." My mother slapped my sister's wrist as she reached for her weapon. I snorted a small laugh.

"Shut up, Dancy," Marla said, as she threw a dirty look my way.

"Look," I said, when I saw Chick tearing down the target display. "What's he doing?"

"I don't know." Momma held her hand up over eyes to block the sun so she could see him better.

"I was gonna shoot," Marla whined as she watched her precious targets disappear one by one.

"Shh," Momma said, walking out a few feet so she could see better. "He's moving the target out farther," Momma laughed and then pointed playfully at Marla. "He's gonna see how good you really are, girl."

I nudged Marla. "Think you can still hit 'em?"

"I dunno, maybe," Marla's reply sounded a little unsure. "I guess we'll see."

Chick was panting for breath as he trotted the last few feet to where we were standing. "Okay, gal," he took two hard breaths so he could finish his sentence, "let's see what you got."

"How far is it?" Marla squinted her eyes to see the setup better.

"'Bout seventy-five or eighty feet," Chick had finally caught his breath enough to speak like a normal person.

"Hmmm." Marla studied his words like a professional marksman setting some sort of internal measurements.

"Go on, honey," my mother said, urging Marla to step up to the challenge.

I looked at Chick with one eye squinted against the sun.

"She'gn do it," Chick said, winking at me.

I heard my sister let out a loud sigh and then watched as she leaned her body into the stacks of hay bales. BOOM, BOOM, BOOM, BOOM, BOOM, BOOM!

Even though they were farther away, I could still see the cans jump and the bottles shatter. Again, she had hit them one by one in perfect timing with the exception of the jug on the right side. It was still sitting there, untouched.

"Wow," Chick said. "Not bad, not bad at all."

"I missed one." Marla was disappointed.

"I wouldn't worry about it, kid," Chick patted her on the back. "I think most people would be pretty darned satisfied if they only hit half what you did today."

"Mmmm," Marla said as she nodded her head. "I guess so."

"What about you, kid?" Chick turned his attention to me. "You ready to try?"

"'Bout damn time," I said, trying to kick some dirt up with my shoe.

"Dancy?!" My mother attempted to scold me for cussing but I paid no mind to her. "Let's do this," I said, punching Chick on the arm.

"Come on, you guys, let's reset this target," Chick invited us to come with him to move the hay bales back to where they were. As pissed off as I was about Marla's newfound sharpshooting skills, I was equally annoyed with my mother, or Unna. My mother obviously didn't want us know anything and evidently didn't want us to be a part of her life with Chick and the others. I had read enough books to at least hold my own in an inquisition, so I began to pry as much as I could.

"Wow, Marla," I was able to muster up some faux happiness for my sister. "You're a good shooter. I hope I'm as good as you."

My sister shot me a look that was rife with suspicion. "Yeah, uh thanks," she said, hesitantly. Marla was no fool. She knew something was up.

"When we get home, let's see if Daddy will take us to the library, and we can get some books on shooting. Maybe there's a little murder mystery out there about a girl your age that shoots guns as good as you."

From the look on my sister's face, I wasn't going to win an Oscar for this performance, but it did get my mother's attention.

"No, Dancy." My mother stopped us both in our tracks as she grabbed us both by a shoulder. "I don't think your father would understand about this," she said with a serious tone. She motioned with her head for Chick to go on in front of us.

"Girls, I want you to be safe even when your daddy's not around, like for things that happened yesterday. I don't want you to go around shooting people, but I do want you to feel powerful and not afraid."

I knew this weaponry enterprise was going to be a secret, somehow, from the moment I first saw Chick holding the gun. Surprisingly, Marla agreed with my mother for perhaps the first time in years.

"Yeah, Dancy, I don't think Daddy would understand."

I rolled my eyes at Marla, not because I disagreed but because I knew her underlying motive for siding with Momma.

"I know, Momma," I said, ignoring my sister's obvious agenda. "This is no worse than throwing horseshoes or shooting craps." These were both things Daddy had taught me and my sister.

"Well, it's a little different," Momma said, wincing. "But even so, we'll just keep this to ourselves."

"So, we don't get to take our guns home?" Marla seemed devastated.

"No, honey," Momma said, with a chuckle. "I will keep them 'til you're old enough to carry them."

"Shit," Marla blurted out.

"Marla?!" Momma shook her head and rolled her eyes. "You girls and that language! I don't even want to think about what you're learning over at that school."

"I'll keep the gun in my panty and sock drawer," Marla pleaded. "Daddy would never look in there."

"No, Marla. The guns will stay with me for now," Momma said adamantly enough for Marla to stop whining.

Momma turned and started walking toward the targets again. "We can come here and practice with them all we want."

I was relieved that Momma wasn't going to let Marla bring that thing home. My sister was terrifying enough in a fit of rage armed with a simple random shoe she'd found lying around the house. Marla with a gun would have added a whole new dimension to surviving in the Wilder house when Daddy was at work.

Unna had bested me at my attempt to draw her out with that bit about the library. But now it was my turn to shoot, and Unna would have to wait until I thought of another clever line that would expose her.

Chick and Momma had pulled the bales of hay about forty feet closer. An obvious advantage over Marla's original shooting point. Even though I wasn't looking at my sister I could feel her smirky grin burning into the back of my head. My six targets were in plain sight, and if Momma and Chick thought I hadn't been keeping track of Marla's shots, they were mistaken. If my math skills served me correctly, she had pulled off eighteen rounds, and I was going to get my dozen more after this setup, too.

BOOM, BOOM, BOOM, BOOM, BOOM, BOOM!

I heard the tink of at least two cans, or at least I imagined I did.

"Three down, Chickpea, not bad for first time," Chick patted me on the shoulder.

"Fuck!" I yelled.

"Calm down, Dancy," Momma snapped. "Three is unbelievably good." My mother's eyes were wide, and her smile ran all the way across her face. "Have you girls ever done this before?" My mother continued to be in a state of disbelief that we were both naturals.

"Give me that gun, and I'll go setup another round," Chick took the gun from my hand. My eyes were set on the three targets I'd missed. "Fuck!" I said again, lower this time so Momma wouldn't hear, but loud enough to make myself feel better.

I watched with intensity as Chick constructed a new setup, all glass bottles this time.

"Ready to go," he was breathless again as he walked back to where we were standing and handed me the gun.

BOOM, BOOM, BOOM, BOOM, BOOM, BOOM!

Certain I heard glass shatter, I was pleased with what I had done.

"Two down, Chickpea."

"Son-of-a-bitch!" I yelled. Momma didn't even scold me this time. Everyone, including Marla, was now acutely aware of my frustration.

"Slow down," Marla said as she walked up to stand next to me. I gave her a quick shove with my elbow.

"All right, all right, suit yourself, Dancy," Marla said, as she cautiously backed away.

Maybe she was right. It did all seem to be going too fast.

"You girls are out of this world," Chick said, turning a stray bucket over and taking a seat. Trying to catch his breath again, he began to cough through is words, "I—can't even hit—two, Dancy." He then cleared the phlegm from his throat.

I didn't care if Chick thought my shooting was good. I had to at least do as good as Marla on the next targets, better even. I was rattled, and I knew it. I had to focus on hitting those targets and not on beating Marla. Along with math and social studies, Mr. Montel had taught me this, "don't let 'em rattle ya," he had said after Kevin Mark Cunningham had just beaten me at an impromptu free-throw contest on the playground. "You've got to develop a dialogue with your opponent and begin to look at things from his perspective," he said. To which I responded, "I'm not gonna talk to that creep."

When my teacher was finished laughing he explained that he was not asking me to talk to Kevin Mark but rather to examine the basket I was trying to hit. "The basket is your opponent, not Kevin Mark." Although I begged and begged, Kevin Mark Cunningham would never agree to another contest with me. I'd like to think it was because I had gotten inside Kevin Mark's head, but I knew the real reason was because his friends made fun of him for challenging a girl to a free-throw contest.

"Want me to get this one?" Momma asked Chick, who was still on the bucket, but now looked a good two inches shorter as the rim had sunk into the soft dirt.

Chick motioned a tired hand toward the target, letting her know that yes, she could take care of this one. She took the gun from my hand so I wouldn't accidentally shoot her while she was walking out and headed to the targets.

"I'm coming with you," I said, skipping behind her.

"Is he going to be okay?" I looked back at a wheezing Chick.

"Yeah," Momma turned for a moment and then kept walking. "Chick smoked a good twenty-five years before he quit."

When we got to the target, the four bottles I hadn't hit were standing there like a toothless grin. They mocked me with their glare as the sun gave them sparkle. I walked around behind the bottles to look at the shooter's spot. From there, the shooter's setup didn't seem far away at all. I could even hear Chick and Marla laughing. Momma rustled around in the garbage cylinder to find two more targets. "Bottles or cans?" she asked.

"Bottles," I said firmly, making a statement that I would not be defeated by these miniscule translucent objects. I grasped each one in my hand and then set each back down on the straw. I even dug them into the hay bale to be sure they had a good fighting chance and would be knocked over only by a bullet and not some wimpy afternoon breeze.

"What you doing, Dancy?" Momma leaned down to look through the bottle with me.

I never looked up. This was between me and those bottles and had nothing to do with her.

"I'm having a dialogue with my opponent," I said with not even a hint of little girl tenor in my voice. "I'm ready now. Let's go."

Momma rose up from the close view of the bottles and followed me back to the shooter's area. I walked faster than her, and when I found my spot my concentration was broken but only for a second. I had forgotten that she had the gun.

Chick started to say something to me, but I refused to listen, putting my finger on my lips, I shushed him. Momma handed me the gun, and I whispered to those shiny bottles one last time.

"Here we go you sons a bitches," I said quietly. BOOM, BOOM, BOOM, BOOM, BOOM, BOOM!

"Whoohoo!" Chick gave a yell. "Looks like you got 'em, Chickpea."

"Hell yeah!" I yelled in celebration.

Marla held her hand out so I could slap her five. "We're both pretty damn good, Dancy."

"Yes, we are," I said, holding my hand out to give her some more skin.

"Let's get some root beer for these sharp shootin' sons a guns." Chick opened the back door for the three of us.

"Drink up, girls, we got to get you home," Momma said, taking a sip from the bottle Chick gave her.

"It's only three o'clock," Marla said, pointing her bottle toward the wall clock shaped like a clipper ship.

"Well, we have some other business to take care of in town," Momma said, winking at us. "A trip by the bank and then, well, some other things."

"You're not gonna," Chick started to speak and Momma quickly shushed him. "Ugh," he said and then shook his head. "I told you I'd take care of that."

"But I want to," Momma's tone was serious now.

"Want to what?" I asked.

"Never mind him." Momma threw up her hand like she was shooing Chick away. "It's a girl thing. He'd never understand."

Chick disappeared back into the kitchen when the phone rang and reappeared a few minutes later wearing his Chick's Kitchen apron. It didn't look nearly as dirty when he put it on as it did hanging against the white kitchen wall.

"Comp'nies comin'," he said, tying the long apron strings in the front. "Gotta get some supper on. You girls come back and see ole' Chick. Next time I'll have a target you can't hit."

Momma laughed. "Sounds like an invitation and a challenge all in one, girls."

Momma let us get on the bike first, Marla in front and me in the middle just like before. I didn't argue about having to ride in the middle. Momma's bike still made me feel a little uneasy, exposed even. So being sandwiched in between the two of them suited me just fine.

We went in with Momma when she stopped at the Stig County National Bank in Johnstown. I had passed through Johnstown before with Daddy, but he had never stopped. Daddy said the whole town sat inside a crater made by a falling meteor tens of thousands of years ago. From the highway it looked like a hole with a lot of little buildings and people; sort of like a dollhouse.

As we pulled up on Momma's bike, I worried at first that the bank employees might think we were there to rob the place. The three of us certainly looked like the bank-robbing type at first glance; Momma in her leathers with her proudly displayed tattoos, and me and Marla in our bandanas and almost-shredded denim. We were now also the proud owners of two fine leather straps, compliments of Chick. He had showed us earlier how to tie them to our legs to keep the exhaust pipes from Momma's bike from get too hot against our legs as we rode.

"You girls sit down there," Momma said, motioning to the burgundy colored waiting chairs.

It felt good in there. Cool as a fall breeze in the morning. The freshly dusted furniture and stair railings, along with the perfectly pressed bank employees, brought my attention to how dirty I was. I wiped some lingering sweat beads from my upper lip, which prompted Marla to grab a tissue from a box on one of the desks.

"You've got a black streak," she said. "Here, let me get it."

As Marla licked the tissue and then wiped the bottom of my nose, I could hear people talking to Momma like they had known her all her life.

"So how's Chick and the rest of the gang doing?" The teller who was counting out money for my mother chattered as she worked.

"Good, really good," Momma said to her as she silently counted the one hundred dollar bills along with her. "We just came from there," Momma said, pointing to us in the waiting chairs.

"Oh my goodness," the bank teller said in a sing-songy voice as she came out from behind the counter. "Is this, really, it can't be. Marla? Danielle?"

We instinctively nodded as she said each of our names.

"Look at these girls, they are beautiful, Louise, just like you always were," the woman grabbed two suckers from a nearby desk and gave each of us one. It was like we were toddlers the way she was talking to us.

The overly-friendly bank teller went back behind the counter and started counting Momma's money again, still chattering on. I heard my mother sigh from all the way across the room. "You girls don't know this, but your mother and I used to be the best of friends in school. Well, I could go on all day, but it looks like you're in a hurry, Louise."

"Yes, Ramona, I kind of am, but it's always so good to talk to you," Momma said, animating her motions just like Ramona had when she had been talking.

Marla and I looked at each other when Momma held up a stack of cash at least an inch thick. "Can I get an envelope or something for this," Momma asked Ramona as she flipped through the cash like a deck of playing cards.

"Oh sure, Louise," Ramona said, shaking her head. "I'm sorry. I should have done that to begin with."

Marla and I watched in amazement as our mother stuck the stack of cash inside the leather pouch that sat at her waistline.

"See you later, Ramona," Momma said as she left the counter. "C'mon girls," she said to us even though we were already right behind her.

Momma waited as Marla mounted the bike. "Were you really best friends with her?" Marla asked the question before I got the chance.

"No, she was kind of a bitch in high school," Momma chuckled. "I couldn't stand her."

"So why is she so nice to you now?" Again Marla asked the question I had in my head.

"She's a suck up," Momma said as she climbed on the bike behind me. "Thinks I got something now."

"You mean *Unna's* got something," I said quietly to myself.

"What did you say, Dancy?" I had forgotten my mother's keen sense of hearing but was reminded of it as soon as she snapped at me. I didn't answer. Marla turned and looked at me with her trademark *what the hell?* expression.

"What did you say, Dancy?" My mother repeated her question, this time with a more terse tone than before. "You think you might know something? Let's hear it," she demanded.

Unna was obviously someone my mother had no intention of introducing to anyone, and I was instantly sorry I had breezed into the topic of her existence so casually.

"Nothing, Momma," I answered my mother but didn't turn around. "I didn't say anything," I said a little louder to try and kill the lump in my throat.

CHAPTER NINE

Girl Talk

I lost count after a dozen or so Benjamin Franklins hit the surface. Some had caught air and floated dangerously close to the edge of the other side of the counter, before they began to stack themselves neatly. Momma's lips were loosely puckered and a tiny whistling sound accompanied each bill she sent forth.

"May I help you, Ma'am?" What looked similar to a woman, but I really couldn't be sure, with a sheriff's badge hanging on her belt loop walked over and stood in front of the stack of cash. Momma looked up for the first time since we'd arrived at the barred window, stopped counting and whistling, and held her index finger up, signaling that she didn't want to be interrupted.

When the faint whistling started again the woman looked at Marla and me. I instinctively pulled the bandana from my head and attempted to fluff my hair, which now seemed to be glued to the surface of my scalp.

Marla was still watching Momma's every move and probably knew exactly how much cash she was laying down. My sister paid no attention when the woman spoke.

"How are you girls today?" the woman asked and then smiled, revealing one tiny dead tooth among a picket of pearly white healthy ones. I knew if I spoke loud enough for her to hear me, there'd be an echo. There was too much marble, stone, and metal and too little furniture. I was aware that a squeaky sound like my voice had the potential to bat around the room for at least a second or two, so I nodded and then looked away, pretending to read the names from the embossed plaque hanging on the wall beside me. I even moved my lips in case there was any question that I was otherwise occupied and, like my mother, I didn't want to be interrupted.

"There's five-thousand dollars." My mother's hands were finally empty. She had managed in seconds to rid herself of every bill from her leather pouch. "I'm here to gather Ms. Loomis. She was brought in yesterday, I believe."

Finally, Marla turned around to look at me. I had been standing there next to her the whole time. My sister had been so firmly attached to Momma's leg as the money was being counted that she didn't notice I was there. We both shrugged our shoulders at one another. "Who's Ms. Loomis?" Marla whispered to me.

"Beats me," I said and then shushed my sister so we wouldn't miss any part of the conversation.

"Would that be Linda Loomis?" The woman questioned my mother as she looked at the pile of cash before her.

"Yes," Momma's voice was monotone.

"That'll be five thousand dollars, Ma'am," the woman with the black Chicklet tooth said as she presented some paperwork from behind the counter.

"Yes, I know," my mother's smartass tone sounded a lot like my sister at that point. "That's why I brought five thousand dollars."

The woman nodded her head and began counting the bills.

"Family?" The woman questioned my mother as she counted.

"No," Momma's voice had no fluctuation.

"Good friend, then?" The woman pressed further.

"No," Momma's voice was a little louder.

I watched as the little black tooth was revealed once more, and the woman's face lit up like Bob Barker had just called her up onto the *Price Is Right* stage. "Oh, you must be a bail bondsman," she said, smiling. "I've never seen a woman bail bondsman in here before. You must be new."

"Not a bail bondsman," my mother reluctantly responded as the woman's black tooth went back into hiding as she continued counting the money.

"Well, looks like it's all here." The woman stacked the cash next to her and then slid some papers halfway under the barred window cutout. "Just sign here, please, and then you can go across the street and get her." The woman drew an "x" next to where Momma was supposed to sign.

Marla and I now stood on each side of Momma, crowding ever closer so we could get a look at those papers.

"Girls," my mother scolded and then elbowed each of us. She then signed and pushed the paperwork back under the bars, trading them for a receipt. The woman smiled, walked back to her desk and picked up the phone. "Ted. Marty here, sheriff's office," she said. "Get Loomis ready. She's bonded out."

Marla and I now knew what Momma was there to do: get Hot Ginger out of jail. It was the 'why' aspect of our mother's action we were both silently struggling with. We kept looking at one another hoping to gain some insight into why Momma would do such a thing. After the Unna comment back at the bank I wasn't about to open my mouth again. It was Marla's turn to find out the answer to this puzzle, but she wasn't taking it.

"C'mon, girls," Momma said as she led me and my sister to the exit. Once there, she stopped abruptly like she had forgotten something and then turned toward the woman behind the bars.

"Hey," she half-yelled to get her attention. I saw Black Tooth's badge bouncing in rhythm with her steps as she came back to the counter.

"In case it's just killing you to know, she's my husband's girlfriend," Momma said, paused, and cocked her head to one side, her long hair flipping around her shoulders. "You must be new."

As we left the building I pulled my sweaty bandana from my jeans pocket and tied it around my head. We left the motorcycle parked in the grass near the steps of the building and walked to the jailhouse. Marla and I flanked Momma like bookends as we strode like the MOD Squad across the steamy concrete. I saw the ends of Marla's bandana wiggle in our wake as we walked. I wondered if mine was doing the same.

Me, Daddy, and Marla had passed by the jailhouse every time we'd come to town, but I'd never seen inside. The windows in the rooms where the inmates stayed were too high for me to see anything. It looked like maybe the jail birds were kept on the third or fourth floor, but I never received visual confirmation. The iron bars on the windows were a dead giveaway, even if I never saw anyone's hands wrapped around them or any faces smashed between them for a bit of fresh air.

I had almost forgotten about Ginger. It seemed like a lifetime ago that we were at the mall. My guts twisted thinking about all the things I'd done since I'd last seen her, not giving her a moment's thought.

I stopped wondering why Momma was going to get Ginger out of jail and decided that I was just glad that someone was getting her out. Even when I saw the police take Ginger away, the reality of where they were taking her never registered with me, until now. The earrings she had stolen for me, now laid somewhere between the pervert and Mrs. Tollet's house. Things that only yesterday had consumed my thoughts, I had carelessly forgotten. I thought about what Mamaw said about such things as this: "You know what they say?" Mamaw would say. "Outta sight, outta mind." If there was ever any question about it, I knew for sure now that Mamaw was right.

Daddy said once that it was the inmates who actually built the Rayes County Jail. As Momma, Marla, and I walked up the front steps, I tried to imagine how many of them it took to lift those boulders into place. There were eight solid rocks at least ten feet wide; no mortar holding a bunch of little bricks together, just solid pieces. Those rocks weighed a good ton each. I pictured the inmates working from within the walls of the jail, building the structure, piece by piece until they had finally enclosed themselves completely with the final rock forced into place, breaking the only light from the beaming blue sky that looked down into their prison.

Momma moved quickly across the corridor once we entered the doors. There were four rows of what looked like church pews on each side of the room. The aisle down the middle of the room led straight to a barred window. The entire setup looked exactly like the service window at Black Tooth's office. A few people were sitting in the pews. I would have counted them but was distracted by a girl with a tattoo of a snake that ran nearly all the way around her neck. The tail came around the front of her throat and ran down her chest and through the middle of her cleavage. The head was just under her ear. The snake's forked tongue was wavy and red, and his eyes looked straight ahead.

"Stop it." Marla saw me staring at the weird snake girl and smacked me on the arm. "She'll come back here and kick your ass, and I don't blame her."

Somehow we had managed to seat ourselves right behind snake girl and Momma was already at the window presenting her copies of the paperwork she had gotten from Black Tooth.

"Fuck you, Marla," I said, finally coming out of my trance. "I'll do whatever I want."

"Suit yourself, Dancy. I hope she breaks your arm," my sister whispered just before scooting at least three feet down the pew from me. "If she comes after you I'm going to act like I don't know you."

"Fuck you, Marla," I said again, this time louder.

I was so focused on shooting dirty looks at Marla I didn't notice that snake girl had turned around and was looking at me. I jumped, startled by her piercing blue eyes contrasted with black liner at least a half an inch thick.

"That's awfully foul language for such a little girl." Her voice was thick and soupy.

I couldn't speak. The snake was looking right at me, and I was now entranced by its eyes. My mouth was as dry as the dirt path running through Chick's back yard. If I had spoken right then dust would have clouded the room. I looked at Marla, who had turned her head toward the wall to keep from acknowledging me. Momma was at the window and had her back turned to me. I was on my own with Snake Girl.

"What?" Snake Girl asked in a tone sarcastic. "Did I hear you say something? More big words from little you?"

I shook my head vigorously. I had been petrified from looking into the snake's eyes too long. It was the only movement I had control over, or maybe it had control over me. Either way, I wanted to get the point across that I had nothing else to say.

"That's what I thought," she said, cocking one painted-on eyebrow. She then brought her arm around with a snake-like motion, holding her index and middle finger together like the fangs of a reptile. "Ssss, Ssss," she made the sound of a snake as she thrust her finger-fangs toward me. "Now, have a little respect."

As she turned around to face the front of the room again, I let out the breath I'd been holding since the moment she first looked at me. I felt a tiny squirt of pee warm my underwear. My heart was racing.

Seeing a bathroom door on the opposite wall where the empty pews were, I took the opportunity to get away from Snake Girl and take a much-needed piss. I got caught in Momma's peripheral vision, and she turned from the window. "Everything okay, Dancy?"

I nodded, and she turned back to the window. Snake Girl gave me a salute with her two fang fingers. I quickly got inside, shut the door, and unfortunately took a deep breath.

"Ulk," I gagged as the odor of old urine hit the back of my throat and came up through my nose. My eyes watered as I held my breath and pulled down my pants, hovering as best as I could over the pape-and-pee-filled commode. I didn't wash my hands. There was no time and the sink was nastier than anything I could have touched throughout the duration of the day. I slammed the door behind me as I collapsed myself over the nearest pew.

I welcomed the stale and humid air of the jailhouse waiting room as fresh and crisp, taking in as much of it as I could in one breath. Snake Girl was now standing next to a man about her same age with a matching tattoo around his neck. I smirked at her as they passed me, no longer intimidated by her or her finger fangs. If my choices were down to facing her or going back in that bathroom, I'd have to come to terms with Snake Girl breaking my arm.

Momma had finished filling out even more paperwork and was now sitting with Marla. When she saw I had come out of the bathroom, she got up and walked by me, patted me on the head, and then went into the ladies room, a loose term by any standards.

There was no time to warn her, and I was still panting for breath. She was in there so long I started to wonder if she'd passed out, run out of oxygen, and was now lying on the damp, mold-riddled tile floor.

"Momma?" I knocked on the door to check on her.

"Out in a minute," she replied, not sounding at all like the breath had been squeezed from her. "I'm washing my hands."

Finally, my mother emerged and shut the door behind her.

"It's pretty awful in that bathroom," I said, crinkling my nose and shaking my head.

"Eh, I've used worse, Dancy."

I followed as Momma went over to take a seat next to Marla.

"When is she coming out?" Marla had managed to find a magazine and was now flipping through it.

"In a few minutes," Momma said.

A formerly white door, now alabaster, slowly opened. "Bet that's her now."

Seeing Ginger brought the events of yesterday rushing back. She was still wearing the same clothes as when the police took her from the mall.

"Girls," she said, excited to see us. We got up to meet her as she began walking toward the pews. She looked *wollered* as Mamaw would've said had she been there. Thank God she wasn't. I imagined a brawl between the likes of Momma, Mamaw, Ginger, and the snake girl, had she not made her exit in time. It might have been interesting, but the aftermath would have landed us all in a cell.

Faded lipstick and flakes of mascara had replaced the well put together Ginger I used to know.

"Are you okay?" I asked Ginger carefully, afraid to hear the answer.

"Of course, I'm okay," Ginger said and then hugged me.

Marla stood nearby but hadn't said anything yet. Momma stayed in the pew watching.

"Oh, I'm so glad to be out of there," Ginger took a deep breath. "I just want to go out that door and never look back. Where's your father?"

"He's not here," Marla offered immediately.

"How did you girls manage to get down here?" Ginger's eyes darted around the room for any sign of our chaperone.

It pissed me off that she seemed more concerned about our mode of transportation today than she did about how we managed to get home after the mall incident yesterday.

"Momma came to get you," Marla turned and looked at our mother.

Momma rose from her pew with cautionary moves and approached Ginger like she was a wild animal.

"Hello, Ms. Loomis, I'm Louise," she said in as soft a voice as I had ever heard come out of my mother.

"So Everett sent his ex-wife to pick me up?" Ginger looked confused and now a little angry.

"No, I came on my own to get you," Momma said, then stopped, allowing Ginger the opportunity to be a bit grateful.

"Well, when Everett gets back from work I'm sure he'll pay you for your trouble." Ginger smiled sweetly at Momma.

"I'm sorry," Momma said. "You don't understand. *I'm* here to get you, to help you. Everett has nothing to do with this."

"No, no. I guess I don't understand," Ginger stuttered and then looked to Momma for answers.

"I'd like to invite you to come and stay at Chick's Place," Momma offered a hand to Ginger as she spoke. Between her fingers was a tiny tan card with some writing on it and, at the bottom, what looked like a phone number. "It's a place where you can go without being judged and deal with your addiction."

Ginger, who had started to take my mother's hand, immediately snapped it back like she was about to pet a rabid dog.

"I'm not addicted to anything." Ginger laughed almost maniacally. "That'd be you, honey. Everett's told me all about you, Lou."

Ginger stressed the name Lou, letting my mother know that she had been a topic of discussion between her and my father. Momma's attention was now on the woman behind the counter.

"Everything okay out there, ladies?" The woman banged a night stick on the iron bars as she spoke.

"C'mon girls, let's go," Momma said, grabbing us both by the top of a shoulder and nudging us toward the door.

Ginger followed close behind us, her heels making quick clicks and echoing along the walls.

Once outside, we watched as Ginger rifled around in her handbag and then produced a pair of dark sunglasses.

"So how about it, Linda?" My mother ducked her head down to try and look Ginger in the face. "Chick's Place?"

"You're crazier than you look, lady." Ginger stretched her neck so she'd seem a little taller. "I'm going home," her indignant tone didn't faze my mother in the least. "And when Everett gets home I'll talk about this with him, and we'll see to the girls, Lou. You can go now."

Marla and I winced at the same time when we realized that Ginger had just dismissed Momma, in essence telling her to go away. We both took a couple of steps away from the two women in anticipation of what might happen next.

"Listen, I've tried to be nice, do the right thing, get your sorry ass out of jail, and get you some help," Momma's voice got louder and she annunciated her words more clearly the longer she spoke. "But I leave you here, Ginger, and my girls will be going back home with me and Everett, who by the way, was going to leave your sorry ass in jail," Momma said, presenting the card she'd tried to give Ginger earlier. Momma then threw it on the ground in front of Ginger.

Ginger said nothing, but her stance, hands on hips and foot tapping on the ground, emitted anything but a general acceptance for what my mother was saying to her.

"Whether you're an alcoholic, a drug addict or a KLEPTOMANIAC," Momma said, yelling the last word. "You need the same kind of help, and when you're ready, Chick's Place is open."

Ginger looked around frantically; obviously afraid someone had heard what Momma said.

Momma turned to leave, and just as Marla and I were about to follow her, she turned around.

"And one more thing." Momma pointed a finger at Ginger. "There is no 'ex' standing here today. I *am* Everett's wife. I let him have his little playthings, but at the end of it all we're together, me and him. And all the little playthings he's picked up along the way, well, like all toys, they get handed down to someone else when the boys are done with them."

I watched my mother's face as she spoke. I had never seen her fight for anything, especially not for my father. I'd heard her say things like, "Take him," "Youc'n have him," "if you think you won a prize, you got another thing comin'," but never anything like what she seemed to be saying now: "He's mine, and you can't have him."

As we were crossing the street, walking toward the motorcycle, I couldn't help but turn to look at Ginger. She was watching us walk away. As our eyes locked, just as they did the day before at the mall when the cops were taking her, she raised a hand to her face, wiped a tear I couldn't see and gave a small wave goodbye.

CHAPTER TEN

Oh, Hell. It's a Silent Wilder

Momma bought a few things, some pants, only one pair of jeans, a silky blouse and even a dress, which she never wore while she was at our house. She now had a small section on Daddy's dresser that was home to some eyeliner, lipstick, rouge, and mascara. Just when I was beginning to think Chick was wrong and Momma *was* ready to come home this time, an eerie kind of hush fell over our house. I found myself wishing for the first time that the yelling, cussing, flailing of arms, and shattering dishware would soon recommence.

I had done my part, and I think Marla had too; trying to make sure Momma never answered the phone or the door, or even collected the mail.

It was that summer that the gnats were thicker than rain. Looking out over the field, I saw circular, black-spotted clouds of the tiny bugs in various spots. The gnats might have been too small to see, but the swarms of them were unmistakable as they hovered like spacecraft over the tall grass. The black and gray pockets of bug larvae moved quickly from one location to another. It was like counting stars, the more I saw, the more I saw. I had eaten more of them than I cared to count, stuck in a piece of bread from my sandwich or floating as they drowned a red death in my Kool-Aid. Of course, those were the gnats I had spotted before consumption and flicked away. No telling how many of their brothers and sisters I had digested. Always inspecting my food carefully, I still knew it was impossible to spot all the gnats before they became a permanent part of my cellular structure. Keeping half-eaten tomatoes and apples out of the house was a challenge during the most humid summer on record in Rayes County, Tennessee. I never knew if the tiny winged creatures were attracted to the heat or the humidity. The answer was impossible to determine and also irrelevant as the heat and humidity always traveled together in the mountains.

Daddy's women, like the gnats, seemed to find themselves restless in the vapors of the summer heat. It seemed like there were more phone calls, impromptu visits, and sweet-smelling cards in the mail than usual, but maybe not. I had never really attempted even a half-ass accounting of Daddy's female contacts until now. It helped that Momma was disinterested in the phone and the mail, but she was always eager to answer the door. Four of them came that summer. Of course, they waited until Daddy's car was home before tapping on the door.

On the first two occasions, Momma was cooking dinner, and Marla and I were able to jump in front of her before she could even get out of the kitchen. The others went away quietly, and one saved our asses when she brought cupcakes. We lied and told Momma it was Mrs. Anderson and that she would sometimes bring dessert for us.

"How nice," Momma had said. "I wish I could've said hello."

"She had to go, Momma," Marla had offered quickly. "You know, her grandkids keep her busy now that they moved in next to her." My sister then outwitted Momma's questioning by talking about the boys and retelling the story of the bike crash.

In each case, the women all had a familiar quality about them, a certain southern sweetness that soured quickly when me or my sister would say simply, "Momma and Daddy are back together," then shut the door. The same one-sided conversations took place over the phone.

Then Ruth Potts followed Daddy home. She worked at GiGi's Market where he stopped to fill up his gas tank every other night and grab a gallon of milk, which he spent the rest of the night consuming alongside a plate of peanut butter and syrup.

Ruth had cone-shaped boobs, not like other women. Me and Marla used to call them beehive boobs and wondered if she knocked things off the shelves behind her when she reached for a pack of cigarettes from the Marlboro display. She always wore a floral printed A-line dress with a tight belt. She was either trying to accentuate her small waist or draw attention to her large breasts, probably both. Either way, Daddy never seemed interested but would flirt with her anyway just to be nice.

This summer wasn't the first time she had followed him home. Her visits were always under the guise of bringing something for me and Marla. Her first sentence as she got out of her car would always be, "When I saw you at the store it reminded me that I had some things put back for the girls." She had brought us each a hair brush, comb and mirror set, tiny bottles of perfume, flavored lip balm, and once she even brought false fingernails and helped us put them on and then paint them.

Now, there would be no open invitation inside our house, no matter what goodies she was carrying. I tried to be sympathetic as my father let Ruth down easy, but it became obvious rather quickly that he needed a quick assist. Daddy had let Ruth walk all the way to the front of his car, talked pleasantries with her for a few seconds, and was almost to the front door with her when Marla and I intercepted what was about to be a major fumble and certainly a game changer within the walls of the Wilder house.

"Ruth," Marla and I shouted, startling her as we jumped in front of her. "Momma and Daddy are back together," I yelled.

"And she won't like it if you're here," Marla finished our sentence for me.

Instantly, Ruth's eyes darted from the front door to my mother's bike sitting just under the porch overhang.

"Oh," she said, her eyes blinking nervously. "I see."

"Now, girls," Daddy said trying to shame us for upsetting Cone Boobs. He placed his hand on the small of Ruth's back. "Your mother would probably love to meet Miss Ruth."

I saw Marla about to protest, and I had plans of joining my sister when Ruth diffused the situation by pivoting to her right, straightening her spine, and quickly walking back to her car.

"Now, Everett," she said, trotting quickly as he followed her. "You tell that little lady of yours that I just stopped in to give the girls a few treats." Ruth motioned for us to follow her back to her car. "You know that's the only reason I ever stop by, just to see *Darla* and *Nancy*."

Marla and I looked at each other and rolled our eyes. When we got to the car, Ruth reached her hand inside a paper grocery bag and pulled out a box of chocolate chip cookies. "Here you go, girls," she said in a shrill, sing-songy tone. "I know they're your favorite."

She was right, but who wouldn't have gotten that right? Everyone loves chocolate chip cookies, even *Darla* and *Nancy*—whoever the hell they were.

"Now, I'm off," Ruth was inside her car with the door shut before we had even determined how many cookies were in the box. She waved as she sped out of the driveway.

"You girls need to give your mother a little credit," Daddy said, placing a hand on each of our shoulders as we walked up to the porch. "I don't think your Momma would be bothered by Ruth Potts bringing you cookies."

"Yeah, if that's *really* why she came," Marla quipped.

"Hey now, girls, behave." He gave each of us a light finger-flick to the back of the head.

Marla and I both fabricated a giggle, but from the nervous-looking smile I saw on my sister's face I knew she was thinking the same thing I was. Daddy was not taking Momma's newfound jealousy seriously enough.

I was glad my mother finally gave a damn about my father again, but at the same time keeping him out of shit was exhausting. He hadn't seen Momma's reaction to Ginger and he hadn't seen her handy work after she kicked the shit out of the pervert. He was walking around oblivious and unaware. Whether he knew it or not, his situation had changed.

"Who was that tiny little thing with the big tits?" My mother stood in front of the kitchen table holding a serrated knife. She stuck the serving fork into the brisket and started sawing at the meat like the dead, brown slab was attacking her. My father didn't respond.

"So, who was she?" Momma asked again, ceasing her stabbing motion and looking up at us.

"J-just a lady who works at, uh, the store," Daddy's answer was splintered but his voice still confident.

"Oh," Momma said, accepting his statement but sill needing some affirmation. "You girls know her?"

"Yeah," Marla was the first to speak. I simply repeated what my sister said.

"Yeah, at the store," I managed to get the words out over the lump growing in my throat.

"Go wash up for dinner," Momma said and then pointed the knife toward the hallway.

"Everything okay?" I heard my father ask my mother as Marla and I crept toward the bathroom.

Either Momma didn't answer him or I was too far away to hear what she had said. Either way, Daddy soon joined us in the bathroom, waiting in line like a school boy sent to wash his hands by a ruler-wielding teacher.

"Girls, it might be a good idea not talk to about Miss Potts while your mother is upset," he said as he looked up from scrubbing his palms just as we were about to leave the bathroom.

"Yeah, I know," Marla responded. I nodded.

At dinner Momma ate about half the brisket on her own while the rest of us shared the other half, with some left over. She consumed two baked potatoes in the time it took Daddy to finish one, and she drank two tall glasses of milk. She didn't talk a lot, but with the way she was shoving it in, it was safer she didn't speak.

"After dinner I thought you might take me for a ride," Daddy said to Momma.

"Eh, I'm not much up to it," Momma slid back away from the table as she picked beef from her teeth with one of the prongs from her fork. "I'd just as soon stay in, but you're more than welcome to it." She unlatched the keys from her belt loop and slid them across the table at him.

"I'm sure one of the Everett Wilder groupies would love to take a spin." The chair screeched across the tile as she got up and scooted it back. She dropped her fork into the empty plate with a clang and walked away from the table.

"Let me know when you're done and I'll clean up," she said as the door swung closed behind her.

Marla and I watched as my father got up from the table, picked up his plate, and raked the remains in the bowl of scraps sitting in the sink waiting to be delivered to Cricket. "Finish up, girls," he said as he took the bowl to the porch room. I could hear Cricket's toenails tapping on the floor as he danced for his dinner.

We waited for Daddy to come back inside but he never did.

Instead, Marla and I went out to the porch room and pretended to play with the dog, so we could see where he had gone. The empty scrap bowl sat on the shelf next to the back porch door. Flies swarmed with delight that Daddy had left something for them, too.

"Shoo, take this in," Marla handed the bowl to me. "Run some water in it and let it soak," she ordered.

In the spirit of anxious curiosity I did what she asked quickly so I could return to our search for Daddy. After we doted on Cricket for a few more seconds we trekked outside toward the barn to see if that's where he was.

"Girls," we both jumped when we heard his voice coming from somewhere behind us. When we turned to look, we saw him sitting in the car.

"You'd better get in the house and visit with your Momma some," Daddy said, like we hadn't much time left with her. We did what he asked and went back inside where we found

Momma with her boots off and her feet up on the couch. "*Dallas* is coming on," Momma said as our shadows broke through the living room doorway even before we did. "Do you ever watch that show?"

Marla and I nodded. "Every week," I said.

"I thought so," Momma said, smiling. "It looks like a show your father would be interested in, women and money," she laughed, and so did we.

"Let's watch," Momma said, patting her palm on the empty seat cushion next to her. Marla bounced in beside her as I stood there with a hand on my hip, smirking.

"It's all right," Momma said, getting up from her seat and plopping down in the middle of the couch, scooting Marla to one end, making room for me. "Now, this is better."

Even as many times as I had seen the intro, it was still just as gripping every week, the mirrored skyscrapers, the horses racing across the open fields on South Fork, and kind Miss Elly's face, staring at us from the screen contrasted by her eldest son, the evil JR. Daddy had never missed an episode.

"Want me to tell Daddy it's on?" I asked, readying myself to make a run for the back door while the first round of commercials played.

"No," Momma patted the seat I'd vacated. "He'll come in if he wants. I'm sure he knows it's on," she said quietly.

Even though it felt against my nature to do so, I left my father in the car. He was sure to be talking on the CB to some woman out there, someone with a handle even sexier than Hot Ginger.

*

I awoke to the sound of applause coming from the living room. Marla was still asleep. It was only three more weeks before school started back and my sister had been sleeping until almost noon all summer, leaving me with no other choice than to tug at her blankets and beg her to get up. I saw no need for waking Marla this morning so I decided to let her sleep. I had someone much better awaiting my company.

The sound of Phil Donahue's voice prompted my stealthy escape from Marla's bed without waking her. My pants were still right where I left them, so I pulled them on and then tiptoed out of the room, shutting the door so there was only a sliver of air between it and the frame.

Momma was on the couch and it looked like she hadn't moved all night, in the same spot, wearing the same clothes.

"Did you stay out here?"

"No," she said, smiling. "I'll go make your bed after the show," she said pointing to the television for me to watch.

That wasn't what I wanted to hear. She'd slept in my bed and not with Daddy.

"Why do you look so sad this morning?" Momma asked.

"Mmm, I dunno."

"Here, have some of these," Momma said, handing me a bag of Cheetos and her half-full bottle of Pepsi.

"Cheered me right up." She licked her fingers and then wiped the leftover residue on her jeans.

I accepted it as breakfast and sat down to see what Phil had to say.

"Eileen Tate is joining us this morning," Phil said, touching his glasses with the hand that held his notes and holding the microphone with the other. "She's the senior editor for Glass House Publishing, the folks that brought us, *The Fat Lady Can't Sing*." Applause erupted, and Phil smiled as he gave his audience a salute with his forefinger, still grasping his notes. He tried to speak, but the applause drowned him out. I watched as Phil struggled each time to interrupt the clapping without success. The camera cut to Eileen Tate. She stood and nodded to each side of the audience. The applause got louder. Phil laughed into the microphone, but I barely heard him over the clapping.

"Geesh," I said. "Good God, stop with the applause." I looked at Momma and rolled my eyes, thinking she would be in agreement and turn the channel.

"Shhh," she tapped her forefinger to her lips. I let out a loud sigh but the applause stifled me, just like Phil. In protest, I sat back on the couch and crunched Cheetos as loudly as I could, chewing with my mouth wide open. The camera panned across the audience. They were standing and still applauding. I tried to crunch louder but was met with a firm tap on my leg.

"Shhh," my mother put a finger to her lips again, this time with a forceful nod to emphasize her point.

I stopped crunching so loudly and began drinking the Pepsi, while making squeaking sounds with my mouth as I blew and sucked on the bottle. My mother paid me no mind.

"As most of you obviously already know," Phil said as he finally got to be heard when he spoke into the microphone, "*The Fat Lady Can't Sing* has women all over the country in a frenzy." The applause started rising again but fell just as quickly as Phil did his own version of a "Shhh" by holding his hand parallel to the stage and then inching it downward four or five times. His tactic actually worked.

"So what does this book, written by a woman, we assume," Phil said, nodding toward Eileen as he posed the question of the author's gender. Eileen nodded in return, indicating his accuracy. "So, what exactly is it about this book that seems to be taking the country by storm? Eileen, I ask you," Phil said, pointing his microphone at Eileen and cuing her to speak.

"*The Fat Lady Can't Sing* has given women all over the country permission to stop doing what's expected of them and start doing whatever they want," Eileen said and then tried to expand the description. Eileen was met with unrelenting applause and a standing ovation. The camera cut to the audience and then to Phil who once again did his version of the "Shhh." Again, the audience settled down and Phil was able to be heard.

"Please continue, Eileen."

"Yes, please continue, Eileen," I mocked Phil, sighed as loudly as I could and then rolled my eyes in the direction of my mother. Obviously, she didn't understand the bond that had formed over the summer between me and Chuck Woolery, who was on another channel right now solving a puzzle. Chuck might of well had been in a parallel universe for all Momma cared.

"Dancy," she scolded me. "If you don't want to watch, then go in another room."

I was out of Pepsi, and my mouth was now coated with powdered cheddar, so I did what she requested and headed toward the kitchen. Just as I was about halfway down the hall, I heard that name, a familiar name—Unna.

"Unna Everett, our author," Eileen paused knowing the audience's reaction would be once again explosive, and it was.

"Listen," Phil, now sounding more like a parent and less like a talk show host, scolded his audience like Momma had just scolded me. "I appreciate your enthusiasm, but if we're going to have the show, we've got to let our guest speak." He pointed the microphone back to Eileen. I stood, barely breathing, at the doorway to the living room. I looked over at Momma, her eyes locked tightly on the TV screen.

"As I was saying, Phil," Eileen stopped and gave a quick smile to the audience. "Our author, Unna Everett, prefers to take her seat behind the scenes." Phil nodded to show that he and the audience understood what she was saying. "She is now working on a sequel called, *The Thin Lady Dances.*" Phil shot his audience a stern look as they began to applaud. The sounds of clapping immediately ceased. Phil turned and looked at Eileen. "Please continue," he said.

Unna Everett, could this be, I wondered. I looked at my mother for answers, but she was still glued to Phil, Eileen, and her overzealous audience. I didn't dare ask, at least not right then.

"So, while we are here celebrating her success, she is out there pounding that typewriter to bring us another masterpiece. I am anxiously awaiting its arrival," Eileen said.

"So Eileen, tell us a little about the first book for those who haven't heard of it," Phil laughed a little at the noticeable omission of the book's title. I was sure the talk show host was fearful of the reaction and the precious moments it stole from his guest. "And then tell us how the book transitions into the sequel."

I looked at Momma. She was completely immobile. I turned my attention back to the TV. Just as Eileen was about to speak, Phil interrupted her. "Hold that thought." He then turned to the camera and said, "Don't go away. We'll be right back after a word from our sponsors."

Trying to ignore the perky girl holding a can of Arrid Extra Dry deodorant, I walked back over to the couch and sat next to Momma.

"Boy, people sure do like that book," I said, sounding like Cindy Brady quoting a script.

"Yeah," Momma said, offering nothing else.

"Wonder what it's about?"

"I guess if we watch then we'll find out," Momma said, not giving an inch.

"Her last name is Everett. That's weird," I pointed out the obvious.

"Not really," Momma said, never looking at me. "It's a very popular last name, just not around here."

"Oh," I half-heartedly accepted her answer, especially since I was getting nowhere with my inquisition.

"And, we're back," I heard Phil reintroduce his guest. I watched my mother for any sign of extreme emotion, excitement, sadness. All I saw was more of the same, eyes locked on the screen.

"Get us a Pepsi," she said, never moving her eyes from Phil. All morning I had been trying to get out of watching Phil Donahue and now that I was finally interested in this old geezer, she wants a Pepsi.

"Sure," I said. "Be right back."

I walked partway and then ran the rest, holding my elbows up to the swinging doors as I stormed into the kitchen. The bottles clinked together as I held them in one hand and searched for the bottle opener.

"Shit, shit," I said, pulling out drawer after drawer. "Stupid, stupid shit," I said as I found the opener and quickly popped the tops.

I stopped for a second as I sped down the hall to see if there was any chance my lazy ass sister might be awake. "Pft," I forced out a breath between tight lips and then rolled my eyes. I could've woken her but I'd have to explain the whole story, the whole Unna thing, and there just wasn't time. And besides, I didn't want to hear any of her negative bullshit about how I tended to make things up in my head. I ran as quickly as I could without spilling the contents of the bottles. I could hear Eileen talking. I couldn't get there quick enough.

"Thanks," my mother said, taking the bottle and still never moving her eyes from the TV screen.

"Ms. Everett is lucky to be alive," Eileen said, obviously in the middle of her story. "Women are the subjects of a lot of pressure to be perfect. No one can be perfect. No one can ever measure up. Like many women, after Ms. Everett was married and had children, she gained some weight. But in her case it spiraled out of control. Then, she learned her husband had an obsession with other women. In her book she describes an internal conflict many women face—the stigma of divorce and the fear of being alone versus keeping an ever-present smile and showing a happy face to the rest of the world. Because her husband's interests seemed to be elsewhere, she assumed it was because she was no longer attractive. She never realized until later that her husband had an addiction—albeit an acceptable one in our society, but an addiction nonetheless. In Ms. Everett's book, she chronicles a life of perfect imperfection that begins with over-eating and a weight problem, then transitions into becoming addicted to the pills her doctor gave her to battle her ever-increasing weight."

"Oh, I see," Phil said, looking into his now-wrinkled notes. "Now, wasn't there some sort of a tragedy with one of her children that pushed her into what came next?"

Eileen smiled at Phil and then at the audience. It was like Eileen was a beauty pageant contestant. "Yes," she continued. "She had lost the weight but then couldn't stop taking the pills. She was out of control and even though her doctors knew she no longer needed the medication, they continued to give it to her. Well," Eileen paused, "they gave it to her because she continued to ask for it. She now had two children, one was an infant and the other was only two years old. Ms. Everett slept in one morning and woke to find her oldest had climbed onto the kitchen countertop, managed to break into the bottle of pills. The toddler opened one of the capsules and was eating the tiny colorful pellets that had spilled out all over the kitchen counter. It was then that Ms. Everett decided her children would be better off without her. Ms. Everett's thought process was that her children would be better off with a parent who was addicted to women rather than one addicted to drugs. Ms. Everett made the hardest decision of her life—to leave her family and go through the process of trying to become drug free."

The audience gasped as the camera cut to row after row of middle-aged women, most of whom now had a hand clasped firmly over their mouths, some of them now crying. I looked at Momma to see if she had any reaction. There was none. Maybe she wasn't *this* Unna, I thought. After all, Marla *was* still alive. I just heard her buzzing between the covers in her room.

"So, what happened then?" Phil now had the audience trapped in the emotional clutches of his talk show.

"The child was fine," Eileen smiled sweetly at the hundreds of distraught women sitting opposite her. They all sighed, and there were a few audible words like 'Jesus,' 'holy,' and 'praise' that came from the crowd of pastel and platinum. "But then Ms. Everett tried to fight the addiction on her own. She beat the pill addiction but then turned to alcohol."

"Why don't you just call her Unna, please?" My mother spoke for the first time since she asked me to get her a Pepsi.

I snapped my head in my mother's direction, looking for any sign of an admission that she was Unna. Nothing. My mother was already back in her comatose state, mesmerized by Phil and Eileen.

The camera cut to a close up of Phil. "Come back and find out how the elusive Unna Everett began her writing career just after she began the addiction recovery process after these messages from our sponsors," he smiled and wiped his forehead.

The Arrid girl came on again and then the Alka Seltzer couple who had just come from a party where they had Mexican food. I had my doubts that anyone would invite that couple to a party, and especially not the wife with that whiny, high pitched, nagging tone. I watched my mother again for any outward signs of a confession, a tear, a flushed neck line. Again, nothing at all to indicate that my mother might be Unna Everett. I had my doubts, but how many Unnas in the world could there be?

"What are you guys doin'?" My sister made her sleepy appearance standing in the entryway to the living room with a yawn and a stretch.

"Oh, not much," Momma said as she immediately got up from the couch, walked over to the television, and turned it off.

Outwardly startled that my mother, who was just seconds ago so engrossed by the *Phil Donahue Show*, that she could barely form words, I looked at Momma for answers. Momma smiled at me. "I think we've had enough TV, don't you, Dancy?"

I felt my mouth drop open slightly and my eyebrows squeeze together. Both seemed to be automated functions I had no control over.

"What?" Momma asked, throwing her hands up in the air. "First you don't want to watch the show, and now you want to watch?"

I closed my mouth and widened my eyes to loosen my forehead muscles, getting them back to their normal position.

"No, that's fine," I said, pretending not to be confused by my mother's sudden shift in focus.

Marla turned and headed back down the hall. With the television shut off we had no reason not to just follow. I placed my two empty Pepsi bottles in the carton next to the fridge and the empty Cheetos bag in the garbage. My sister was fumbling around the cabinet trying to reach the cereal. She placed a knee up on the countertop and then lifted herself up so she could reach the top cabinet more easily.

"Get down from there," Momma said and then went over to her. "You're going to fall and break your neck."

I watched the two of them fumbling around the counter and tried to imagine a little Marla breaking into the cabinets and eating diet pills. She was certainly acrobatic enough now, but I wondered if she could've really pulled that off when she was a toddler. Possibly, I reasoned, with the help of a chair.

"What the hell are you looking at?" my sister spat at me.

"I wasn't looking at you, dumbass," I responded with a few spatters of my own.

"Girls!" Momma shouted. "Stop it."

Marla was never a pleasant person in the mornings. But the venomous outbursts like this one were normally spared for when she was really pissed off at me, not for just the usual "stop looking at me" fight.

Marla and I were both more tired than usual, but even after the crazy week we'd had that was no excuse for my sister to attack without proper provocation. I decided that was it, I wasn't telling that bitch Marla anything, not about the *Phil Donahue Show* or Eileen Tate, and certainly not about Unna.

"Bitch," I said, under my breath. I always felt better getting the last word, even if no one heard me.

"Girls, listen," Momma sat down at the table. We did the same. "I have to leave tomorrow."

I instinctively looked at my sister. Marla turned her head away from Momma and over to me with a look that was different than any I had ever seen on her face before. She was daring, no, double daring me to cry. So I didn't. She was as solid as a statue, though somehow her movements were free and easy.

I watched Marla get up from her chair and begin rifling through the cabinets again, ignoring completely what Momma had just said. All the while I was convinced that inside my sister had turned to stone.

The lump in my throat was tiny and disappeared quickly as I swallowed it away.

"Marla," my mother said. "I'm leaving tomorrow."

"Big deal," Marla said but never turned around. "So go. Why wait 'til tomorrow?"

I looked at Momma. She had tears in her eyes. She then turned her attention to me.

"I'll still just be at Chick's. I can come and visit more often now and the two of you can visit me there as much as you want."

She must have read my thoughts. Daddy never liked for us to go to Chick's, so I knew Momma was exaggerating when she said we could come and see her as often as we liked.

"Your father says coming to Chick's is okay," Momma assured me. "As long as it's on the weekend and it's just Chick there and not the others."

I nodded my head. I liked it at Chick's Place and I liked that I actually knew where Momma was, an actual place, not just some fog-filled space that my father liked to describe as "away for a while." Until she got to Chick's, that's where she stayed often—"away for a while."

"So, you're *not really* leaving this time?" Marla questioned as she turned back toward us.

"No," Momma shook her head. "Not this time. I'll be around now more than ever."

Marla nodded a satisfactory gesture, which made me feel less like crying.

"I'm working my way back here, but I have some things to do first," Momma said. "I'll be back in this house before you know it."

I smiled as I remembered what Chick had said. He was right, Momma wasn't ready and if she really *was* Unna Everett, then I was almost certain I knew why she had to go away again. I was sure it had something to do with *The Thin Lady Dances*.

"You girls want to go over to Mamaw's House and get some breakfast?"

"Yeah," I said, without even waiting for Marla's approval.

Marla nodded. "I'll go get dressed."

Momma braided my hair and put on my bandana. I was excited to get to go on the bike again and just as excited to see Mamaw.

"I want to see her," Momma said when I questioned the purpose of our visit. "I've talked to her on the phone a lot, but I haven't seen her in over a year." My mother tightened my braid. "Besides, I miss her gravy and biscuits," Momma smiled.

The sound of those words, gravy and biscuits, made my mouth water even after I had just devoured an entire bag of crunchy, cheese goodness and a bottle and a half of Pepsi.

"Yeah," was all I could say as I thought of brown crunchy biscuit bottoms dipped in Mamaw's off-white gravy speckled with pepper and bits of sausage.

Marla emerged from the hallway fully dressed. She seemed certainly more chipper than during our last encounter and even in a better mood than I had expected, considering we just got the news that Momma was leaving. Maybe my sister, like me, had noticed that Momma *was* different this time, more assured, more certain, like someone with definite plans.

Marla had already placed the bandana around her head and braided her own hair, not waiting for Momma to take care of it.

"When we get back from Mamaw's I'm going to take off," Momma said as she wrapped the rubber band around the end of my braid. "I need to ask you to do something now in case I forget later."

"What?" I turned around, almost slapping her with my fresh braid.

Although Marla didn't respond verbally, she lifted her chin in a very cool biker chick kind of way to casually gesture the words, "Tell me."

"I need for the two of you to keep these women around here beat off your father 'til I get back," Momma said, smiling at the two of us. "It'll get easier," she said, noticing the panicked look on my face. "Don't worry," she repeated herself, now with a smug look on her face. "The older he gets, the easier it'll get."

I nodded. "I gotta go pee and I'll be ready," I said and then trotted down the hall to Daddy's room instead. I carefully inspected my mother's end of the dresser. All her new things were still there. I then thumbed through the clothes in the closet, touching her unworn dress that was hanging there with the price tag still on it. I was satisfied that she'd be coming back, but I had to be sure. I tiptoed over to my father's nightstand sneaking about like someone could hear me. I then carefully opened the top drawer. Ah, there they were, still in the box, the handkerchiefs that Marla and I got him for Father's Day. I felt a little guilty stealing one. We were with Ginger when we got them, so we probably hadn't paid for them in the first place. Now, one was about to be stolen again but this time with the best of intentions. I quickly spritzed a bit of my father's cologne on the small white cloth and then stuck it in my pocket.

As I slammed the front door I turned to see Momma and Marla sitting on the bike. Marla was giving me her, "What the hell took you so long," look and Momma was taking a quick drag off a cigarette.

The blub, blub, blub of the motor got inside my chest and rattled me just like it did the first time I rode, but this time it was different. It was a good rattling somehow, like the difference between when I got scared butterflies and excited butterflies in my stomach.

Just as I was about to hop on the seat, my sister, who less than thirty minutes earlier I had dubbed a stupid bitch, did something unexpected.

"You wanna ride in front?" she yelled over the engine's roar while pointing to the empty space in front of her.

"Thanks," I yelled over the roar of the motor.

Momma revved the engine, took a few more puffs of her cigarette, and then flicked the butt into the field. Momma put Marla's hand on the handle bars and then, placing her own hand on top of my sister's, she revved the motor again. Marla shook her hands out like she was shaking water off them. Momma then took my hands and placed them on the handle bars and revved the engine just like she had done with Marla.

"Feel that?" Momma asked. "That's the power of freedom."

As we rocketed down the road I wondered about Unna, and if she wasn't Momma, then where was she right now? What was she doing?

CHAPTER ELEVEN

Mamaw's House

The sight of that old faded sign made me smile. It covered the entire space from the top of the porch to the roof. *Mamaw's House* was all it said, but the enormity of the letters more than made up for the simplicity of the title. There weren't many cars there, probably because it wasn't breakfast time and it wasn't lunch time either. Momma, Marla, and I had arrived somewhere in between. The two big windows at the entrance had new flyers taped to them since the last time we were there. Marla and I always made it our business to read every word like there would be some message waiting there just for us.

Our eyes moved in unison as we pored over the words on the flyers together.

"Aww," we both said at the same time when we saw a Polaroid of a Weiner—*Missing Dog. Answers to the name of Baby.*

I turned to see if Momma was coming. She was taking her time with that cigarette.

When Marla and I had all but finished reading the messages: tractor for sale, babysitter for hire, yard sale Saturday, yard sale Friday and Saturday, seamstress services, we both jerked as we spotted a large blue eye looking at us through the other side of the window, just between a picture of a Dodge pickup and an index card advertising free kittens.

"Shit!" Marla yelled at the window.

I squealed out what was almost a scream.

The metal Nehi soda sign stuck to the screen door began to move and the rusty spring behind it pulled tighter, making a bawling sound.

"Best advertising you can get for little or nothing," Cousin Sadie said, as she came out onto the porch.

"Dammit, Sadie," Marla said, putting her hands on her hips. "You scared us half to death."

"That's what happens when you come peeping around my windows when I'm wiping down tables," Sadie said, pulling the cheese cloth towel from her shoulder and snapping it at Marla.

"Ouch," my sister instinctively twisted her body so the towel missed her.

"What do you mean, 'Ouch.' It never even touched you." Sadie popped the towel at her again. "What are you girls doing here all by yourself?"

"We're not," I said, pointing to Momma, who had just flipped the butt of her cigarette across the lot.

"Holy shit," Sadie said, as she watched Momma get off her bike and walk toward us. "Your Momma's here."

"Yup," Marla said, turning to watch as well.

"Son of a bitch," Sadie said to Momma as she came upon the porch. "I can't believe it."

"Girls got in kind of a scrape. Needed their Momma," my mother said as she hugged Sadie.

"Damn you," Sadie yelled as she pulled herself out of my mother's grip. "You could'a told somebody you were comin'."

"Eh," Momma shrugged her shoulders. "I'm here now."

"I can see that, dumbass," Sadie popped the towel on Momma's butt as she reached to open the door.

"Wait a minute," Momma said, shutting the door and stepping back a few inches. "What's this?" She ran her hand over the slightly raised white letters. Stuck to the window, placed strategically so patrons were forced to read every word before entering and big enough so it could be seen even from the road, "A Little Bit of Everything With Some Good Advice, Whether You Like It Or Not."

"Now that's new," Momma looked at Sadie for an explanation.

"Well, just the last part is new," Sadie said, running her index finger underneath the last line.

"Yeah, that's what I mean," Momma pointed to the line, "Whether You Like It Or Not."

"You can thank your old man for that," Sadie said. "I guess Mamaw told him what he didn't want to hear. He left out of here in a huff. Day after, Mamaw added that line and said next time he comes back, he'll know what to expect."

Momma shook her head and rolled her eyes. "He's just a big ass baby," Momma said as she opened the squawking door and motioned for us to go through. "Your father, girls. I swear," she said rolling her eyes again.

I could see Mamaw through the counter window, or at least I saw the top of her head bobbing around as she cleaned. When Marla and I walked toward the counter, Mamaw looked up to wipe her forehead with the back of her hand.

"Well look-a-here," she said as we plopped our bottoms on top of the high seats at the counter.

"Hey, Mamaw," I yelled over at her. "What are you doing?"

"Scrapin' this infernal grill," she said as she came out from behind the window. "What are you girls doin'? I thought your Daddy had clean run off with you girls. Ain't seen you in a couple of days."

"Yeah, it *has* been a few days," Marla said and then looked away like she was counting the days since we'd been in there last.

"I see your Momma's home," Mamaw said, looking over at Momma. Sadie was still chewing our mother's ear off.

"Yeah, she came in the other day but she's leaving today again," I said and then waited for Mamaw's reaction. I got a simple nod of understanding but nothing else. "She's leaving today," I said it again to be sure she had heard me right.

"Hmm," she nodded again. "Is that right?"

Mamaw's thighs knocked open the tiny swivel doors that split the counter as she came through them.

"Lou, get your ass over here and let me take a look at you," Mamaw's commanding voice broke even Sadie's chattering. In fact, Sadie was forced to stop talking mid-sentence. I think Momma was glad. She never looked back, just headed straight into Mamaw's open arms. Mamaw hugged Momma once quickly and then pushed her back so she could look at her.

"Well, you look real good, Lou, just real good," she said and then hugged Momma again. She led Momma over to a counter chair next to Marla. "Sit down here and I'll get you girls something to eat," Mamaw said. "I still got some biscuits and gravy from breakfast."

"You're making my mouth water old woman," Momma said, slapping an open hand on the counter and making a loud pop.

"You watch your mouth, you little shit," Mamaw pointed a crooked finger at Momma. "Same goes for you, girls, watch your little potty mouths in here. Biscuits and gravy?" Mamaw asked, looking at me and Marla.

"Yes," I said before my grandmother even finished her sentence.

"Oh yeah," Marla said, nodding and raising her eyebrows up and down like she was being turned on by the thought of heavy breakfast.

Mamaw nodded at Sadie, and pointed her thumb back toward the kitchen. Sadie saluted as she came through the swivel doors and then disappeared into the kitchen. I watched through the counter window as Sadie put Mamaw's apron on and tied it around her tiny waist.

"So what are you doing here?"

"The girls ran into a little snag and needed some help," Momma said, looking over at us. Marla stared straight ahead, never moving.

I flushed red as I thought back to the pervert and the penis. That seemed so long ago, and like it happened to someone else or something I had only heard about it. But now, with the threat of Momma telling Mamaw, it became real again.

"I heard something about that," Mamaw looked at us and winked to show her approval of our decision to call Momma. "Chick took care of it?" Mamaw asked, obviously knowing the answer already.

"*We* took care of it," Momma said, nodding slowly.

"I heard you got Ginger out of jail." My muscles relaxed when I realized Mamaw wasn't going to continue talking about the pervert and penis incident.

"I did," Momma answered. "How'd you know?"

"Hell, you know how it is around here, Lou. News gets around fast."

"Guess I forgot." Momma nodded, as she looked around the empty restaurant.

"The place fills up and before you know it, everybody knows everything. It's better than anything you can read in the *Rayes County Gazette*." Mamaw flicked an old newspaper that had been flung on the counter. "And it's certainly more accurate."

Sadie came out of the kitchen balancing three plates on her left arm and carrying a pitcher of orange juice in the other. She placed the juice down next to me and then scooted the plates, one by one over to their rightful owners. The over-easy eggs jiggled as the plates knocked against the counter. I was glad to see Sadie had brought us the works, fried potatoes and a small helping of grits, too. Like a magician pulling a hundred scarves from his sleeve, Sadie's right hand disappeared under the counter for less than a second and then produced three glasses.

"How's that," Sadie asked after she had filled the last glass. "Pretty damn good, huh?"

"Eh, you did okay," Momma said. "I could teach you a thing or two." Momma smiled and winked to let us know she was only playing with Sadie.

"You stuck up bitch." Sadie quickly pulled off her apron, wadded it up and threw it at Mamaw.

"Girls, girls! Stop that infernal language in front of these young 'uns." Marla and I laughed as Momma had to apologize to Sadie.

"You are an excellent waitress," Momma said, reaching over the counter pulling at Sadie's arm.

"Better than you were, right?"

"Yes," Momma admitted with a simple nod. "Much better than I *ever* was."

Our plates sounded like musical instruments as the stainless steel forks continued to hit against the ceramic plates. Marla and I went after our breakfast with a vengeance.

"I told Everett that woman was trouble," Mamaw continued talking about Ginger, paying no attention to the interruption. "He got pissed off and stormed out of here."

"Sounds like him," Momma said between bites.

"Well, I won't say I'm glad about what happened." Mamaw poured a glass of juice for herself. "But I was right and that's a fact. That woman is trouble and everybody knows it, even stubborn-ass little Everett now."

An intermittent breeze from the oscillating fan blew a few straggling gray hairs away from Mamaw's face. She took a deep breath as the wind hit her.

"What I can't figure is why in the hell you saw fit to go get her out of jail. She ain't even from around here," Mamaw said, insinuating that not being from Rayes County was much worse than being a kleptomaniac.

Momma chewed the bit of food she had just put in her mouth, swallowed hard, and then took a gulp of juice from her glass. Mamaw waited for an answer.

"It was the right thing to do," Momma said, placing her hands at either side of her plate as she awaited Mamaw's impending judgment.

"Shew," was the only sound the old woman could manage. The sound accompanied a shake of her head.

"Everett wasn't going to help her," Momma said, confident that she had stifled Mamaw. "Somebody had to. Ginger isn't a bad person. She just has some problems."

"I can handle a drug addict, an alcoholic, and just about anything else," Mamaw said. "But a liar and a thief can go straight to hell as far as I'm concerned."

"Well, that's your opinion," Momma said, holding her glass up to Mamaw for a toast. "An addiction is an addiction. It's all the same. Only the vice is different."

"Shew," Mamaw blew again.

"Everett is done with her. I was just tying up the loose ends." Momma's tone was certain. She was done talking about Ginger and Mamaw knew it full well. My grandmother held her lips tight to try and hold back the next smartass remark. That didn't last long.

"I didn't raise him that way," Mamaw defended her parenting. "I don't know what happened to Everett to make him so fickle with women. Maybe it was all the pretty girls who came in and out of his life. The waitresses here always took a special interest in little Everett. I think he was in love with them all," Mamaw said. "I guess when he was a little boy he just got used to having beautiful women coming in and out of his life all the time."

Momma shrugged her shoulders and shook her head.

"At least I know he won't keep 'em for long," Mamaw smiled at Momma. "You're the only one he loves, Lou."

Momma never looked up from her food.

"He seems to be getting better with age," Mamaw continued with her closing argument. "And the women he chooses seem to be a little less crazy—remember that dirty Beatnik?"

Momma looked up and nodded as she smiled. "Yeah, that was fucked up," Momma chuckled a little.

After only a few bites I was starting to get full. My reflexes slowed and my eyes wandered around the restaurant. My gaze landed, as usual, on the no less than thirty-one pictures that bordered the tops of the restaurant walls. Mamaw took the framed photos down to clean once a year. It was always on the Sunday following Labor Day, which was the same day she would take another group picture of her current staff. There were twenty pictures on the wall from the view of the counter.

Momma was in four of them, standing not quite in the center of each group but not at the end either. Daddy was in all of them. I guess I had never noticed before how many of those pictures included pretty girls kissing my father on the cheek as the rest of the staff smiled for the camera man. Daddy was so little then, elementary school-aged.

Mamaw had eleven more pictures hanging on the top of the right-hand wall. She was sure to run out of room soon and have to start another row. I was glad that the pictures of Momma and Daddy together were visible from the counter. That way all the customers got to look at my parents. I always worried when Mamaw took the photos down for cleaning because I wondered how she remembered where they all went.

"They're numbered," Mamaw had said, like it would be common knowledge that the pictures would never change places. "They all have a place and that's where they'll stay til I'm dead and gone from here."

None of the four pictures that included both Momma and Daddy showed the two of them standing together. In two, they were on opposite ends of a row and in the other two they were in different rows. It was funny to see them so young. Daddy had a thick head of hair then, blond and straight. Momma's hair was dishwater blonde and wavy, like Mamaw's thick-cut bacon.

"Mrs. Gardner was in here the other day." Mamaw's mention of mine and Dancy's other grandmother nudged my thoughts out of my parents' past.

Momma began to fidget with her fork and began tapping it on the side of her plate.

Mamaw put her hand on my mother's arm. "Don't worry, she didn't ask about you."

Momma let the fork fall to her plate and put her hands under her legs to gain some kind of control over them.

"I'm surprised she'd step foot in here. Might damage her lily white reputation with the ladies at the club." Momma's voice was tense and a bit shaky.

"She just ate a sandwich and left," Mamaw said. "I think it's a step."

"I doubt it," Momma said, releasing her captive hands and pulling a cigarette pack from the inside pocket of her vest. She tapped the end of the pack on the counter several times.

Granny and Pappy Gardner had moved to Royalton, about an hour and a half away. Probably one of the reasons why Momma was so shocked to hear Granny Gardner was anywhere near Mamaw's Place.

Marla and I visited Granny and Pappy Gardner a few times a year. Daddy would always take us early on a Saturday and pick us up late on a Sunday. Granny Gardner was one of those sophisticated older women who could be described best as dripping with jewelry and money. I knew the club my mother spoke of well. Marla and I were paraded around that place at almost every visit. Granny Gardner would ask about Momma sometimes but both Marla and I noticed that when she did Pappy would always think of a reason to excuse himself.

When Pappy wasn't around other people at the club would come over and talk to us about Momma. There were pictures of our mother in the club's debutant archives. All the girls who had their coming out parties at the club held a place in its history albums. Momma was high society, complete with beehive hair and red lipstick. Granny Gardner's friends would tell Marla and me how much we favored our mother.

"She's getting older. Hell, we all are," Mamaw said, referring to Granny Gardner. Mamaw hesitated, waiting for a response from Momma. When she got no reaction, the old woman continued. "But even at her age, she looked younger somehow—confident, formidable even. Not at all the way I remembered that weak and frail woman you used to call mother, Lou."

Momma stretched a tight smile across her face. "I guess I *would* like to see her. Everything has changed so much since then. The last time I saw her was when my father was unloading my things at your house, Mamaw. I'll never forget the look on my mother's face," Momma said, looking down at her plate. "I think she wanted to go with me."

"Your Momma was afraid for you," Mamaw pulled my mother chin up with a crooked finger. "Wanted you to have the best of everything and saw you headed down the wrong road, Lou. She panicked when you got pregnant. She fell victim to being subservient to your father—a good Baptist woman, and your father was a victim of his pride."

Momma and Mamaw were talking about the Wilder son that my parents never had. I had heard of him often. Mamaw had told me and Marla that she knew it was a boy by the way Momma was carrying him; low, amidst her hips. Momma had lost our older brother at seven months when she wrecked the car on Plack Hill curve. Matthew Wilder was buried at Crest View Cemetery.

Momma and Daddy took us to see his grave once. I wondered but had never asked how a baby that was never born gets out of its momma's belly and placed into a casket. Sometimes I'd think about what it would be like to have an older brother. I guessed he'd probably look a lot like Daddy did when he was younger.

Momma and Mamaw were silent for a good minute and then finally Momma spoke again. "So you say my mother looks different?"

"Yeah," Mamaw nodded and looked over at the table where Granny Gardner must have seated herself when she came for that sandwich.

"That's good," Momma said.

Sadie's face suddenly appeared between mine and Marla's heads. "Hey, you girls want me to read your fortune?" She whispered so she wouldn't interrupt the tense moment between Mamaw and Momma. The cards were already set up in our favorite booth, just next to the pinball machine. Three sodas were waiting there as well.

"Cut the cards, Marla," Sadie demanded. "Now you, Dancy." I made the second cut.

"Now," Sadie began, her eyes sparkled with anticipation as she turned over the first card. "This is the first card and belongs to Dancy since she cut last. It's the Seven of Cups and represents choices you will make."

As usual, I hung on every word. The future was the one thing I could count on to always change, especially when Sadie read my cards.

"So, Sadie," Marla's smart-ass tone broke my trance. "Last time, *I* had the Seven of Cups that came up first, choices, choices, choices. Whatever will we do?" Marla looked at me, crossed her arms and rolled her eyes.

"Shut up, Marla," Sadie and I responded to her sarcasm almost at the same time.

Outnumbered with no other choice but to go along with the reading, Marla settled in.

"Now, Marla," Sadie continued. "Your first card is Strength."

Although my sister had uncrossed her arms and was trying, except during short bursts of failure, not to roll her eyes, she was still skeptical, seeing no fun at all in a harmless card game about the future.

"Hmmm. I don't think I've seen that card before," Marla quipped. "Is it new?" A tiny facetious laugh escaped her lips.

"No," Sadie scolded. "None of them are *new*, smartass. The craft is ancient."

"Yeah, yeah, go on," Marla interrupted Sadie's explanation.

"You will have to be strong," Sadie said and then pointed to a symbol on the card that was placed just above the head of a figure depicted strangling a lion. It looked like the number eight, only sideways. "Infinitely strong, Marla," Sadie tapped her finger on the symbol.

CHAPTER TWELVE

The Fairest of Them All

"Steak and lobster," my voice shot up an octave as I spoke to the judge. The moment the words left my lips I wanted to take them back and replace them with something honest.

"Well, Miss Wilder," the judge spoke into the microphone, his back to the crowd. "We grill a mighty fine steak here in land-locked Rayes County, Tennessee but to get a lobster for dinner you'd have to travel a ways to get that, now wouldn't ya?"

"Yes, yes sir, I would." My voice began to quake again. Still, I raised my shoulders and smiled sweetly as I panned the audience. There was Cee standing behind the back row, lifting her palm in the air in tiny inch-like increments. That was the signal for *speak up, I can't hear you*. And it wasn't the only one. A salute meant that I needed to stand up straight, an index finger to the nose meant that I was not making eye contact with the judges, hands on the hips and shoulders dancing meant that I had not maintained equal strides as I walked across the stage.

Although I had been out there for less than a minute, it seemed like an eternity. I was sure it was much like the way one might feel in hell. Every minute expanded and stretched to infinity, giving the sinner time to reflect on a life of ill deeds.

As I stood there in the lights, smiling like my life depended on it, I wondered what my sin had been. Was this my hell, and why had it come so soon? I suddenly felt a tad Catholic and began to confess to God telepathically, of course, all the things I might have done, bad things. Was I finally reaping what I had sewn? I had let three boys play with my boobs since the ninth grade, not all at once, of course, at separate times but in the same movie theatre.

Since Marla had left a month early for college so she could participate in some do-gooder ramp building for the handicapped, I had spent most of August at home alone and naked. Every morning as soon as I heard Daddy's car pull out of the driveway, my clothes came off. Sitting on the couch watching my game shows, my soap operas, making a sandwich, all of it I had done naked. I worried that maybe I was becoming a nudist and would have to live like those people over in Jake's Nest, a nudist colony somewhere around Knoxville that no one ever talked about.

It might have been an urban legend or it might have been true, no one really knew for sure. But the story of Jake and the creation of his nudist colony sounded like something right out of the Bible. Five years ago, a man and a woman who had been heartbroken by unrequited love, were united in a mission to create a place where people could live peacefully and where everyone would be in love with everyone else. Jake, who owned an enormous amount of property put an eight-foot fence around the perimeter and turned his acreage into a small community where the residents grew their own food, made their own medicine, smoked tons of reefer, and had a lot of sex, so I had heard.

Jake's Nest triggered convenient amnesia in many circles if the topic was ever brought up in polite company. No one wanted the news of a nudist colony smack dab in the middle of a conservative state like Tennessee to get out. I was sure the Puritan-like souls in Rayes County considered being naked in front of others a sin. Maybe this had been my sin—I was secretly a nudist.

Then, there were those times that I went out in the back yard and laid out in the sun naked. Slipping into my Baptist upbringing I started to wonder if I had tempted the boys with the bowl haircuts next door. Only two weeks ago I told Dickie Gates he could sneak in my bedroom window, just to see if he'd do it. He walked the four miles from town well after midnight only to find out I wasn't offering much more than a smooch for his troubles. God, he was pissed.

Whatever my sins had been, individually or collectively, the reaping had begun right there on that stage. Even my telepathic confession to God Almighty and his Son, Jesus Christ, didn't stop the judges from, well, judging me. I thwarted the inquisitors with rehearsed answers that in most cases didn't even apply to the questions.

"So, Miss Wilder, do you intend to go to college?" the bald man asked as the yellow glare of the spotlights absorbed into the peach skin on top of his head. It looked like he might get beamed up into space and not a moment too soon for me. I waited, but when the aliens didn't take him I had to form some sort of an answer.

"College is important for young women," I heard the voice coming out of my mouth but I was convinced someone else must have been speaking. "It's a very important thing to do."

This was my answer, the only answer he was getting, so to punctuate clearly and let him know I was done, I smiled and panned the audience as Cee had instructed.

Finally, the words I had longed to hear, "Thank you, Miss Wilder." Then with a synchronized nod of the three heads sitting before me, every muscle in my body relaxed. I turned, shuffled across the stage, and poured myself into a waiting chair. Becoming full-on Baptist again I began making promises to God of all things I'd never do again if he'd just get me off that stage.

The taste of nail polish remover was still present on my tongue. Cee must have manicured her nails just moments before she smeared the glob of Vaseline across my teeth.

"Smiling doesn't come easy for some girls, you know," Cee had said. "I'm not saying you are one of those girls, but it's possible you might be one of those unfortunate contestants that could use a little extra incentive to be happy. Now, open up."

Her bony little hand squeezed my cheeks while the free one was busy digging lubricant from the translucent jar sitting on a not-yet-occupied folding chair next to me. When she was done, she dabbed my lips with crimson-colored lipstick. "Now, rub them together gently," she scolded me even before I had squished my lips onto one another.

"Ugh. Glll," I had tried to grunt in defiance but my throat was clogged with petroleum jelly.

"Now, now, little Dancy Wilder," Cee had said as she pushed my boobs together with her tiny hands. "Beauty is always worth it."

I looked beyond the seated guests and saw her standing next to my father. Even in her heels she didn't come close to meeting his shoulder. My smile became effortless when I imagined her as an Oompa Loompa from Willie Wonka's Chocolate Factory, orange skin and all. Cee was holding her hands up over her mouth and it looked like she was either crying or trying like hell to cry. She kept waving at me incessantly, knowing I couldn't respond. I looked at Daddy, who was gazing at the stars in the sky and yawning. Cee turned to shush a crying baby and its mother as my name was announced.

"Danielle Lynn Wilder is our fifth runner up," the speaker squawked across the fairgrounds. A nervous laugh trilled from my throat but over the applause I managed to play it off as profound shock and excitement.

Laura Owen, the bitch from sixth grade who had stolen Kotex from my purse during recess, was now sitting next to me in an evening gown. She was teacher's pet, stayed inside every Monday to help grade spelling papers. She had opened the pads one by one and strategically placed them on the floor forming an arrow pointing to my desk. She had laughed as I gathered them up in both hands, everyone watching, and took them to the restroom to throw away.

Now, I actually felt sorry for her as I got up to take my place on the stage. I figured the only thing worse than competing in Fairest of the Fair would be actually giving a shit about winning and then watching someone like me take the stage, even as fifth runner up. I really *did* wish it was her instead of me, and I hoped God was listening to all my generosity and forgiveness and wasn't busy still tallyin' up all the stupid shit I had done. The anticipation on Laura's face was begging the speaker to call her name. I could almost hear her thoughts: *maybe I got third, maybe second, maybe I won the whole damn thing.*

Dickie and his minions were now standing along the fence watching, laughing and pointing. My stage fright immediately subsided, turning instead to rage as I mouthed the words, "Go to hell," and pointed my bouquet of roses in their direction. A stinging sensation on my thigh made me turn. "Now, Miss Wilder just a few more minutes," the pageant director had left her seat on stage and glued herself to my hip, pinching a hunk of flesh out of it in the process.

"Ouch," I complained but applause for the third and fourth runners-up covered up my words.

"I'll pull your little ass off this stage and beat you with those thorny roses if you embarrass me." The little red-haired woman pinched me again. The fierce nature of the pageant director's glare and the solid grip she now had on my arm made me a believer. I focused my attention on Cee, who was still either crying or trying real hard to cry. From that distance I couldn't tell.

Maybe Cee had been right all along. "No one wants to hear the truth, Dancy," her long, black eyelashes had waved at me as she spoke. "They want to hear what makes them feel good, what makes them feel important. Not the truth, never the truth."

"But I've never even had lobster," I had argued with Cee.

"That's not the point, Dancy," Cee ran her fingers through her long, platinum curls as she sighed in aggravation. "Every girl out there is going to say she loves pizza. You're all fifteen years old. Of course you love pizza. You have to say something different so they will remember you."

"So, I'll be the lobster girl? That's a promising future."

"Now, stop that," Cee snapped at me. "All you have to do is place. You'll get your picture in the paper, and if you win the crown then you get, well, you'll get that crown."

Cee didn't understand why I couldn't completely envelop myself in the pageantry of it all. For one thing, I knew there was no chance in hell that a girl like me could win, and I had always heard that the winners were chosen even before the week of the fair. If that was the case, then competing was a farce as far as I was concerned.

Cee had placed in every pageant in the state at some point in her life, even in the Miss Tennessee contest.

"It's all in how you think of yourself," Cee had said. "Confidence is everything. If you believe you are beautiful, other people will believe it too."

As I looked at the small red-haired woman who had now left my side, trusting me to my own devices, I remembered how sweet she had been on the first day of sign-ups. Now, this pageant director was the bitch from pageant hell and a stage gargoyle. Cee was right; no one wants to know or cares to know the truth.

The Fairest of the Fair pageant wasn't one of my proudest moments as I stood there in the pink satin formal Cee had picked out for me. But it meant a lot to Cee. I finally turned to face Cee and blew her a kiss. Like the crickets chirping in a humid August nightfall, she could get a bit annoying but would be sorely missed during a quiet winter. Cee caught my kiss in her tiny hand, added one of her own and sent it back. Daddy held up a pair of jeans, a polo shirt, and my favorite Bass sandals, letting me know that it would all be over soon and I could enjoy another year at the Rayes County Fair, no frills, no lace, and no Vaseline on my teeth.

Cee would be the talk of the congregation tomorrow. I knew it and so did she. This time, though, it would be for taking that poor little, mouthy Wilder girl and turning her into a beauty queen. Not for breaking up anyone's marriage and maybe not for pulling her skirt too high in front of the reverend during Sunday school service. Cee could sit proudly tomorrow in what she considered to be the most coveted spot in our church: second pew, first seat. It was that exact spot where Cee could shine the brightest. It was just behind the church Deacons, so Cee was still considered subservient and true to her faith, but in front of the rest of the congregation so the people could admire her as she showed up strategically three minutes late, gliding down the aisle like it was her personal fashion runway.

I began to refer to the woman who had become my pageant coach and my tormentor over the past two months simply as Cee, with her permission of course. Her full name was Christian Cate, however she had also been known as Isabella Catelyn Bleufield Maymore Jacobson Claxton Perryworth. These were all names collected throughout her many marriages. All were good names, many of them old money names in Rayes County. Some of the men had been widowed, some divorced, and some still married when she met them. Their marital status before Cee met them had been temporary, of course.

It was really only a matter of time before Cee got around to Daddy. Over the years it had just been mere happy coincidence that their union hadn't happened sooner. Every time Daddy was free and single, Cee was either working on her next marriage or just finishing off the last one. By the time Cee was once more available to mingle, Daddy would be otherwise engaged, either with Momma or the latest piece of ass he'd managed to find wandering about.

Of course, a relationship, solid or not, never stopped Cee if she saw a man she really wanted. Cee would explain her actions away as divine intervention or something that was just meant to be. My father was always attractive and seemed to get even more so with age. But for Cee, Daddy may have been a little too light in the wallet up till now.

Rayes County social climbers, especially those like Cee who carried tiny golden shovels in their designer handbags, began to notice that the Wilders were doing a lot better these days, a new car every year, college for Marla at the best university in the state, and some much-needed designer labels for the youngest of the Wilder clan. If not for those labels, I might have actually become a nudist, but there was something about Izod, Aigner and, Calvin Klein that made me feel like getting dressed might be worth the trouble.

I was sure we all had Unna to thank for our newfound wealth, although there was no way for Cee to know that. I don't think it would have mattered to Cee that the money was actually my mother's. Even if Cee had found out the money was all Unna's she probably would have started blowing *her* kisses if not for strict religious guidelines. God knows Cee was running out of rich men to choose from. It *was* a small town, after all.

If Cee thought for a minute that she was going to add the Wilder name to her extensive collection of stolen, borrowed, and bequeathed surnames, she had another thing coming. Momma could've crumpled Cee like a paper wad and thrown her in the trash, but for some reason she hadn't. My mother's inaction indicated to me that she was unconcerned about Cee being a part of my father's life for very long.

I knew Cee wasn't going to make it into next week. My pathetic exhibition on stage was nothing compared to the scene playing out behind the crowd. Cee had smacked Daddy in the stomach at least four times for scratching himself and kicked him with the side of her six-inch heel each and every time he had spit on the ground.

My father knew how to behave himself in public: no spitting, no scratching, no yawning. It appeared Daddy was making a rebellious statement by doing all three while Cee stood proudly next to him. Like me, my father had grown tired of her unreasonable expectations: the perfect meal, the perfect dress, the perfect hair, the perfect family, the perfect day, the perfect man, as she had sometimes referred to my father.

Cee was so busy striving for perfection that even in those fleeting moments when she had damn near achieved it, she didn't recognize it.

Cee was simply one of my father's diversions as he awaited my mother's return. I wasn't worried that I hadn't kept my promise to Momma. Cee was no threat to our family. She was nothing more than a participation trophy, one of those little awards that are given out to anyone who bothers to show up.

I held my dress up to my knees and jumped off the stage. I could hear Dickie and the other idiots from school cat-calling from somewhere that was a safe distance away from my father. I didn't even turn around to see where the boys were. I simply flipped them the bird and kept walking.

"You did great, Dancy," Cee was gushing over my victory. "Now, next year we're getting that crown."

I wanted to tell her that there would be no next year, that I would not take that stage again unless it involved climbing up there to full-on French kiss Andy Gibb—a long shot, considering the vocal talent for Fairest of the Fair each year consisted of barber shop quartets and gospel groups. But the pride in Cee's little round face wouldn't let me steal her moment. I took off my fifth-place-runner-up sash and put it over her head, placing the Fairest of the Fair logo carefully in full view just atop her bulging cleavage.

"Here, you hang onto this for me. My friends are waiting for me to go on the rides."

Cee swiveled her shoulders back and forth, showing off the sash to everyone, but no one in particular.

"I'll put my dress in the car," I said, taking the clothes and two twenty dollar bills from Daddy.

"Proud of you," my father said, and then pecked a kiss on my forehead.

CHAPTER THIRTEEN

Blood, Sweat, Tears, and Other Shiny Things

My hands fit perfectly around the hard plastic finger grips and had molded into the wheel, becoming a part of the white, red, and chrome that surrounded me. The speedometer and the RPM gauges were like big round eyes, so excited to see me.

"It goes up to 180 miles per hour," I said, touching my finger to the number.

"Sure does," Daddy said. "But that doesn't mean you have to take it that fast!" He directed my finger more than halfway around the dial and pressed it hard on the 50 mph mark. "That'd be more like it."

"Pfft," I puffed out in disgust and rolled my eyes at my father. As Daddy walked to the front of the car I defiantly moved my finger to the 80 mph mark. "Now, that'd be more like it," I winked at the wide eyes staring back at me.

"This is going to be an awful lot of work, Dancy." Daddy poked his index finger inside each and every dent, taking inventory of how much time would be spent pulling each one back to the surface.

"I'll help," I said in defense of Shiny Girl, a name I had already given the car that I knew would be mine if I begged my father in just the right way.

"Damn right you will," Daddy said, looking at me through the windshield. As my father spoke the words, I released my fingers from the grips of my newfound freedom and took one last look at my inch-long, wine colored nails. Who had time to manicure nails on Friday nights anymore, certainly not me. When sixteen rolled around I'd be cruising town with the top down, Leroy riding shotgun. I looked over to the empty seat next to me and imagined my handsome Leroy looking back, his shirt half open and his chest a bit wet from exposure to the summer heat, his tight faded Levi's hugging his muscular thighs, his lips coming toward me, his hand on my knee

"Give me your nail clippers," I said, getting out of the car and walking toward Daddy.

"Don't cut 'em too close, you'll need some of those. Paint and bondo are tedious work." Daddy handed me his clippers without even so much as a hesitation and watched as I tore at my fingernails with the blade. Now my father would know I was serious.

I watched as a bit of plaid eclipsed my peripheral view of Daddy as he began pacing in front of the car.

"I've got a list of restoration guys who'd love to work on this baby," the salesman smacked Shiny Girl's hood. My father was still watching as I publicly butchered my nails.

"No restoration guys. If she wants this car, she's gonna earn it."

I stopped the massacre and looked up. It had worked. My father was going to buy this car and it was going to be mine.

"Sure you don't want to take one last look at the front line?" the salesman asked, pointing to the new cars placed near the highway. "Right off the factory line, what all the kids are driving."

"No," I said, interrupting my father before he could speak. "I don't want what everybody else has; I want her," I nodded toward Shiny Girl and then took my hand and softly rubbed it over the space where the salesman had just moments earlier smacked her.

"Well, at least she's saving you some money," the salesman clicked his tongue and winked at my father.

"I doubt that," Daddy sighed as we walked back toward the sales office. "It'll still cost me."

I handed Daddy his clippers and he returned them to his front pocket. "Thanks, Daddy." He didn't speak but nodded.

"These are the last of the hail-damaged cars at Johnny's," the salesman pointed to a row of dinged up cars. As we walked, the plaid-clad man continued referring to himself in the third person. I was just happy he didn't start talking about Big Johnny, the name marked on the hand-written tag dangling from his lapel. Big is not a word that this Johnny would have ever been tagged with. He was plenty shorter than me, and Daddy towered over him like a skyscraper. "Got you quite a deal there, Mr. Wilder," Johnny said, rapping his knuckles against the hood of a brown Isuzu that looked like it had leprosy.

As I thought back to the event that had beaten most of the life out of all these fine machines, the event that made Shiny Girl mine, I couldn't help but smile. The tornado of 1982 had been vicious. It killed two people and destroyed countless homes and businesses, yet there I was smiling like some evil genius who had orchestrated the world's weather patterns for nothing more than a precious car.

I had often wondered over the past year if that tornado wasn't somehow a necessary event in the town's history. The old, faded buildings were now new and modern, everything freshly painted, repaired, and in some cases entirely rebuilt. My restoration began that fall as well, one week after Fairest of the Fair and almost in the same moment I had decided I was no longer going to be a paper doll for Daddy's women. My father would just have to find some other way to entertain the ladies. It was then that the wind started to blow.

My father and I cowered in the basement; once I had convinced him that if he didn't stop looking at the tornado coming toward us and seek shelter that he would surely be killed. We were only under the house for fifteen or so minutes, but it seemed like an eternity. Cricket came with us and, like a Geiger counter during an earthquake, quivered with each thunder clap.

When Daddy, Cricket, and I emerged from our hole we were relieved to find our house, the barn, and the well-house all intact. The only thing that had changed was the lighting all around us—it was brighter than I had ever seen it. The trees, which had for all my life shielded our property from the sun and other elements, were gone. The only tree left standing was the one Daddy had sworn he was going to cut down. "It's too close to the barn," he had said. I had heard him curse that tree time and again. However, after the tornado of 1982 all that my father had to say about the tree he'd sworn to murder was, "Well I'll be a son of a bitch."

Daddy had assured me that UT's campus never got the storm we did and that Marla was safe. It was strange my sister

214

wasn't with us. Normally, Marla and I would talk about an event like the tornado for days, but she wasn't there. I reluctantly made conversation with my father instead as we recalled the day over a Big Boy burger and fries. I think Daddy realized then how much I missed my sister. My father began talking with me about spending some time on campus with Marla. In a year or so I'd be leaving for college, though I didn't know where I'd go or what I'd do, especially if I wasn't going to follow Marla.

I wondered if all the changes that had occurred in my life and in Rayes County would have still taken place even without the interference of a tornado. Without the fierce weather of 1982 would I have just kept on being batted back and forth between the interest and whims of the women Daddy brought into and out of my life? It was a question I couldn't answer, but it didn't matter because things *had* changed.

Watching Marla leave for college made me believe that I could leave too and that there was a different world out there waiting just for me. It never occurred to me that I could stay at Marla's dorm when I visited. The thought of trying my legs on a college campus excited me much more than visiting my sister, although I never confessed it to my father.

I recalled the day when we moved Marla into her dorm room at UT. I had rerun the events over in my head several times, every action, every reaction, and every emotion.

"Oh wait," I had said to my sister as she stood in a strange room with the stringy blonde stranger she now called her roommate. "Your flute is still in the trunk."

"Never mind," Marla waved a dismissive hand as she spoke. "I don't need that here; just take it home."

My sister had carried that rectangular case to school every day since the fourth grade. It was like a third arm to her.

215

"Oh," I had responded, trying not to appear shocked as I looked appraisingly at my sister's new roommate, whose eyes were rimmed black like a raccoon. "I'll take it in when we get home."

Even though we had left Marla there two months before classes began, she didn't return home to visit until the Thanksgiving holiday, Fall break, as she referred to it. Although it had only been a couple of months, the girl that came home was someone else in Marla's body, it seemed. My sister had come home with a new haircut, new opinions on politics, history, and the spiritual unrighteousness of religion.

Marla had found her freedom, but she found it in some way that was strange to me. Seeing the new Marla and what leaving home had done to her gave me a prophetic picture of what was waiting for me.

Marla was seventeen before Daddy bought her car, yet I was only two months prior to sweet sixteen, and my freedom machine had been purchased without even a mention of my age.

Marla and I had traveled as a pair all our lives and for so long had been referred to simply as "the girls." It was hard to imagine there were any rules set aside just for me. And now that Marla wasn't at home, there were no rules for her, and it seemed like there were none for me either. Marla had been the trailblazer, and I was following so close behind her that no one noticed me riding her coat tails.

She was sixteen before she was allowed to go to a concert, even supervised; yet, I tagged along with her at fourteen. I had been unofficially dating since fifteen. Daddy had tried placing an age allowance on boys, but it really hadn't been necessary for Marla, she never showed much interest. It was different with me, though. I was interested—very interested.

Brought back to the present by a slap on the back, I was startled by the invasion of my personal space as the salesman practically yelled in my face.

"Looks like you're the proud new owner of that pretty thing out there," the salesman said, pointing to Shiny Girl.

I wanted to hug the annoying man in the plaid suit out of sheer instinct of happiness, but I refrained and hugged my father instead. After all, Daddy was the one who spoke those magic words: "We'll take it."

I wasn't allowed to drive Shiny Girl home; Daddy had it delivered the next day while he was at work. I started it, sat in it, and opened the top as I imagined myself cruising the strip with Leroy at my side.

I looked in the rearview mirror and saw Daddy pulling in the driveway.

"You ready to get started?" he asked as he slammed his car door shut and then retrieved his lunch box from the trunk.

"Sure am." I pushed the heavy car door open and followed my father into the house.

"You'd better go change clothes, Dancy."

"Why?"

"You'll figure it out," he said, pointing me in the direction of the hallway.

I pulled some bleached-out jeans from the back of the closet and put them on and found one of Marla's old band T-shirts. As I saw my manicure kit laying open on the dresser, I looked at my freshly murdered nails and grieved for a moment.

"Ugh," I muttered, pushing my fingers into a fist to hide what was left of my nails. My elbow brushed the curtain as I pulled my hair back into a ponytail, but when I saw Shiny Girl sitting there in driveway, I gave my nails no more thought.

The storm door slammed as I ran down the steps of the porch. Daddy had already moved the car into the barn.

"This is for you," he said, handing me a rubber hammer. Instinctively I grabbed the end of it and tried to squeeze the black rubber.

"What's it for?"

"Give me your hand."

Daddy stuck my hand under the open trunk lid. "Feel that?"

I felt a tiny bulge, like a bulge about the size of a tennis ball protruding through the underside of my new car's trunk.

"Now take this," my father said as he grabbed the rubber hammer. "And hit this." Daddy held the trunk lid up with his other hand and gently thudded the underside of the trunk.

"Let's hope we can get most of these out this way," he said, looking at the top side of the trunk to see if he had made any progress.

"What if we don't?"

"Well then, we'll use that," Daddy said, pointing to a long metal rod, with what looked like a plunger at the end, lying next to an arsenal of other tools that I had never seen in our barn before.

"Where'd you get these?"

"Buddy of mine from work restores cars."

"Why didn't you bring him home with you?" I laughed.

"This is *your* car, Dancy. *You* need to do the work."

"Are you still upset that I didn't get a new one?"

"No, I was never really upset," Daddy said, walking to the front of the car. "Just a little surprised at you."

"Why?"

"Never figured you'd go for the classics," Daddy said, admiring the front grill. "I think this is gonna be fun."

"Yeah," I said, bumping the hammer against the metal tennis ball-like protrusion to show my father I wasn't afraid of the work now facing me.

"Easy, easy," Daddy said. "You want to try to not crack the paint. Less touch-up we have to do, the better off we'll be. Red isn't a color you want to try and match up if you can help it."

"How long do you think it'll take?" I asked, already anxious to show off my new car in public.

"Eh, about a month or so if we work on it as hard as we can."

"Just in time for my license."

"Yep, and then you're gone forever," Daddy said, as he blew out a long breath and pulled a can of Pabst Blue Ribbon from the barn fridge.

"What do you think you're doing?" I scolded my father for leaving my side.

"Supervising," he said, dragging a stool up next to the car. "I've worked all damn day."

He popped the top from his beer and leaned back against a wooden beam in the center of the barn.

"Where's mine?" I asked, reaching for his beer.

"In the cooler, Dancy," he said pointing his can toward his stash.

"Seriously?"

"Hell, no," my father said, laughing. "But if you finish this car all by yourself we'll sit down and have a beer together, I promise."

"Sounds like you think I might not finish it," I said, putting my hands on my hips.

"Well, you're not off to a real good start," Daddy said, pointing to the trunk I had let close with my rubber hammer locked inside.

"Here," he said, handing me the keys to retrieve it.

I watched my father as he read the paper, cleaned his nails, and worked on the crossword puzzle.

"You can go in if you want," I said, pissed off that he hadn't lifted a finger to help me yet.

"No, that's okay," he said, getting up from his stool. "I'm going to go make a sandwich, but I'll be right back. You want one?"

"Yes, please," I said, my mouth watering at the thought of any food touching my lips. "And some water!" I yelled after him.

As I heard the back door slam shut, I fell to the ground, sobbing into my now red and swollen hands.

"Fuck," this is stupid, I said, slamming an already-sore fist into the trunk. "Dammit," I said under my breath.

"You can do this, Dancy. You can do this, Dancy." I kept saying to myself over and over. "Don't let him see you cry."

I grasped my hand onto a tail light and pulled myself up. I climbed into the trunk, and slammed the rubber mallet into as many protrusions as I could see, as fast as I could, growling each time I hit one. When I had hit them all at least four times each, I could feel my wrath start up again.

I climbed out of the trunk to take a look. This time, some of the dents were gone. An adrenaline rush pushed my arm down to slam the trunk lid shut so I could admire my work. I ran my hand over the finish. Some of the knots were still there, but I could see some of them were gone.

"That's my girl," I said to my new car. I licked a dirty finger and swiped the spit over a spot that once was a dent.

My hand was bleeding from a cut I couldn't locate and a bead of sweat fell through my eyelashes as I gave up the search.

I took the bottom of my T-shirt and shined one of the perfect spots I had just fashioned.

As I heard the back door close, I turned to see my father carrying a tray. Cricket danced all around him trying to get a whiff, a bite of something.

"Get down, Cricket," Daddy yelled. "Dammit, get down."

"Come here, Cricket," I yelled for her but her focus was human food, nothing else.

"Damn dog," Daddy said, blowing out a long breath.

"You all right?" Daddy started to place the tray on top of the closed trunk but I smacked at his arm.

"Fine," I said, pointing to my victory.

"You did that?" He placed the tray on the roof of the car to examine it further.

When I nodded, he said, "You sure?" He held his head close to the no-longer-existent ding and closed one eye to get a better perspective.

"I'll be a son of a bitch," my father said, smacking me on the shoulder. "You got one."

I unwrapped a bologna sandwich from a paper towel and took the thermos from the tray he had brought.

He took a sandwich as well, grabbed another beer from the fridge, and sat down on his stool.

Cricket, relentless in the pursuit of our food, conned me out of a good half of my sandwich with her soulful stare. I sat in the dirt, leaned against the car, and ate the other half. It didn't matter that the white bread was dirty from my hands; in fact, it felt good to be dirty, tired, and sweaty. It felt good to be my father's equal that night in the barn.

"Good job, Dancy." Daddy's mouth was half full of sandwich as he spoke. He swallowed and then took a gulp of beer as he got up from his stool to take another look at the pump knot I had just banged out of my new car. "Really," my father made it a point to emphasize his compliment to me. "Nice job."

I got up from the ground and stood next to Daddy. When my father finished his sandwich, he wiped a bit of blood off the car trunk with his leftover paper towel.

"Blood, sweat, and tears, little girl," he said, grinning at me and shaking his head. "You ready for some help now?"

I had to smile and roll my eyes at Daddy. My father was always so damn corny.

I wadded my paper towel into a ball and put it in my pocket, saving it for future cuts and abrasions. "Yes," I responded with a nod. "I could use a little help."

My father patted me on the head and winked. "Don't worry, we'll get this done, you little grease monkey," Daddy said, wiping his thumb over my forehead.

CHAPTER FOURTEEN

Bad, Bad Leroy

It was too cold to put the top down, but weather didn't matter. Leroy was in the passenger's seat wearing those ass-hugging jeans I was so fond of. If it were summer, he might have opted for some loose-fitting shorts and I would have been sorely disappointed.

"Damn, this is a cool car," Leroy said, tapping his hand on the dash.

"You've said that like a thousand times, Leroy."

"I know, man, but it's *cool.*"

My wrist rested casually on top of the steering wheel, my hand dangled like a rag doll as I cruised Shiny Girl, stopping at the red lights on the strip. Everyone was checking out me, Shiny Girl, and undoubtedly, Leroy.

For my birthday, Marla had an airbrushed vanity plate made for the front of my new car. It read: "Shiny Girl." Until my sister pointed it out, I didn't realize that the name Shiny Girl could have referred to the car or the driver.

Leroy was right. Shiny Girl *was* a cool car, and she made me cool. I no longer had to worry about sounding cool. My new car spoke volumes for me.

Leroy's friends hailed us into the Rexall parking lot, amazing prestige for a mere sophomore in high school. Being pulled over into a pocket of twenty-somethings was unheard of on the strip—not bad for a first night out on my own.

"Sweet ass car, Le-boy," a tall lanky man with a beard grabbed Leroy's hand in his fist and pulled it as they playfully arm wrestled through my passenger window.

I saw a few snowflakes fly past the streetlight as I got out of the car to join Leroy and his friends.

"Yes, she is cool," Leroy patted the top of the car and slid his tight ass onto the hood. Just like a scene from a James Dean movie, he lit a cigarette and took a long drag as he leaned forward, resting his arms on his knees. I stood there nodding and patting Shiny Girl's hood, validating what my man, Leroy, had just said about my fine new machine.

I had pulled into the lot and then backed around so that the front of the car would be visible to the cruisers on the strip. Lined up there next to the other cars, Shiny Girl's frame stood out like the Queen of Hearts at the Mad Hatter's table. I positioned myself carefully, squeezing my hips between Leroy's legs, facing traffic so everyone would know I was with Leroy and that the coolest car on the lot belonged to us. Puffs of smoke came out from around my face. I felt his warm breath on my ear.

"You cold, baby?"

"No, not too bad," I said, pulling my coat tighter together and pushing myself closer to his warm body.

I watched as the rest of the sophomores, juniors, and seniors from Rayes County High School drove past us in their new Celicas and Mazdas.

I rolled my eyes as Kenny Watson tooled by in his mother's new Chevy Caprice. Kenny didn't look our way, but I know he saw me and Leroy. Everybody saw me and my man standing there in our full frontal coolness.

Kenny had been asking me to the movies since the second grade, just after Mrs. Smith allowed me to paddle him for taking some pencils off my desk. Kenny had tormented me all year, teasing me about my frizzy hair, my big ears, and my manly-looking shoes. I often thought Mrs. Smith was just waiting for the right moment to seek vengeance on my behalf. So when she saw Kenny take the pencils, she allowed me to paddle him in front of the class, taking me aside first to tell me not to hit him too hard.

When I had finished giving Kenny the five licks Mrs. Smith had requested of me, he didn't turn around from the board right away. When I walked by Kenny to see if he was okay, he winked at me.

Kenny was red-faced and humiliated as he walked the full length of the class and slid into his back row desk. I sat back down in my seat, second row, second chair, and began to question my memory of the winking incident. Maybe I had imagined it, a hallucination, I thought, brought on by the extreme stress from the taunting and teasing. I carefully turned to the back of the room, holding my head low so Kenny might not notice. I jumped when I saw him staring at me. Kenny winked again, raising and lowering his eyebrows like he had been turned on by the paddling. I quickly turned around in my chair, thinking that maybe Kenny had suffered a brain injury.

Maybe the pencil thief had conked his head against the blackboard too hard when I was wailing on him.

Whatever happened that day, Kenny never recovered. With the exception of the one time that Kenny asked me to go roller skating with him, he had managed to ask me out every Friday of my life that was spent in the county's public school system, right up to yesterday.

Kenny had asked so many times he could have just recorded it and played it every Friday at 3 p.m. But he didn't. Each time Kenny asked, the invitation would have a bit of added creativity. Yesterday's invitation included ice cream and a movie, of course. I had simply rolled my eyes at him.

Kenny may have been a bit of a bad boy in the second grade, but he had changed. Those beady little eyes were now rimmed with black plastic and covered with thick lenses. Kenny had eaten a few too many Cheetos and was a little blubbery in the tummy. Rumor had it that Kenny was going to be our class valedictorian. When he made his run for class president last fall Kenny also announced he would be a student at MIT when he graduated high school and shortly after would be writing programs for new video games, maybe even holographic ones that our children would be playing in the future.

When Kenny wasn't spending his time studying or asking me out, he could be found at Pizza Palooza in the arcade, putting his initials on every game after he had cracked the code. Kenny's initials could be found on the winner's boards of both the games I liked, Star Wars and Pac Man. That just pissed me off at him even more. I could never beat him and never get his whiny ass voice out of my head. *Go to the movies with me, Dancy, How about it, Dancy, Me and you, Dancy.*

"Ugh," I said to no one, as I watched Kenny pass in the dorky Caprice.

Other than the occasional comment to Le-boy, a nickname Leroy's buddies had bestowed upon him long before we ever met, or a grunt from my man, the crowd was silent, taking their cues from those passing by, waving, yelling, and blowing their horns.

ZZ Top told the passing crowd we were untouchable and Led Zeppelin screamed at them to leave us alone.

Leroy put his cigarette to my lips, his face close to mine. "Go ahead, it'll warm you up."

I nibbled on it a little and puffed but didn't inhale.

He pulled the cigarette from my lips, spun me around, and kissed me, his whole mouth covering mine. He clasped his hands around my butt cheeks and squeezed them rhythmically to coincide with the faint moaning I heard and felt coming from his throat.

Horns were blowing but I didn't care. It sounded like a parade passing down the strip behind me.

"Woohoo! Go Le-boy!" someone yelled. More horns blew. When he had finished kissing my mouth, he moved to my neck. My now-wet lips were exposed to the cold air. I knew they'd get chapped. I didn't care. I could feel the sucking on my neck getting stronger. It no longer felt passionate. It felt like Leroy was on a mission.

"No," I yelled and pushed myself away from him.

"Too late," he said, laughing and pointing to what was sure to be a huge hickey. I didn't even have to look at it. I knew it was enormous. I could tell from the effort he'd put into it; even his own lips were purple.

"Damn you," I said hitting him in the chest. "My father's gonna see that."

"And what's ole' Everett gonna do?" Leroy laughed and the others joined in and began to rub their eyes like crying babies.

"My Daddy's gonna be mad," Leroy's friends mocked, each with his own version of the sentence as they mimicked child-like voices.

"Fuck you!" I yelled at Leroy's friends and flipped them the bird. "Let's get out of here," I said as I walked to the driver's side of the car, Leroy was standing right behind me. "Come on," I said to Leroy again and opened the door, hoping he'd get the message this time and get in.

Leroy held the door with one hand and cupped a hand over my ass cheek with the other.

"You should let me drive, baby. You're a little upset," his breath was hot on the back of my neck as he spoke.

"But, but, I don't think," I started to speak but Leroy interrupted me.

"But what?" Leroy asked sarcastically. "Oh, *I've* got your butt," he said, squeezing my butt tighter and now he had both his hands on my ass.

I turned around and kissed Leroy. "You be careful with Shiny Girl," I said and reluctantly handed him the keys.

As I walked around the front and got in the passenger's seat, Leroy said his good-byes to the crowd, hand smacking, arm pulling, and back slapping, boy stuff.

"Past her bed time?" one of them yelled over at us as Leroy got into the car.

"See you guys later," Leroy responded and laughed at the comment.

"Fuck you!" I yelled, flipping a bird from both hands at Leroy's friends as we pulled out of the parking lot.

"God, Dancy, calm down," Leroy said as he squealed tires. I smelled the rubber as I rolled up the window.

"Slow down, dammit," I yelled.

"God, you're such a little baby," Leroy paid no attention to me as he fidgeted with the stereo and gear shift simultaneously.

"Where are we going?" Leroy had made a right instead of a left at the end of the strip.

"Friend of mine is having a party, and we're invited," Leroy said, as he punched the gas pedal. "Let's see what she'll do," he said, intending to take full advantage of his time behind Shiny Girl's wheel.

"These friends?" I questioned Leroy. "The ones from back there?" I asked, pointing my thumb to the road behind us.

"It's not their party, but they're coming," Leroy answered, adjusting the rearview mirror.

"You gotta be fuckin' kiddin' me," I shouted.

"Dancy, you'd better calm down," he said, as the car accelerated to 90 mph. "They're okay, babe. They're my friends, and you're gonna have to get used to them."

I turned to look behind us as headlights followed close.

"That them?"

"Yep," Leroy smiled and winked at me. "I look pretty good over here, don't I?"

I smiled and slid over next to him, looking into Shiny Girl's big round eyes as her glowing needle passed 90. She didn't look happy. I thought of Daddy's pressing my finger into the 50 mph mark the day we had bought the car. I closed my eyes and laid my head on Leroy's shoulder and finally gave into the thrill of the fast ride.

I opened my eyes as the car started to slow. I heard gravel popping but could only see ten or so feet ahead.

"Where are we?"

"Yeah, I know. These cats live in Bum Fuck," Leroy concentrated on the road ahead of him. "Ah," he said as a utility light came into view.

The faded trailer sat on concrete blocks and had a tow bar connected to the front end. It wasn't really a travel trailer but was almost small enough. I counted seven cars parked in the field and two in the drive. That wasn't taking into account mine and the others that had followed us.

Leroy and I got out, waited for the rest of his friends, and walked to the front steps of the little trailer in a group. The trailer was just a short distance from where we parked, so there wasn't much time to reflect on what had happened at Rexall.

Leroy slapped on the door with an open hand. We could feel the bass coming from the loud music inside as we stood on the small wooden deck.

"They can't hear us," one of the idiots behind Leroy noted. "Let's just go in."

Leroy pulled the door open easily. No one even noticed we had entered the trailer for a few seconds or so. The room was thick with a blue haze. I recognized that smell immediately.

"Hey, Leak." An older man sauntered toward us and Leroy slapped him on the shoulder.

"Le-boy, where the hell you been?"

"Here and there, Leak."

Leak only had one good eye and would have looked a lot better if the bad one had been covered with a patch. Leak's good eye moved as he spoke, and the other eye tried to move right along with it without much luck. The movement was more of a nerve-like twitching than actual, purposeful motion.

To stop myself from staring at Leak's eye, I moved a few feet from Leroy's side and began scanning the room. The couch was full. There were six people sitting on it. The chair next to it was also full, three people there. A few were sitting on lawn chairs that had been brought in from outside and the rest of the people were sitting in the floor.

The women partying inside the trailer were mostly older. One was sitting straddled on her man so I couldn't see her face, only her long, brown hair that reached way down past her ass. She held a bottle of beer in one hand and a cigarette in the other. She appeared to be riding him like a horse as she bounced up and down with her arms crossed around the back of his neck. When she raised her head to take a drag from the cigarette, I screamed, "Mary!"

Mary looked around the room like she had heard something but wasn't entirely sure what. As Mary turned to take another drag from the cigarette, she saw me. I saw her mouth moving but couldn't hear her words over the loud music. I winced a few times as I watched Mary try to walk over and almost fall over the people in her path, still holding the bottle in one hand and cigarette in the other.

"Oh my God, you bitch, Dancy Wilder," she slobbered her words as she put her face next to mine in what was meant to be a hug, but wasn't. "What the hell are you doing here?"

I had stopped trying to communicate over the music so I just pointed instead to Leroy, who was still standing pretty close by.

"You two," Mary slobbered again. "I thought you two might hit it off."

She had actually introduced me and Leroy. I saw her at the state park one afternoon last summer with a group of her friends. Leroy was among them.

"How 'bout I give you a call, little Dancy," he had said, brushing my arm with his finger. I gave him my number and after that, the park became *our* place, the only place I could meet him without Daddy finding out.

Mary pointed a now-empty beer bottle over to the couch. "That's my Big Jim," she slobbered her words at me again.

I had already inspected the man Mary had been sitting on and taken note of everything about Big Jim so I could call Marla the minute I got home and tell her all about what Mary had been up to. Big Jim's beard was unkempt to say the least. The mess of hair stuck to his face looked filthy, like it had bits of something in it. Big Jim was wearing an Army jacket. Most of the men in the room were wearing camouflage. He was balding and had wisps of gray hair protruding out from under a bandana just above his ears. Big Jim's wrinkles were deeper than the fine lines that Daddy had on his forehead.

Like she sensed my judgment of her, Mary said, "He's older, but he takes care of me." Mary held onto my shoulder for support. She unwrapped an index finger from around the empty bottle, kissed it, and pointed it toward Big Jim, who really wasn't that big from what I could see. Big Jim paid no attention to Mary; he was staring straight ahead just as he had been when she was bouncing all over him.

"He's a very serious guy," Mary slurred, trying to explain Big Jim's aloofness toward her. As she leaned in to talk to me her hair melted into the cigarette she had been holding too close to her once-glorious mane. I moved the cigarette away from her hair and rubbed the melting pieces out between my fingers to make sure any fire was extinguished.

"Oh, that happens all the time," Mary said, referring to her melting hair. She then laughed and wiped a long strand of spit off her chin that had escaped from her mouth.

Much like Kenny had been a constant source of aggravation for most of *my* life, Mary had been my sister's tormenter for most of hers. Moneybags Mary, as Marla and I used to call her, was one of the biggest spoiled rich bitches in Rayes County. Her father was a heart surgeon and the running joke was that he had taken her heart out and sold it for their mansion-sized estate.

I remembered at Marla's graduation that Mary had listed news anchor as a future profession, same as Marla had listed. Daddy and I clapped as loud as we could, though he wouldn't let me yell. He said it was rude. In any case, my voice was no match for the screaming, yelling, and foot stomping when it was announced that Money Bags Mary would be attending journalism school to pursue a career as a television news anchor.

I smiled at Mary now, thinking how pleased Marla would be that I had found her arch nemesis in a backwoods trailer spending time with an old hairy man.

Out of the corner of my eye, I saw an older woman had taken Mary's place on Big Jim's lap. I pointed in that direction.

"Son of a bitch," Mary yelled, though no one but me heard her. Mary then threw her empty beer bottle, hitting the old whore dead center in the back. The old lady's squawk broke the crowd's chatter and someone turned the music down. As Mary staggered over the other drunks to get to Big Jim, the old whore, who was now madder than hell, was heading our way. Everyone at the party who wasn't already standing came to their feet, encircled the two women, and then the chanting began. "Fight, fight, fight!" they yelled.

I shuffled to my left, strategically trying to put myself between Leak and Leroy, but Leak had already sprang into action. Within two great strides, Leak had managed to grab Mary and the old whore by the hair and pull them apart. I could now see Big Jim in full view, staring straight ahead, reacting to nothing.

With robotic motions like he had done it a thousand times before, Leak shoved the women back into their original seats.

Mary's was, of course, on top of Big Jim's lap, which appeared to make her happy. Leak pushed a couple of other people out of the way, walked toward us, and continued the obviously half-finished conversation he had been having with Leroy.

"Can't do it, man," Leak said, looking at me with a suspicious eye. "I ain't gonna say it again." Leak opened the front door and stepped out onto the porch.

"What if she smokes one with us man?" Leroy yelled after Leak. "That's proof she ain't no nark."

I looked at Leroy. The loud music had resumed, so I used body language to ask, *What the hell?*

"Doesn't trust you," Leroy yelled in my face. "Thinks you're trouble."

I knew Leroy toked. He had made no secret about it. I had confessed to Leroy that I had smoked it once, though I didn't say when or who with.

The cold air hit my lungs as we followed Leak outside. I coughed and hacked. Doubled over, trying to catch my breath, I heard Leroy pleading again. I spat over the railing and took another deep breath, which brought on another coughing fit. No one seemed concerned.

"C'mon, man, just a dime bag," Leroy begged.

"I didn't survive eight months in the jungle to be put in a cage over a little chicken tender," Leak pointed a freshly-lit cigarette toward me.

"If she smokes one with us?" Leroy was pathetic. Even I was tired of that question.

"Light 'er up," Leak handed Leroy a tiny roach.

Even before he lit it, I shook my head.

"I'm not gonna smoke that, Leroy," my voice was weak from all the coughing. "You don't know whose lips have been wrapped around that thing." I looked toward the trailer door in disgust, hoping that'd be enough for Leroy to stop trying to prove I wasn't a nark.

"Oh, c'mon, baby," Leroy held it to my lips.

"No," I yelled. "Now, stop it."

Leak finished his cigarette, flipped it over the wooden railing and looked at Leroy. "Get her gone, and maybe then we'll talk."

"C'mon," Leroy said, pulling my arm.

Anxious to get out of there and back to my car, I followed without even sending what had become my trademark "fuck you" at Leak.

"Why do they call him Leak?" I asked, as I scooted across the seat getting as close to Leroy as I could.

He laughed. "I haven't thought about that in a long time," he said, laying his arm over the back seat to back the car around. There were almost a dozen cars in Leak's field now and I held my breath waiting for the screeching sound of metal on metal.

"When Leak was in 'Nam, he got shot in the head," Leroy said, as he managed to successfully navigate the car out of what looked like an abandoned demolition derby behind us.

"Oh my God, really?" I was sure I had never met a real Vietnam Veteran.

"Yeah, shot in the head," Leroy shaped a gun with his hand and pointed it at the windshield. "Pop," he played with the sound placing special emphasis on the letter "p."

"Holy shit," I said, amazed that anyone could live after being shot in the head.

"Yeah, they bandaged him up and sent him home," Leroy said, starting to accelerate faster now that we were out on the open highway. "When Leak left state-side, he was a math genius and now he can't even find his own way home."

"What?" I asked shocked. Leak seemed normal enough, gross and dirty, but normal.

"Yeah," Leroy chuckled. "Funniest damn thing, he can find a weed the size of his thumb but he can't remember where he lives. That's why he stays out there in the trailer. It's the coolest place in Rayes County if you ask me."

"So why do they call him Leak?" I reminded Leroy of the initial question.

"Oh yeah, that." Leroy nodded. "He says when they shot him in the head, some of his brains must have leaked out."

I was relieved to see the lights from town quickly coming at us as we drove, but I got nervous again when Leroy passed the downtown turnoff.

"Where the hell are we going now?"

"Pizza Palooza," Leroy said, smiling at me.

"You gotta be fuckin' kiddin' me." I pushed myself away from Leroy so I could see his face better. There was no way he was serious.

"Well, *you're* going to Pizza Palooza," Leroy said, patting me on the leg. "I'm going back out to Leak's to get that dime bag and then I'll be right back to get you."

By the time I could react, Leroy had already pulled in front of the doors to let me out. I didn't move.

"C'mon, baby," Leroy urged with a nudge to my arm. "The sooner you let me go, the sooner I'll be back."

I looked through the double glass doors into the arcade. The place was full of losers and geeks.

"I don't want to go in there." I crossed my arms and didn't move.

"Fine, dammit," Leroy was pissed now. "I didn't sign up for this, Dancy. Just take me back to Rexall and I'll get a ride out to Leak's. You go do whatever it is that sixteen year olds do."

His words hit my stomach like a fist. I could see headlights from the cars now lined up behind us, parents waiting to let their kids out.

"I think we're holding up traffic," Leroy smoothed his hair in the rearview mirror.

"Fine," I said, finally scooting away from him to get out of the car. "But I'm not going in. I'll be waiting on that bench so you'd better not be more than twenty minutes. It's kind of cold out."

"That's my girl," Leroy said as he winked at me, and then grabbed my hair to pull my head back and kiss me. His breath stank like cigarettes and beer and either his hair or mine smelled like the blue haze from Leak's trailer.

"Thanks, babe," Leroy put the car in drive before I could even shut the car door. I watched Shiny Girl's tail lights get smaller as Leroy took her out of the parking lot and onto the highway.

When I walked over to the bench next to the double doors at Pizza Palooza I realized I'd be more visible outside on the bench than if I just went inside. There was already a line of a half a dozen or more cars waiting to drop off kids and that bench was in full view of everyone whether they were coming or going. I decided to go inside and find a table where I could keep an eye on the front door.

The sounds of the arcade sent my eyes darting all over the building. It had been at least a year since I'd been inside Pizza Palooza. Either I had forgotten what the arcade sounded like or new games had arrived in my absence, along with new sounds. I took off my jacket and sat down at a small table pressed against the front window. I was still visible to onlookers but there was nowhere else to go where I could still keep an eye on the parking lot.

I wiped a flake of mascara from my cheekbone as I looked at my reflection in the glass. The purple mark on my neck was about the size of a walnut, about what I had expected. I pulled my jacket off the back of my chair and put it back on, lifting the collar to hide Leroy's sucker. I could feel my face turning red as I wondered who else had seen it since I came into the building.

The crowd was sparse but getting thicker by the minute as more game geeks were dropped at the sidewalk. It seemed later than it was. According to the Pizza Palooza clock I had only been out for two hours. It seemed like it should've been midnight already.

"Anybody who's out past 11:30 is up to no good, Dancy," my father had said. "Be home by 11:15 just to be on the safe side."

I didn't argue. It was a small battle, really, not worth the fight. Instead I decided to humbly agree with his curfew and gain an additional fifteen minutes each month. By the time summer rolled around, when it really mattered, I'd be out 'til 12:30, easy, with Shiny Girl's top down.

Tiny snowflakes were becoming more visible under the street lights. Mamaw would have called it "a little skiff of snow."

"Excuse me, Miss," a girl wearing a black and red Pizza Palooza T-shirt interrupted my gaze out the window. It was odd to see a woman that old with such long hair. From a distance she had looked no more than mid-twenties but now that she was up close I could see she was well into her thirties.

"Yes?" I replied, questioning her appearance at my table. Order and pickup at Palooza was strictly up to the customer. The snack bar had no real waitresses to speak of, unless occasionally wiping down tables counted. Yet, this waitress carried a tray with a drink and two slices of pizza.

"The gentleman over by the Asteroid machine asked me to bring this to you," she turned and nodded her head in the direction of the arcade.

"I don't see who you're talking about," I said to her after I was sure I had thoroughly scanned the place. Asteroid games dotted the place like stars in the sky. Asteroid was the most popular game in the arcade.

"There he is," she put the tray down and pointed to tall, skinny, red-headed boy, who I recognized right away.

"Should've known," I said as I watched Kenny trying to look cool gliding across the carpet and onto the tile, almost tripping over the transition but managing to save the soda he was carrying. While I had been busy scanning the arcade for the chivalrous gentleman offering me pizza and soda, Kenny was already making strides toward my table.

"Hey, hot stuff," he winked at me and then sat down without being invited.

Grabbing a slice of pizza from the plate, he commented before taking a bite, "Don't mind if I do, Dancy. Thank you for asking."

"Help yourself," I said, scooting the plate closer to him. "Have them both."

"So where is Prince un-Charming?" Kenny looked out into the parking lot.

"Very funny, Kenny," I rolled my eyes.

"So, where is he?"

"He had to run an errand."

"Without you?"

"Yes, obviously without me, smartass."

239

"No need to get hateful," Kenny said, grabbing a napkin and wiping a bit of sauce from the corner of his mouth.

I sighed, pulling the plate back toward my side of the table and took the other slice of pizza. I *was* starving after all. Leroy's promise of pizza had yet to come to fruition, and I hadn't eaten since noon.

"I knew you couldn't resist," Kenny took another bite as his eyebrows danced up and down on his forehead.

"If you're talking about not resisting the pizza then you're right. Everything else I could take or leave," I said, smiling.

"Oh, so you don't want this," he said, pulling the drink out of my hand.

"Yes." I pulled it back, sloshing a bit over the edge.

"Now look what you've done." Kenny looked around nervously like someone was going to come after us. "We'd better get this cleaned up," he said, swiping the table with his hand. "There, now try to be more careful."

I couldn't help but laugh in the midst of Kenny's witty sarcasm.

"I'll do my best," I responded.

Although I tried not to show it, I was glad Kenny had sat down with me.

"I like your new car," Kenny said, starting to show signs of someone who wanted to converse rather than flirt with me.

"Yeah, she's great, just unbelievable."

"Shiny Girl, I like that name," Kenny said nodding approval.

"Yeah, it fits her," I said. "Marla bought the name tag for my birthday."

"Looks real good," Kenny said. "How is Marla, anyway? I heard she's at UT."

"She is; left last August, just me and Daddy now."

"You got Shiny Girl," Kenny sung his words.

"Yeah." I instinctively looked out toward the parking lot wishing I'd see Shiny Girl there. I began to chatter nervously as I saw Kenny scanning the lot for her as well.

"So are you still the top scorer on all the games here?" I asked Kenny, not waiting for an answer. "You always were the best at all of them. Used to make me so mad."

"Where is it?" Kenny interrupted my aimless rambling.

"What?" I tried to stall.

"Your car?"

My gaze fell to the table but I held my shoulders high as I answered. "Leroy's got her," I said, looking Kenny straight in the eyes now. "He'll be right back, really, any minute now." I looked at the clock. Twenty minutes had already passed. "He'll probably be pulling up any second. You might want to make yourself scarce." I looked toward the window and then back at Kenny.

"I see," Kenny said, nodding slowly and then getting up from the table. His face was like an open book. I could tell he was skeptical about Leroy. "Really, he'll be right back," I repeated myself.

"Well then, good night, Fair Dancy." Kenny pulled my hand from the table and kissed the back of it. "I'm off to save the world from asteroids," he said, flinging a stiff arm in the direction of the arcade. Kenny then spun around on one foot and walked toward his war machine to complete his mission, fighting for control of the universe.

As I sat there for the next hour and a half waiting for Leroy to return from Leak's, Kenny kept poking his head out of his Asteroid game every so often to give me a salute. My eyes continued to dart nervously back and forth from the highway to the parking lot and then over to Kenny. Any time I'd catch a glimpse of red and chrome my I'd lose my breath only to find it again when I realized it wasn't Shiny Girl.

"Want to play a game?" I heard Kenny's voice from behind me. I had seen his reflection in the glass come toward me several times and then turn and walk away. This time, he had found enough courage to tap me on the shoulder.

"No, I'm too worried."

"Oh," Kenny said, sitting down in the seat across from me. I didn't look up. "What time do you have to be home?"

"Around 11:30," I said, trying to stretch my time as far as I could.

"Me too," Kenny said, rapping his knuckles on the table. "We'll just wait and then if Leroy doesn't show by then I'll take you home."

Kenny's solution was sweet but lacked common sense. I looked at him and nodded my head but then went back to trying to mentally will my car into the parking lot with Jedi-like force.

"I can't go home without my car, Kenny."

He nodded and pressed his lips together. Obviously, the thought of how much trouble I'd be in if I went home without my car had not occurred to Kenny until I mentioned it.

"I see," Kenny said and then got up from the table. "I'll be right back, gotta make a phone call."

"Yeah, right," I looked up at him and smiled. "That's what the last guy said."

"Good one," Kenny said and then laughed. "I *will* be right back."

If Kenny was nothing else, he was dependable. I could always count on him to be there when I didn't want him around. But now I really did want him there, so I was happy he was sticking with me. I spent the next few minutes continuing

242

to look out at the parking lot and then back at the clock in what seemed exact intervals, two minutes allocated to each.

As I watched the second hand make another round, I turned to see where Kenny had gone and spotted him in the far corner of the arcade talking on the only pay phone in the building. I smiled as I watched him. The conversation was animated and full of energy.

I turned back to the window as he hung up the phone, giving me a thumbs-up as he did. There was still no car, no sign of Leroy.

"R and B are coming," Kenny said confidently like he had just announced that the FBI was going to walk through the door and begin a thorough investigation into the case of my missing car. "They'll be here in a minute." Kenny looked at the door.

I furrowed my brow at him and shook my head. "Why?"

"We're going to get your car back."

I said nothing, but my mouth gaped open.

"You *do* want your car back, *don't you?*" Kenny spoke to me slowly. "Or did I misunderstand? Have you been worried all this time about Shiny Girl or has it been Leroy you've been missing?"

I looked out at the parking lot, now almost empty, and then back at Kenny.

"I'm worried about my car, smartass, and yes I want it back. But what good are Roger and Barry?"

R and B, as they had become known at Rayes County High School were bigger nerds than Kenny. Roger and Barry were math and science freaks and could usually be found setting off an explosion in one of the school labs, if they weren't playing Atari and fantasizing over girls who wouldn't spit on them even if the two boys had caught themselves on fire.

Somehow R and B had managed to attach themselves to RCHS's only computer nerd, Kenny. There was speculation that the three of them were trying to build an atomic bomb and launch it toward the Soviets, but it was far more likely they were just playing video games most of the time.

"They have a car," Kenny said, defending R and B and tapping his index fingers like drumsticks on the table. "We can cover both ends of town that way."

Kenny was proud of himself for putting together the dream team he was sure would find Shiny Girl, and I hated to take the wind out of his sails, but I wasn't about to go on a completely unnecessary wild goose chase in a nerd-mobile.

"I don't think Leroy is in town," I said, shaking my head and rolling my eyes. "He went to a friend's house."

"Oh yeah," Kenny said sarcastically and then looked at the clock to prove some kind of a point. "His *errand*." Kenny rolled his eyes at me and shook his head.

"R and B, right on time," Kenny pointed to the parking lot.

Roger and Barry were always easy to spot. They traveled together so much of the time it was hard to know who really owned that Gremlin. I had seen both of them driving it, separately and together.

"So whose car is that anyway?"

"It belongs to both of them," Kenny said. "Not many people know this but R and B are brothers."

"What?" I was shocked. "You're kidding."

"Nope, brothers," Kenny said. "Don't let the variation of colors fool you. They have two different fathers, same mother. She was a bit of a rounder, sordid past, you know the type."

I thought I knew everything about everyone at Rayes County High School. This was new information. Barry was as white as a coal miner's ass cheeks in the winter, and Roger was about as black as a miner's face at the end of a hard day digging nine inch coal. Although R and B were both the same height, the only trait the two of them shared was that they were short, a good eight inches below the top of Kenny's head. I watched R and B with interest as they walked toward the double glass doors, still amazed that they could be brothers.

"I'll be damned," I said, mesmerized by R and B and what I had just learned. "I'll be damned."

"I know," Kenny said, taking note of my epiphany. "Freaky."

Like robots, R and B grabbed a chair each and slung them under the small table where Kenny and I were sitting.

"So, what's the plan?" Roger looked at Kenny and then back to me while Barry's eyes seemed to be locked onto my boobs.

"What the hell are you looking at?" I scolded Barry.

"Way to go," Barry said, reaching over and slapping Kenny on the back.

Roger joined his brother as they both glared at my boobs. "Give me a five on that," Roger flattened his palm and held it out for Kenny to slap, never pulling his eyes away from my chest.

Kenny remained calm, signaling to me by pointing to his neck. By the time I realized they weren't staring at my boobs and it was the big, purple, hickey that had gotten them all out of sorts, Kenny's face was already blazing red. R and B turned to Kenny to confirm the sucker on my neck was his handy work. He shook his head vigorously and signaled a cut-throat motion until they finally got the message.

"Oh," Barry said, pointing to my neck. "Not yours?"

Kenny interrupted with a sharp, "No."

I could feel my face getting hot and my stomach felt queasy.

"So, we're looking for Dancy's car," Kenny said, ignoring the distraction. "I want you guys to start looking on this end of town. Dancy and I will take the north end."

R and B nodded with robot-like movements.

"When you've looked in every parking lot, every alleyway, and up and down every road then we'll meet back at Burger Queen."

The boys nodded again.

"Dancy's car is easy to spot. Red, white, and lots of chrome, Chevelle SS," Kenny's authoritative instructions were admirable but unnecessary.

"He's not in town," I said to Kenny again. "He's at a guy's house, named Leak."

"Care to wager on that?" Kenny stared me down. The boys remained silent, awaiting my answer.

"No," I said and then crossed my arms. I had nothing to wager with. My car was gone. Leroy was nowhere to be found and I was at the mercy of whatever these nerds wanted to do.

"Let's go." I relented, knowing I could talk Kenny into taking me to Leaks once he realized Shiny Girl wasn't in town.

The Caprice smelled like somebody's mom, Kenny's I suspected.

"Smells a little girly in here, I know," Kenny apologized right away.

"I kind of like it," I said, breathing in deep as I watched the Gremlin pull out in front of us.

"Good thing," Kenny said laughing, "'cause it doesn't go away."

The rear road leading into the Pizza Palooza shopping center was always a hub of activity for those who wanted a bit of anonymity as they hung out in town. Kenny took that road first.

"Leroy's not here," I crossed my arms and glared across the car at Kenny.

"So, about that bet," Kenny overlooked my smartass comment.

"There is no bet," I said.

"If we find your car in town," Kenny continued to talk, ignoring my reasoning. "Then you go out with me one time." Kenny then hesitated to gauge my reaction and when I had none, other than rolling my eyes, he continued. "And if we don't find your car in town then I'll never ask you out again."

I wasn't entirely sure my existence would be the same without Kenny constantly pestering me to go to the movies, but I did like the possibility of escaping school some Friday in the future without having to break his heart.

"Sounds like a fair bet," I said confidently. "You've got thirty minutes."

Kenny seemed unconcerned even after he had spent fifteen of those precious minutes just cruising the main drag, glancing every now and again to the parking lots on either side of the strip.

"I'm going to head up on the highway," Kenny said, casually wheeling the Caprice over the railroad tracks.

"Go ahead," my tone was sharp. "You've got ten minutes."

Kenny took a long, deep breath. "Ever heard the expression, oh, something about a gift horse?"

"I'm just saying that he's not in town, Kenny. It's not that I don't appreciate your -," I stopped mid-sentence when I saw Shiny Girl sitting at Burger Queen.

"Oh shit!" I pointed.

Kenny said nothing as he pulled into the parking lot right next to my car.

"Hang on," I said, opening the door to get out before Kenny had even geared down to park. Melting snow had run off the warm concrete and into the ditch. My shoes filled with water as I sloshed through the sopping grass. I moved faster as I saw movement inside my car.

"Leroy!" I yelled when he didn't see me standing in front of the windshield. "Leroy!" I screamed again as I leapt to the driver's side window.

I felt like someone had ripped my heart from my chest and was holding it out in the frigid air. I was speechless as I watched Leroy hold his index finger up to the window, asking me for another moment of ecstasy with the brunette whose head he appeared to be devouring, mouth first.

Beating a fist on the window, I screamed Leroy's name again. Enraged to find my car door locked as I tugged the handle, I beat a fist on the windshield. When Leroy finally forced his lips to detach from who I now recognized as Money Bags Mary, he turned to me and smiled. The window began to come down inch by inch as I watched his arm move, slowly cranking the handle. The night was silent as the snow fell between us. I could see every red vein in the whites of his eyes as he sat there grinning at me like the Cheshire Cat.

"Cool car, Dancy," were the first and last words Mary slurred at me.

"Get the fuck out of my car," I growled through gritted teeth. Leroy threw a cigarette out the window.

"Okay, okay, Dancy," Leroy's breath stank like rotting eggs. I turned my face away. "You don't have to be such a bitch about it."

I couldn't speak and I couldn't recall how I got there, but I somehow ended up on the passenger's side of the car, demanding that Mary open the door. I saw her mouth moving but heard nothing as she opened the door and started to talk to me. Before another slur could find its way into existence I grabbed Mary by the throat and pulled her from my car, shoving her into the grass. Once inside, I opened the glove box and placed a shaky hand on my revolver.

"Goddammit, Dancy," Leroy started to lecture me but took one look at my .38 Special and got out of the car. I slammed the passenger's door shut, then locked both doors and quickly put the gun back in the glove box.

My body trembled as I recalled Chick's words, "There's only one letter that stands between anger and danger. Don't be a dummy." It was such a stupid thing for Chick to say, such an old man riddle. Ridiculous. I knew now how the lines were blurred, and I wasn't entirely sure if I had been angry or in danger. For now, they both seemed one in the same. It didn't matter now. I had done it, I had pulled my gun on someone but at least no one had seen.

I looked up from the steering wheel and into the rearview mirror, Leroy's scent still hung heavy in the car. I watched the piece of shit that only hours earlier I had referred to as "my man" as he walked through the parking lot, getting smaller as he strode away. I turned around to see Leroy's coat lying in the back seat. Now R and B's Gremlin was parked behind me. I hugged the wheel and sobbed into the chrome and hard plastic. Shiny Girl's round eyes were wide with fear and question. Not only had I abandoned my precious car, I had slammed a now-bloody fist into her driver's side door.

A light tapping on the window pulled me momentarily from my grief.

"You okay?" I saw Kenny mouthed the muffled words through the window.

I looked around to see R and B staring at me through the passenger's side window. It wasn't bad enough that my car had been stolen, I had been cheated on, and that the long-haired whore, Mary, who cuckolded me was now lying helpless in front of my car. A small crowd, in addition to Kenny, Roger, and Barry was starting to form.

"Jesus Christ, I look like hell," I said, glancing in the rearview mirror. I pulled myself together enough to grab Leroy's coat and get out of the car. "Here," I handed it to Kenny. "Get rid of this for me," I sniffled, my eyes filled with tears.

"Boys," Kenny yelled to R and B, who were now walking around Mary like she was an alien.

"Yeah," Roger was the first to come, then Barry right after.

"Will you do something with this?" Kenny handed Roger the coat. "And take care of that," he said pointing to Mary. "Take *her* home, and I don't care what you do with *this*," Kenny said, holding Leroy's coat out with an index finger.

"We can take her home with us?" Barry had managed an erection even in the frigid night air.

"No, not *our* house," Roger scolded his fair-skinned brother. "*Her* house."

"Mansion on the hill," Kenny said, pointing to a row of lights just beyond Woodland Shopping Center, a place known as Snob Knob to everyone in Rayes County with the exception of the people who lived there.

"Sure thing," Roger said, slapping Kenny on the arm. "Goodnight, Dancy."

"Night, Rog," I muttered as I watched the brothers retrieve Mary from the ditch. As they carried her past me, a cold, wet strand of her hair grazed my hand. I escaped just before I burst into tears again, running as fast as I could toward the glass doors at Burger Queen. I kept my head down until I reached the bathroom. Once inside I sobbed into my jacket sleeve.

Startled when the door flew open, I was shocked to see Kenny. He closed it quickly and locked it behind him. He grabbed me by the waist and hoisted me up onto the sink.

"Dancy, pull yourself together," he demanded. "What the hell is the matter with you? I've seen you eat guys like Leroy for breakfast and spit them out for lunch."

"I don't know," my sobbing had eased a bit from the shock of Kenny barging into the ladies room. "You're in the girl's bathroom," I said, in case Kenny hadn't noticed.

"Yes," I can see that. "And I just want to know one thing," he pointed his finger in my face, appearing to be quivering with anger. "Why is it so damn clean in here?"

When the echo of his voice had bounced off every wall, the bathroom was silent.

I laughed. "God, you're an idiot."

"Have you seen *that* place?" Kenny pointed in the direction of the men's room.

"No, I can't say I have," I laughed again.

I watched as Kenny pulled at least a few feet of paper towels out of the dispenser, rolled them in one-foot increments, and then tore them in half. He wet one half with cold water and left the other half dry. I wanted to ask him what he was doing but my voice was tired so I just watched. Kenny pushed my hair back away from my face and began to pat the cold, wet towel gently on my cheeks.

"How did you know Leroy would be here?" My voice, now weak and weary, sounded like it belonged to someone else.

Kenny kept dabbing at my face and when he was done he wrapped my bloody hand in the wet paper towels. He then took the dry ones and started to pat my face again.

"I made two phone calls, Dancy, one to R and B, and one to my brother. Did you forget he's a cop?"

I nodded and grinned. "I see."

"He put out an APB for the car and reported back to me," Kenny said, unwrapping my hand to take a closer look. "It only took a minute. Like I told the boys, your car is easy to spot. He said it was at BQ. Did you hurt Shiny Girl when you hit the windshield, the door?" Kenny tried to change the subject.

"Oh hell no," I said, wincing as I tried to make a fist. "She's solid, pure metal; not a scratch. I can't even imagine the size of those hail balls that dinged her up last summer."

Kenny laughed. "Well, at least if you did dent her up, you'd know how to fix her."

"So if you knew Leroy was here then why did you tell R and B to come?"

"I wanted somebody to be here in case my guts had to be scraped off the parking lot and taken home to my mother," Kenny said, smiling. "I've watched people piss on that pavement. I didn't want to lie there any longer than I had to. I told my brother to stay out of it. He gave me his word."

"I guess this means I owe you a date."

"Nah, don't worry about it." Kenny dabbed at my bloody knuckles again. "I'd kind of just like to ask you out for the rest of your life, whether you go or not is irrelevant." He smiled.

For reasons I could neither explain nor control I flung my arms around him and began to cry.

"Hey you." Kenny held me tight. "I thought you were stronger than that." He stroked my hair and the rhythm of his breathing comforted me. I could've stayed there forever in his arms but he broke free from my grip. Pushing me back so I could see his face, he kissed my forehead.

"This could never turn out well," he said. "You like the bad boys."

I smiled. "As I recall, you used to be a bad boy."

Kenny laughed and hung his head. "Yes, yes I did."

"Besides, I think you're bad enough already, people just don't know that about you."

"Maybe so," he said, pulling me into his arms. "So, if we decide to do this, and I turn out to be a bad boy, will you promise to give me a good paddling?"

I pulled his arms from around me and as we both laughed, I jumped off the counter. Taking his hand in mine, I reached to unlock the bathroom door but then didn't. Instead I put my arms around his neck and tried to touch my lips to his.

"No," he said, placing a hand across my mouth. "Our first kiss is *not* going to be in the ladies room at Burger Queen, no matter how clean it is," he looked around the room, nodding in approval, "and that," he pointed to the hickey on my neck, "is not going to be the first thing I see when we're done."

CHAPTER FIFTEEN

Another Kind of Greek

He didn't want to hear the truth, I was sure of it. Otherwise he wouldn't have asked the question.

"I think your newspaper's coverage of Congressman Tilly's earmark projects," I hesitated to make sure I hadn't used the word "pork," which was what I was thinking, "was very fair and balanced. I think it represented what good journalism is all about. You didn't follow the herd when they were crucifying him; you stood up for what you believed—that the projects were worth the money spent and that they were for the greater good of the community and the taxpayers."

I thought back to when I had first entered the building and how nervous I was about the interview. Now, in the thick of it, I knew I had been right to be a little shaky.

Just before the *News Sentinel*'s receptionist called my name I had stepped into the executive restroom to freshen my face. I looked in the mirror to take one last look at the *Rayes County Gazette* beat reporter and wish the future *News Sentinel* features editor good luck. I had dabbed a little Vaseline on my teeth to make smiling easier and to add a little sparkle before the interview.

Smearing my teeth with petroleum jelly was something I had vowed in my teens to never do again, but knew my smile was lacking in sincerity. When my lips were spread across my face I looked like a mad scientist luring my next victim into lobotomy surgery, not like someone Dick Robinson would want standing in his newsroom with a cup of hot coffee every morning. So when I saw the tiny square jar in the medicine cabinet, I was dabbing my finger in it and smoothing the jelly across my teeth before I could stop myself. I worried for only a millisecond about who had used it before me but then decided that catching a cold or even a brief bout of stomach virus would be a small price to pay for a successful future in the news business.

I thought briefly of Cee and wondered if she had managed to grow old gracefully or just married a rich plastic surgeon instead.

Now, as I sat before the Editor-in-Chief, I questioned not only my smile but also every word springing forth from my mouth. Peavy, my editor at the *Gazette* had encouraged the interview, but prefaced it by telling me what a tight-ass conservative Dick Robinson was. Marla added to my anxiety with a last-minute bit of advice about how keeping our sister status a secret was paramount. The news station Marla worked for and the *News Sentinel* had a long-lived rivalry that had been around since Channel 18's foundation was being poured.

"In your work as a beat reporter, did you ever, or have you ever, had any misunderstandings with law enforcement?" Dick asked, making me question if he knew something from my past.

I smiled as I debated what my response would be: truth or fiction. Opting again for the latter, I answered, "Well no, sir.

Just like any other reporter," I didn't outright lie, but I believed that I could qualify my answers. "There have been occasions when I have been requested to leave, and I have obliged when I was not on public property, no arguments. I operate by the book."

The incident from the Dently trial immediately played in my mind like an old movie clip. Arm in arm two deputies had me removed from the judge's quarters for suggesting the court was playing to the television cameras, like the judge was in the running for an Oscar. I assured myself that the incident was much too local for anyone to have heard about in Knoxville so I answered Mr. Robinson.

"No."

Mr. Robinson tapped a forefinger to his chin. "What about on a personal level? Any problems there?"

Lying came easier now. "No," I shook my head. "Unless stealing that parking spot from a little old lady out back a little while ago counts. Is the lot always that full?" I tried to change the subject by adding my own brand of levity.

"Yes. Parking is an issue downtown," Mr. Robinson said, nodding in agreement. "Always has been." Unfortunately, Mr. Robinson wasn't smiling at my witty response to his previous question.

I nodded solemnly as well. Then I was smiling again and hoping he was ready to move on to a new line of questioning.

"I love gadgets, always have," Mr. Robinson said, relaxing his arms across the table and leaning in a bit.

I tried reading Mr. Robinson's body language, but came up blank.

"We have a new search system; well, not exactly new," Mr. Robinson corrected himself, "but we've had it in place for a couple of years now."

I nodded and tried to act interested in something besides getting the interview over with and getting the hell out of there.

"It's a database search system for our archives." Mr. Robinson pushed a manila folder across the table toward me.

I smiled, reaching for the folder and pulling it the rest of the way across the table. "May I?" I asked for permission to view the contents.

"Holy shit," I blurted out as I saw the article inside. I didn't excuse my language.

"I do a search on all our candidates," Mr. Robinson said. "I usually get back some interesting sports scores, awards or an honor roll list, but never anything like this."

I pulled my eyes from the copy of the more than five-year-old news article and looked at Mr. Robinson.

"I guess I should leave now," I said, getting up from my chair.

"Why?" Mr. Robinson's voice was commanding. "Sit down! That article is one of the reasons I called you in for an interview."

I looked in his face for signs of sarcasm. When I saw none, I accepted his invitation to stay.

I sighed heavily as I looked at the article again. The copy was crooked on the paper, probably made in a hurry just before I got there by that bitch at the receptionist's desk who asked if I'd like some coffee. I twisted the page counter-clockwise to straighten it out and read the headline to myself: *Sisters Shoot at Local Legislator's Son, Investigation Pending*

Flashes from that night instantly came into full focus. Momma and Daddy had insisted I stay on campus with Marla for a full week before deciding to commit to UT. I had just turned eighteen and told anyone who got in my way that I knew how to handle myself. After all I was eighteen, all grown up.

I had instantly fallen in love with dorm life, Marla's life, and even after the first night I knew I wanted to be there.

Momma made me promise I'd go to class with Marla, but my sister didn't like the idea any more than I did, and she knew her professors would never agree to it. After all, like Marla had said to our parents, "It's college, not daycare."

Marla and I told Momma and Daddy that we would follow their plan and I would stick to my sister like glue, but that never happened.

Each day when Marla was in class I spackled my face with too much makeup, put on the shortest skirt from my suitcase and me and Shiny Girl would cruise Greek Circle, looking for hot college guys. If I saw someone interesting enough, I'd park the car and investigate further on foot. Greek Circle was the one place on campus that Marla forbid me to go, so naturally it was the first place I went every day, staying there as long as I could. A sign for an impending party in front of one of the houses had caught my eye early in the week. "Ladies Night," were the words that drew me in.

Trying to talk Marla into going, I had mentioned the party several times only to be met with, "No. Hell no, and goddammit, Dancy, don't ask me again!"

So I decided to go by myself. After all, Momma wanted me to get the full college experience. I justified my plans to party with the Greeks. I began that Friday afternoon by telling Marla I was feeling sick and instead of waiting until Saturday, I would just drive home that night. Like a typical eighteen year old, I had no plan for what I would do after a full night of partying at Greek Circle. Sleeping in my car was the best scenario I had come up with.

Once there, I learned quickly Greek Circle parties were an exquisite scene. I was pissed at Marla for trying to keep this extraordinary Greek secret from me. Beer flowed freely through the halls of the Greek houses. It was followed closely by vodka, rum, and bourbon. By eight o'clock I was hammered, and as usual I was ready for something to eat. The snacks on the kitchen counter were depleted, so I snuck into the fridge to find some leftovers.

"Hey, hot thing," his voice boomed over me. When I looked up at him as my body was squatted half-in and half-out of the refrigerator, I saw his massive arm, ripped with muscles and tanned just like my teen TV crush, the Hawaiian beach lover Tom Selleck.

"This your fridge?" I had asked him and then didn't let him answer, "'cause there's not a damn thing in it." I tried to be funny. He laughed as I rose from my search of the bottom shelf. It was a friendly laugh, not threatening in the least.

"Yes, that *is* my fridge," the muscled college boy had said, taking a look inside. "Sorry she has nothing to offer you," he said, referring to the fridge and then pushing the door shut. "But I, on the other hand," he punched himself in the chest like a caveman, "can offer you the services of a sober driver who can take you out to get pizza."

Playing sick at my stomach all day had forced me to validate the rouse by munching on crackers and 7-Up that my sister had gotten from the campus snack bar. By this time, the thought of real food almost made me drool.

"How come you are still sober?" I asked, looking around inquisitively at the counters full of empty liquor and beer bottles.

"Game tomorrow," the college boy said, tugging at the number on his shirt.

"Oh," I said, now noticing his football jersey for the first time.

"I'll take that as a yes," he had said, not waiting for me to accept the invitation for pizza.

"What's your name?" I asked the mountain standing before me.

"Kyle," he said, pointing to the name printed on his back. "John Kyle. If you're local you'll know me as John Kyle, Jr."

"Not local," I said, letting him know that if he were famous, I had somehow never heard of him.

"Didn't think so," he had said, looking me over like I was a race horse he was about to bet on. "Haven't seen you before."

"My name is Dancy." I had started to tell him my name.

"Doesn't really matter," he had responded quickly. "I asked you to get pizza, not to get engaged."

That sentence was the first of many red flags I had ignored with regard to John Kyle, Jr.

John's promise of pizza was promptly fulfilled. Neither John nor I had called ahead so we placed the order when we got to the pizza place. We then sat in his car making out for the entire twenty minutes the cashier said it would take to make the pizza.

John and I ate it in the car and made out for at least another thirty minutes. In between bouts of thrashing around in John's Camaro, he talked about how much money his family had and how his grandmother had filled many of the houses on Greek Circle with antique furniture from her massive estate.

As we pulled back into Greek Circle, John Kyle, Jr. asked simply, "Wanna do it?"

Shocked by John's blunt proposal I stuttered, "Uh, I d-don't think so."

"Well do you or don't you," the college football standout asked again.

My answer was more definitive on the second attempt,

"No." I laughed, thinking he was kidding when he responded, "Doesn't matter to me, I always get laid anyway."

"Thanks for the pizza," I said, shutting the car door and heading back toward the house, thinking my football player experimentation phase was over.

Once inside the house, I started drinking again, first bourbon and then beer. The Greeks might not have been keen on keeping food but there was no shortage of alcohol.

"Hey you," I heard John Kyle's voice behind me. "I want to show you something upstairs."

I shrugged my shoulders pretending that I didn't hear him and turned away hoping someone would walk up and start talking to me. Only a couple of hours before, I had thought John Kyle, Jr. the muscular-looking Adonis, was the hottest thing going on in Greek Circle, but at some point in the evening he had started to remind me of a large monkey.

"Hey, I got you pizza," John said, tugging at my shoulder. "Just this one last thing, and then I'll leave you alone."

"Okay," I said, following him upstairs. "What are we doing?"

"I've got some really cool posters up here, and I want you to see them," he said walking toward a door at the top of the stairs.

Once inside his room, he grabbed me like a rag doll and threw me on the bed. "Four-poster bed," he said proudly, grabbing onto the footboard frame and shaking it. I tried to get up but he forced me down, holding my throat with one hand and unzipping his pants with another. I could neither scream nor cry, so I lay there gasping for breath, knowing what was about to happen and praying to God that afterwards he would just let me go. I tried to focus on the only light in the room coming from a utility pole near the window. Then suddenly a bright light flooded the room. I wondered if I had died but then heard John Kyle, Jr. call my sister's name.

"Well, well. Marla Wilder," he said, in a mocking voice. "Come back for more?"

Just as my eyes were starting to get used to the light I was deafened by what sounded like an explosion. The death grip around my throat loosened so I jumped to my feet to see my sister standing there pointing her old .38 Special directly at John Kyle, Jr.

I had never tried to remember that night. In fact, I did my best not to ever think of it at all. Until now I had almost convinced myself that it had happened to someone else, not me. But that one piece of paper that Mr. Robinson had put in front of me brought back every detail of my first college experience—something Marla and I never spoke of again. I looked up at Mr. Robinson knowing full well that my job interview was over.

Mr. Robinson was never going to give me my dream office, with the six-foot windows that faced city square. I was destined to spend the rest of my journalism career looking at the dark paneled walls of the *Rayes County Gazette*. I had accepted that my clothes would be forever glazed in the residue from the smoke emanating from Peavy's generic cigarettes.

I decided there and then that I had nothing to lose, so I cleared my thoughts and just told the whole damn truth.

"And you know what my favorite part of that whole fucking night was?" I had strategically managed to work in the "f" word and then paused to gauge Mr. Robinson's reaction to it.

Dick simply shook his head. I gave him time to respond verbally but he said nothing. Dick's face remained placid, so I continued.

"It was when my sister said: 'Now you get off her. I got three bullets left. One for that big wooden ball." She pointed her gun to the last remaining bed post. "And then two more for those little pink fleshy ones between your legs."

I closed the manila folder with the copied article from my history tucked inside and slid it across the table.

"You know, he shit himself that night," I added proudly, holding my head up straight.

Mr. Robinson sat there speechless, much like John Kyle, Jr. when my sister was finished making him think he was about to die.

"Thank you for the interview, Mr. Robinson," I said, getting up from the table.

Mr. Robinson let me get all the way to the door before he spoke.

"Son of a bitch!" Mr. Robinson railed. "I knew this story was gonna be good."

Startled, I turned when he yelled.

"Get your ass back in here, Dancy Wilder. You're hired!"

"What?" I said, still standing at the door.

"You're hired, I said. I hated that little prick, John Kyle, Jr., in high school, still do," Mr. Robinson said, motioning me to come back to the table.

"Good to know," I said, without a clue of how else to respond.

"Your sister, Marla works over at Channel 18 News, right?"

"Yes," I said, surprised this man had done so much research on me.

"You know little John Junior is the new city manager, right?"

"No, I didn't know that." I shook my head.

"Just happened last week," Mr. Robinson said, leaning his chair back, putting his feet on the table and rubbing his chin. "Bet your sister knows."

"She probably does," I said, crinkling my face in confusion.

"Kyle is a real son of a bitch and crooked as they come," Mr. Robinson removed his feet from the table and thrust his face toward me. "I'll pay you $10,000 more a year than the features editor's position and you'll cover the city beat. Dancy Wilder, I want you on my team."

"Of course," I said as my voice nervously changed octaves between the two words. Unheard of for a small-town reporter to break into a metro-daily city beat on the first try, I began making a mental list of everyone who had ever said I'd never make it out there.

"I want you and your sister to make Kyle shit his pants again." Mr. Robinson threw his head back in laughter.

"Isn't Channel 18 News competition?" I questioned, remembering what Marla had said.

"You don't miss a thing, Dancy. Sure is. But for our purposes, until I tell you otherwise, information sharing is welcomed," he rubbed his chin and glared at me. "Share anything else with her and you're fired."

I swallowed hard when I heard the word "fired" and then squeaked out the words, "Sure thing."

I gave Marla's word, as usual, without asking her first. "We'll handle it."

"I'm glad the real Dancy Wilder finally decided to join us for the interview," Mr. Robinson's tone was sarcastic. "And please call me Dick." He extended a hand. I stood and shook it firmly.

"When should I start?"

"As soon as you can get here," Dick said, slapping me on the back so hard I was nearly knocked off my heels.

As I opened the door to leave, he stopped me.

"Wait a minute," he said, pulling the door closed again. "Just for the record, we were pussies on the Tilly coverage. We bent over, and he screwed us every time we went to press. There wasn't an ounce of ink spilled on Tilly that resembled any real journalism, but all that's about to change," he said, slapping me on the back again. This time I had braced myself, and my feet held firmly to the floor.

I smiled and shook his hand again. "I'm glad the real Dick Robinson finally showed up for this interview."

"Hah," he blasted a laugh. "You're gonna fit in just right around here, young lady."

CHAPTER SIXTEEN

Hot Summer Story

"This is Marla Kaye reporting," my sister said into the mic and then gave a nod to the camera. "Now back to you, Sam."

I searched the background as she spoke, looking for any indication of movement from within the house. I had visually devoured my television screen for the past four hours, along with two full bags of chips, jumping from station to station looking for anything I could find on the Tilly kidnapping. Again, I kept going back to Channel 18, like the rest of the region, waiting for Marla to tell me more.

"Dammit, fuck!" I said, throwing a potato chip at the screen as the station cut to commercial.

"That story should have been mine. Fuck!" I said again. Daisy sat next to me on the couch, watching my every move and wagging her tail. She panted heavily in anticipation of my next outburst, hoping for another potato chip.

"You know that story should have been mine," I said to Daisy again. She tilted her head and snapped her ears to full attention when she heard the sound of crumpling cellophane in my lap.

"C'mon, girl." Daisy anxiously followed me into the kitchen and attacked her bowl as I filled it with crumbs from the nearly empty bag.

I leaned over the counter, waiting for Wally Hickson to shut his mouth. I had heard enough from him about his "real good used cars and more, on 127 North." I was sure Wally bought the late-night time slot because it was cheap, usually not more than a half a dozen viewers at best; now most everyone in eastern Tennessee was watching Wally, waiting for Marla to come back on and give an update on Tilly.

I looked at the newspaper lying on the counter. I had two bylines on the front page yesterday, nothing today.

I went back through the events of the last several hours, making mental notes of all the missteps I had made. I hated myself for those mistakes that had landed journalist Dancy Wilder at home rather than at the crime scene where she belonged. I was sure this story would've been the biggest of my career.

The scanner had remained eerily silent all day. At first I had chalked it up to a slow news day and felt lucky to do some loafing. I walked over to Mad Q's Coffee Shoppe mostly just to fill in some free time.

"What's up, Dancy?" I had been glad to see that Tina was working. At least there'd be someone to talk to even if there wasn't much news. I didn't know much about her, but she always reminded me of a sitcom character, one of those sassy waitress types who was stuck in a dead-end job at a downtown greasy spoon.

Mad Q's was flanked by the state police post and the sheriff's department. Just across the street was the *News Sentinel* building. If the courthouse had been nearby, Tina might have at least stood a chance of meeting a rich lawyer. But as it was, Mad Q's was crammed by working stiffs who barely met middle class criteria, cops and reporters. I knew exactly how she felt.

"Not much," I finally answered her. "In fact, pretty slow for the eve of a holiday weekend."

I was looking out the restaurant window, staring across the street at the *News Sentinel* building. The heat vapors from the pavement rose in waves from the concrete. "That rain didn't cool it down much," I mumbled vacantly.

"I know," Tina said, placing a tall Styrofoam cup in front of me. "Almost like it got even hotter."

My mouth watered as I heard the ice rattling in the cup.

"Yeah, probably did," I said, pointing to the digital temperature sign at First National.

"Holy shit!" Tina gasped as she looked out the window. "A hundred and nine. Now, that's insane!"

"I think I'm gonna call it a day," I said, placing a five on the counter for my soda.

"Don't worry about it," Tina said, pushing it back toward me. "I'm just glad you didn't make me turn on that damn coffee pot. You got any plans for the big three-day weekend?"

"No, not really," I said, opening the door. "Might go to my sister's. What about you?"

"Family reunion," Tina said, rolling her eyes. "It's a Waverly tradition every Labor Day weekend."

"See you later, Tina." The bell rang as I left, just as it had when I arrived. The intense heat stole my breath as the door closed behind me. The humidity filled my lungs too quickly and I began to cough, giving me time to take a closer look at my surroundings. There were no cars at the sheriff's department

269

and none at the state police post, no cruisers, no vans, no K-9 car—nothing.

In the five years that I had spent at the *Sentinel*, I had never seen so much of nothing on Copper Street. It was like a ghost town. I half expected to see tumbleweed cross my path.

I turned around and went back into Mad Q's.

I slung the door open and called "Tina," startling her. "Where the hell is everybody?" I asked and then pointed left and then right, referring to the two law enforcement buildings on each side of the restaurant.

"Beats me," she said. "They took outta here like piss ants in a line just a few hours ago. Real quiet, no sirens, just real sneaky like."

"Thanks, Tina," I said, smiling. "I think my day is about to get a little more interesting."

I walked the fifty or so feet over to the sheriff's department. There was no point in even trying to get anything out of the state boys down the street. State cops were always by the book. But the sheriff's department was a different story. I had some shit on them, and they owed me.

"Where the hell is everybody?" I pushed the door open. It slammed against the wall behind it. "Hey," I yelled back to the counter. "Where is everybody?"

I saw the top of Sherry's head. She was hard to miss, platinum blonde, hair teased to heaven is what Mamaw would've said had she ever met her.

"Out on patrols," Sherry said, standing up when she heard me call out.

I could see the fear in Sherry's face as I walked toward the counter.

"All of them?" I questioned Sherry's statement. It seemed to cause her a bit of anxiety. "Really? All of them?"

270

Sherry rolled her eyes. "Oh, God, Dancy what is it?"

Sherry tried to pretend she was annoyed with me but I knew fear when saw it.

"So sorry to bother you; have I come at a bad time?" I asked sarcastically as I looked around the empty building.

"Sherry, if I didn't know better, I'd swear that you're hiding something from me."

"What do you need, Dancy?" Sherry's nerves were getting the best of her. She clicked her two-inch long fingernails together so that they sounded like castanets.

I looked around the building again to make sure we were alone. "You know how I hate to always have to bring this up, Sherry," I said, not even having to finish the sentence before she interrupted me.

Sherry was a partier, a drinker, a heavy drinker. I had only been at the paper for a little less than a year when I was working late one night and heard some chatter on the scanner. The chatter was followed by complete silence, except for one word. The only word I could really make out was "shamrock."

I had just finished my writing for the night, and I thought I'd head over to the Shamrock Bar and Grill to check it out. I pulled in just as Sheriff Bill Bison was putting Sherry in his cruiser. Her car was lodged in the front door of the bar. The only thing visible from Sherry's car was the blinking tail lights. Except for me, Bison, and Sherry, no one else was in the lot, or even on the street.

As I walked over to the cruiser, Bison held out a hand to block my vision.

"Now listen," Bison said, trying to keep me from getting a good look at his passenger. "We don't have to do it this way, Miss Wilder."

Sheriff Bison looked at me angrily as I pulled out my tiny camera and took a picture. The story, however, that ran the next day showed a picture of Sherry's car and underneath the picture were the words: *Dispatcher's car stolen, crashed into historical downtown bar.*

After that, I got whatever I wanted from Bison and his deputies. I knew that wasn't about to change today.

"Okay, Dancy," Sherry placed her hands on her hips in defiance even though she knew she was going to spill her guts to me anyway. "Congressman Tilly has been taken hostage by some crazy group that calls itself MMO."

The news business had conditioned me to at least try and fake concern when I heard something terrible had happened. But I knew my eyes lit up when Sherry said those words. A Congressman being kidnapped was the story of a lifetime.

"When?" was the only word that I could manage.

"Someone who saw the kidnapping called Bill early this morning," Sherry said.

"The unidentified woman told Bill they took him late last night," Sherry leaned over her desk and wrote something on a notepad. "Here," she said, handing me the slip of paper. "Happy now?"

I looked at the tiny slip of paper: *1684 Toggle Road, Seminole: 14 miles north on 127, turn left at Cole's Quick Mart, 24 miles, turn left on Toggle, 17 miles, dead end.*

"Don't you tell 'em I sent you down there," Sherry demanded as I was heading out the door. "I mean it, Dancy," I heard her yell as I went from a fast walk to a run.

Hindsight is always 20/20, Momma always said. If I had it to do over again, I would've never called Dick. The dumbass gave the story to an even bigger dumbass.

"It's not your beat, Dancy," Dick said, droning on about how it wouldn't be fair to hand it over to me when Don Chester has been waiting a year for a big story.

Don worked on the fringes of the county, small communities like Seminole where news was hard to come by. His last big story was a drowning with no pending investigation, just an accidental death.

"That's my point," I had said, trying to change Dick's mind. "He's not experienced enough for something like this. You're going to let him fuck it up."

I had thought the momentary silence on the phone meant Dick was thinking about how much better I would be at covering the Tilly kidnapping, but I was wrong.

"No, Dancy," Dick said firmly. "And don't you go down there. I'm sick and tired of you showing up at stories that aren't on your beat. It confuses people when we're trying to get an interview."

"Dammit, Dick," I started to argue again but he cut me off.

"No, Dancy. No. No. And if I hear you were down there, you're fired."

"Fuck!" I said and then slammed down the phone.

Don the dumbass had a quite a newsroom reputation. *Send him to cover a fire and if a murder takes place in the house next door, he'll bring back a story about a fire.* People went around saying it all the time because it was true. He was like a robot, no mind of his own and in no way equipped to cover the Tilly kidnapping.

I knew what I had to do, and I had to do it fast. If Dick was going to give my story away, I'd give his story away.

"I need to speak to Marla Kaye, please," I heard my own voice. It was like listening to someone else's private conversation, like someone else had control of what I was about to do.

273

It had been eight hours since I had placed that call, giving Marla the exclusive my boss had tried to steal from me. My sister had been on the air for the last four hours, and no matter how many channels I clicked, only Marla had the story. Thinking of all the news vultures across the region, I began to wonder why no one else was coat-tailing on her Tilly scoop. Was everyone in bed, on vacation, or maybe they just no longer cared about Tilly?

As much as I tried to reason out why no other reporters were chiming in on the Tilly kidnapping action, I was getting a weird vibe. As the Channel 18 News cameras pivoted back and forth between Marla's on-location reports and panning the scene I looked for any sign of Don the dumbass stumbling around in the background. He was nowhere that I could see. However, all the missing cruisers I had taken note of earlier in the day, and even the county's K-9 unit, were lining both sides of the road, all the way back to the dark horizon.

The view from my television screen showed people in Marla's background walking back and forth inside the run-down, white frame house. Marla was only 100 or so feet away. The Channel 18 camera shot close-ups of my sister's reporting, panned out into the yard, then zoomed in on the lit windows. Inside the house it looked like a party. I counted over a half a dozen shadows walking around.

"So far the Millennium Militant Organization or the MMO, as they were called during the height of their activity in the early seventies, have made no demands and, in fact, were not the ones to contact police after the kidnapping." Marla's reporting was impeccable as usual. "A concerned citizen thought she recognized the Congressman as he was being shoved into the back seat of a brown, four-door sedan in the parking lot of the

Marlett Hotel. The car, as reported by the citizen, was driven by a large male wearing a military jacket.

"This concerned citizen, who does not wish to be identified, bravely followed the car all the way to this location before becoming frightened. He then drove back into town and contacted the authorities," Marla's voice and on-screen demeanor was authoritative as usual.

"Taking precautionary measures, police have now cleared the entire 17 miles of Toggle Road, blocking traffic entering or leaving." Marla continued speaking, as the Channel 18 camera panned to the long stretch of highway again.

"There are only two other houses on Toggle Road other than this one, where Tilly is being held captive, and they are considered abandoned property. If the MMO's past criminal endeavors are any indication of what their demands will be, they will soon be asking for money and weapons to help fund their militia as they prepare for their 'warfare of the future'."

Again, I searched for any sign of Don in the camera shots and again he was nowhere.

"Way to go, Marla," I said to the television screen. "Good background work."

I was startled out of my trance-like state by the phone.

"Wilder." Dick's voice made me jump. "Yes, Dick," I said, and then forced a fake yawn to make him think I was asleep.

"Don't fuck with me, Wilder! I know you're watching; I can hear it in the background."

I waited a moment and then muted the television.

"What is it, Dick?" I hoped he got the message that I was still pissed. If he was calling to get me out there to cover that story, he was going to have to beg.

"Don called. They've blocked off the road and won't let anyone else in, Dancy." I could hear Dick's spit hitting the phone as he spoke, placing special emphasis on his p's.

"We're locked out Wilder. Godammit!" he yelled. I heard what sounded like ceramic hitting wood. I pictured him banging his coffee mug on his desk, brown liquid spattering the walls. I wasn't about to speak unless he asked me to.

"If I find out you told your sister about this you're fucking fired, Dancy Wilder! You're fucking fired!" Dick repeated. He slammed the receiver twice before actually hitting the disconnect button.

A lump in my throat began to grow. I swallowed hard to suppress it. I looked at Daisy, who was now sound asleep on the couch. I thought of Daisy and I having to eat out of old potato chip bags from the big green Dumpsters behind the Kroger's near our apartment because I had lost my job and could no longer afford food.

My nerves had barely recovered from Dick's shouting match when the phone rang again.

"Hello," I said slowly, muting the television again.

"Can you get the story from your sister?" Dick's tone was calmer now. "Well, can you?" he asked, not giving me time to respond.

"Sure," I said, nervously. "I'll get right on that."

"Well, you're still fucking fired, Wilder," he said and then paused. "Get that story in as soon as you can."

Relieved that I might not be fired, I grabbed a notebook and a pen and sat down on the couch. I unmuted the television and waited for Wally, the used car salesman, to finish yet another commercial.

"Maybe after this Wally should run for Congress," I said to Daisy. She opened her eyes, raised her head, and then laid it back down.

The phone was now plastered into my palm for fear Dick might call again. Even though I was expecting it, I was startled when it rang.

"I got it, Dick," I said before he had a chance to speak.

"Dancy, it's me." Through static and muttering in the background I heard Marla's voice.

"Hey, shithead," I said, laughing. "Who's got the best damn sister in the world? Huh? Huh?"

"I do, you crazy nut," Marla sounded embarrassed like someone was listening to us.

"You know I almost got fired over this crazy shit. Hell, I might still be fired. Marla, you gotta get me something outta there. Hold back something for me to give Dick. I need something to get me outta hot water or I'm fired!"

"I'll do better than that," my sister paused. I waited.

"The police have the names of the kidnappers, but they won't let us release them."

"Yeah, that'd be great if you could let me have the exclusive on that." My mind was firing out random thoughts on how to save my job and keep Daisy's dog bowl full.

"No, Dancy. They want *you* here. The kidnappers want *you* here," Marla's voice took on a solemn and serious tone, otherwise I would've thought she was joking.

"What do you mean?" I had managed to stop my mind from racing. I was all business now, focused and coherent.

"They sent a note out a few minutes ago," Marla continued. "Here, let me just read it to you. It'll be quicker:" *Send in Marla Kaye from Channel 18 and Dancy Wilder from the News Sentinel, then we'll negotiate.*

I started to speak, but found that I couldn't. The gasp that had escaped my mouth caught my sister's ear.

"I know, it's weird," Marla said and then paused for my reaction.

"Yeah, weird as hell," I responded. "Why us?"

"I looked at the list of names and there was one that caught my eye immediately, Dancy. You're not gonna believe it."

"Who?"

"Terry Hardwick."

The sound of my sister's voice saying that name took my breath away. I caught a bit of fresh air and managed to force out a few words.

"You gotta be fuckin' kiddin' me!"

CHAPTER SEVENTEEN

Ghosts From the Past

Marla fluffed her hair just before a small light on the side of the Channel 18 camera glowed red. The humidity in the air had all but glued her once-bouncy faux curls onto her scalp.

It was after midnight, nearing 1 a.m. and the long hours were evident in my sister's voice. I walked behind the Channel 18 News van and then perched myself atop some equipment cases in front of the grill so I wouldn't distract her.

"Inside the house are members of the MMO, who police have now identified individually. Those names have not been released to us at this time." My sister's fatigue was evident. She had to clear her throat several times during the delivery of just one sentence.

A rusty chain-linked fence was partially torn down at the side of the property and barely visible through the kudzu that had mostly devoured it. The tall grass in the yard was taken over by weeds and rogue vines.

I was sure this little house had once held fond memories for someone, a family, children who used to play in the yard, possibly a grandma and grandpa. I imagined that when the last family member had died the empty house stood for as long as it could.

Then just as the kudzu and weeds had started to claim the little white house, Tilly and the MMO came along, giving the little white frame structure a final fifteen minutes of fame.

Just before I had left the house, national networks were beginning to break the Tilly kidnapping story. I was sure Channel 18 News was making a small fortune selling the live-feed to news organizations desperate to get the story, with Marla at the pinnacle of it all.

Other stations, including radio, as I had heard on my trip down Toggle Road, had begun to interview a string of Congressmen. It was evident that each politician was treading carefully on comments, offering only good thoughts and prayers for Tilly's safe return.

No one was willing to jump behind Tilly's political machine and drive it in his absence until they at least found out the motive behind his kidnapping. I was sure they were thinking what I was thinking: *maybe the son of a bitch deserved it.*

After a near-perfect campaign and landslide victory, Tilly had managed to turn his back on every voter that pulled the lever in his favor. Tilly's campaign strategists had relied heavily on testimonials from the working poor, the sick who had no insurance, and the jobless.

After only six months in office Congressman Tilly managed to lay hands on more pork than the butchers at the Piggly Wiggly. He said that in order to improve health and living conditions for future generations in the region, he would build a fitness facility open to the public, complete with an Olympic-sized ice skating rink.

Health and fitness would be encouraged while Tilly was in office. His administration spent 9.4 million taxpayer dollars on the facility that carried his name on the massive sign that hung above the entryway in full view of interstate traffic.

The day of the ribbon cutting, flyers were handed out listing membership prices to use the facility.

The cost for an annual family membership to Tilly's state of the art facility was $500. No one expected that any of the poor, fat, jobless people Tilly had used in his election ads would ever be able to afford membership.

Tilly's second order of business was to pull funds from twenty-two after-school programs that had been set in public libraries across the region. Instead, Tilly claimed the funds from educational programming and reassigned them to a new television show in which his wife, Angel Tilly, read stories to children from a comfy couch their gated Southern Colonial mansion.

One of Tilly's most successful campaign ads had been the testimonial of a single mother who relied on after-school programs where her children could go while she worked a full eight-hour day. Now the programs that the single mother had relied on were gone, thanks to Congressman Tilly.

The list of Tilly's infractions on his promises was endless. I, like others, was standing there watching shadowy figures pace in front of the windows in the little white house, wondering what the hell Tilly had done now.

Marla's whole body drooped the moment the camera shut down.

"How you holdin' up?" I asked as she walked around to the front of the van. I was already standing at attention, ready to bust into that house and get my exclusive.

"I'm fucking tired," she said, punching my arm with the small bit of energy she had left. "But it's worth it. Thanks for the tip, Dancy."

"Dick the dick has fired me twice already and rehired me once," I said, smirking. "I know the math doesn't add up but at least I still have a job, for now."

"God, Dancy," Marla said, shaking her head. "I can't believe you did that. I'm glad you did, don't get me wrong, but I can't believe you did it."

"Oh well." I gave a shrug. "Dick took my story away from me, so I took his. It wasn't Dick's to take in the first place. *I* found it."

Marla leaned in close to me and whispered, "Keep quiet about Terry."

It was something I knew already, not to let anyone in on the fact that our dad's old girlfriend had requested our presence during her attempt at felonious activity, but even after all these years Marla still felt it was her duty as a big sister to watch out for me.

Marla and I turned at the same time when we saw fluorescent stripes coming toward us.

"Ladies?" Sweat was rolling in beads down Sheriff Bison's face. His hair so wet it looked like he had just stepped out of the shower. "Can't imagine why they want the two of you in there. Is there something I should know about?"

Marla and I both shook our heads. "No idea, sheriff," Marla was the first to speak.

I shrugged my shoulders when he turned to me for an answer. "No idea," I managed, as usual, mimicking my sister's words.

"Guess we'll find out," Bison said as he placed a hand on my back, guiding me forward.

Marla walked in front of us, stopping in front of the Channel 18 News van to get a short refresher on how the equipment worked. I stood close to my sister as Jerry, her faithful cameraman, draped the strap around her neck.

"Damn the both of you," Jerry said as he smacked me on the back. "Wish I could go. You take care of our talent in there; we need her in one piece." Jerry said to me and then hugged Marla. He then shocked both my sister and I when he kissed Marla on the forehead.

"Be careful," Jerry said and Marla nodded. "Roll when you're ready. Don't push them too hard, they might be dangerous."

Bison lifted the yellow tape enough so we could walk under it. "We'll be watching from there," the sheriff said, pointing to the news van."

I found it hard to believe that Jerry had agreed to let a uniformed officer inside his news van, but the kidnappers' unusual request to send a Channel 18 reporter inside the house seemed to have somehow strengthened the strained relationship between media and law enforcement.

The role reversal of the media, now on the front line, and uniforms stuck behind their own police barrier seemed to soften the officers.

I could see the genuine concern in Bison's face as Marla was gearing up. My supplies were less cumbersome, a small tape recorder and my Nikon. I had twenty-four shots, and I knew I had better use them sparingly.

CHAPTER EIGHTEEN

The Naked Truth

"Holy shit," I whispered to Marla as we walked toward the house. Our long strides turned to baby steps as we neared the side entrance. My sister and I locked arms for the final few feet.

When Marla and I reached the door of the little white house, I lifted my hand and balled my fist. Marla quickly pulled it back down to my side.

"Seriously, you're going to knock?" she mocked me and rolled her eyes. "They know we're here, Dancy."

I shrugged and smiled. "You're always telling me to be more polite," I quipped.

"Dancy, Marla, is that you?" The door cracked open no more than an inch and a voice whispered out to us.

"Yes," we both said in unison. Marla and I looked at each other to see if either recognized the whisper. The confused look on Marla's face told me she didn't. Neither did I.

The door's hinges creaked as a bony hand became visible, clutching the edge of the door.

"Give me your hand," the voice whispered again. I looked at Marla as I reluctantly touched my fingers to the bony sticks trying to pass for fingers. Quickly the hand grabbed mine, and the door's opening became large enough to pull me in.

I was immediately shoved into a wall face first.

"Spread 'em," a man's voice yelled at me. "Spread 'em," I heard another man's voice yell from the other side of the room.

"Okay, okay," I heard a bit of sarcasm in my sister's tone.

"They're fine. I told you I know them." I found comfort in Terry's silky voice that had well over a decade ago nauseated me. Terry's voice was an older version of the one I had remembered but still recognizable. I knew it was her.

"These girls are peacemakers," Terry's sing-songy voice made me smile. "They don't believe in killing machines."

"You said it's been a while," a man's voice responded to Terry. "People change."

"Not my girls," I heard Terry say as the man continued to pat me down. "No guns, right, girls?"

"Right," I said and then heard Marla say the same.

I thought of the arsenal of weaponry in the top of every closet at my father's house, the .38 Special under my driver's side seat and the pistol I was sure Marla still packed in her purse.

Finally, I felt the force holding my face to the wall loosen and then disappear altogether. Still a bit shaky, I staggered as I tried to regain my balance.

Terry came to my aid.

"Oh, Dancy," Terry said, hugging me before I had a chance to speak.

It was Terry all right, although her hair was longer now and the yellow and red hues had turned completely gray. She still wore the same rose-tinted, wire-rimmed glasses and still smelled of incense.

As Terry released her grip on my torso, Marla came up beside me, and Terry grabbed her as well for a long embrace.

"You girls have turned out so beautiful. I watch you on TV all the time, Marla." Terry backed away to get a better view. "And you, Dancy, I read all of your articles."

My eyes darted around the room. I was surprised to see we were standing inside a fully functional kitchen, complete with what-nots and painted plates hanging on the walls.

Five men stood around Terry, inspecting us as she spoke. Two more men stood watch at the window. It was like watching the sequel to *Snow White and the Seven Dwarfs*, the Golden Years.

In my mind it sounded crazy, but it was fast becoming apparent that Terry was the ringleader of this operation.

"Sit down," Terry said, motioning for me and Marla to take a chair. The men stood around us as Terry took a seat at the kitchen table.

"You girls are wondering why you're here?" Terry said, patting the table.

Marla and I nodded.

"You're my little messengers," Terry said, smiling. "We're going to share with the world the peace that so many are reluctant to accept."

Marla started to speak but Terry put an index finger to her lips and shushed her.

"Listen to me, Marla," Terry said as she snapped her fingers, looking at one of the men standing near her.

My sister remained silent.

The man quickly retrieved a pack of cigarettes from the oversized military jacket he was wearing and pulled one out.

The sound of metal scraping on flint was familiar to me as he opened the lighter and lit the cigarette that he handed to Terry.

Marla and I watched a look of ecstasy come across Terry's face when she inhaled that first drag and then slowly blew smoke out of her mouth.

"Smoke?" She gestured an arm to the cigarette man and then to us, asking if we wanted a menthol.

"No, thank you," I said.

Marla simply shook her head.

"Congressman Tilly is trying to take our land away," Terry said and then took another drag off her cigarette, inhaling deeply again.

"All we want is to live in peace and love, in harmony," she continued, now getting teary-eyed.

"After your father and I parted ways, I met my soul mate, Jake." Terry closed her eyes and smiled as she said his name.

Terry held her hand out and immediately one of the men grabbed it as she gave his hand a firm squeeze. Tears were now popping through the edges of her eyelids. "Jake was the love of my life," she continued.

I saw Marla's eyes quickly looking around the house, and my eyes were darting as well. Like me, my sister was looking for any sign of where Terry and her band of merry men had Tilly stowed away.

"Jake showed me a way of life that makes everything beautiful," Terry said, looking into her empty hands like something precious only she could see was sitting there.

"The mind is beautiful," Terry continued, lightly touching her forehead. "The body is beautiful," she said, smoothing her hands across her still-flat-as-a-pancake chest. "The world is beautiful."

Marla and I watched as Terry became lost in her thoughts.

"Jake's Nest!" the thought came to me quickly and I yelled without meaning to. Everyone at the table, including Marla, jumped at my sudden outburst.

"Ah, you know about this place." Terry nodded. She seemed pleased.

"Not much. Just what I've heard."

"And you, Marla?" Terry asked.

"Just what I've heard, too."

"Tilly wants it," Terry's eyes filled with tears, but her voice didn't quiver. She held her hands out like she was presenting Jake's Nest to us.

"You mean— Jake's Nest is here?" I looked behind me and out the windows.

"Almost," Terry said. "We're very near."

I had heard for years about Jake's Nest but never really knew where it was located. The nudist colony was one of those things that people joked about and made references to, but no one I knew had ever been to Jake's Nest or knew much about the place.

"So what does Tilly want with Jake's Nest?" I asked, wondering what a Bible thumping Congressman like Tilly would want with a nudist colony.

"Does it have something to do with the crops you're growing here?" my sister asked, letting Terry know she knew a little more than she was letting on.

"Yes," Terry answered. "The problems began with our first crop. They came out here, cut it down, and we haven't grown any since. Tilly said if we promised not to grow any more marijuana he'd keep the Feds from taking the land."

It was completely out of character for Tilly to let anything go that would garner headlines. And the Congressman couldn't have bought better coverage in an upcoming election. Not only would Tilly have gotten credit for taking down the elusive naked sinners we had all heard so much about, but he would have also gotten a pat on the back from the current D.C. administration.

"Why would Tilly-," I started to ask when one of the men standing nearby interrupted.

"Tilly came back a few weeks later and told us that we'd better sell him the land or he'd hand us over to the Feds, and then Uncle Sam would own it."

The man blew cigarette smoke as he spoke. His yellow teeth were barely visible under a moustache that had begun to grow so long that it curved around his upper lip and into his mouth. His tone was harsh, and he emanated anger.

I found myself unnerved by his presence.

"Tilly said he'd give us a hundred thousand for all of it," the man continued his rant. "Market value's over a million."

Terry held her arm up to calm her angry henchman.

He shoved his hands in his pockets and looked at the floor like a five-year old boy who'd just been scolded by his kindergarten teacher.

"We wanted to bring Tilly out here to experience the peace for himself," Terry said. "Then maybe he would understand our mission, a mission of peace and harmony."

I saw my sister fidgeting. I knew Marla had been quiet for far too long.

"So you say you want to extend peace to the rest of the world but you take a man by force, tie him up, and hold him hostage with guns?"

Marla was questioning Terry's sense of integrity. I could tell that my sister was quickly slipping into reporter mode, and that she was about to begin a no-holds-barred interview.

"We don't have guns," Terry said, looking around the room at the men who had spread out a bit.

"Anybody in here got a gun?" Terry asked with a sarcastic tone.

None of the men spoke, but they all shook their heads. Some of them opened their jackets as proof.

"And Tilly certainly isn't tied up," Terry said.

Marla and I looked at one another in disbelief.

"So is anyone in here part of a group known as the MMO?" my sister questioned.

All of them shook their heads in confusion. "Who is the MMO?" Terry asked.

"Never mind," my sister said, rolling her eyes. "This is freakin' unbelievable. Bison is such a dumbass."

"So where's Tilly?" I asked, feeling a little more relaxed knowing the place wasn't chock-full of automatic weapons.

"In there," Terry said tilting her head toward a dark hallway. "You want to see him?"

"Should we start rolling?" Marla lifted the camera. Terry snapped her fingers and pointed at it.

Her right-hand henchman promptly removed it from Marla's hands.

"Hey, wait a minute!" Marla protested. "You wanted us in here to tell your story."

"Let's get some clothes on him first," Terry said in a motherly tone, tilting her head toward where Tilly was being held. "His constituents might not take him seriously if he isn't dressed the part."

Marla and I looked at each other. Both of us rose from our seats in shocked silence.

My sister and I followed close on Terry's heels as we walked down the dark hallway. The music I had been hearing like a faint echo in the distance since the minute Marla and I had been forcibly pulled inside the door was louder as we walked farther down the dark hall.

Terry pulled a skeleton key from her pocket and unlocked a door. I wasn't sure if it was the deafening, rhythmic beat of the music, or the pungent odor of pot smoke that almost knocked me backward. Both were overwhelming.

Naked and bathed in red light, Ben Tilly stood swaying in the middle of the room, completely unaware that we had entered. Terry walked over to a small stereo sitting on a table in the corner and turned off the music.

Tilly was moving a few seconds behind real time and continued to sway like the beat was still popping in his ears. Then, like a balloon with the helium sucked out of it, Tilly slid down the wall onto the floor where he sat, legs crossed, eyes closed, rolling his head around his shoulders.

I had always prided myself on being professional in any situation, naked bodies included, but I knew I'd never be able to look at Tilly the same way again. This image would forever be the only one in my mind, whether Tilly was at the podium giving a speech or throwing out the traditional first home-game pitch for UT baseball.

"The music brings down blood pressure and makes you relax," Terry busied herself gathering Tilly's clothes that someone had draped over a nearby chair. The old Beatnik then laid Tilly's garments out on the bed like a good housewife helping her husband get ready for work. "And the smoke is for, well, Dancy you know what that's for," Terry said, referring to my first experience toking weed with her. "It's the best. Grew it myself. It's pure but potent."

"And the red light?" Marla asked.

"I just like it," Terry said nonchalantly, shaking out the Congressman's pants. "Makes me feel passionate."

Marla rolled her eyes. I could see that she was seriously trying not to laugh.

As smoke billowed out of the room, Terry opened a window just near the bed. Soon the air was clear, and Tilly began to show signs of waking from his stupor.

"Any of this been caught on either of those?" Tilly asked, as he nervously pointed first to Marla's camera and then to mine.

Neither of us answered him.

"Not sure if you remember me or not. Dancy Wilder, *News Sentinel*," I said sticking my hand out for him to shake. He quickly and rudely pushed it away.

"Please, Miss, I think we are past the point of polite pleasantries," Tilly sighed and looked around the room. "And I know who you both are," Tilly said as he pointed a limp hand to me and then Marla.

"Me and these girls go way back, too," Terry said, sitting down next to us like we were all about to have a slumber party.

My sister quickly shot me an "oh shit" look.

This was a game changer for all of us. Now that Tilly knew Marla and I had a connection to Terry, he'd stop at nothing to ruin us both. A long moment of silence concealed our thoughts.

Tilly was eyeballing me and Marla. I knew he was sizing up the situation and our possible involvement in it.

"Anything on those?" Tilly asked again, pointing to Marla's camera and then mine.

"Maybe or maybe not," Marla said, pulling her camera closer to her body. "Guess we'll have to see."

Picking up on Marla's cue, I began making a mental list of what we had on Tilly so far.

"And you two know this woman?" Tilly asked, pointing to Terry.

Terry smiled and winked at me.

"I helped raise these girls," Terry proudly announced. "They turned out pretty good, if you ask me."

"Yes, yes, they did," Tilly was beginning to get some strength back in his voice. I could picture him now at a press conference, playing up the liberal media's involvement in his kidnapping.

"You ladies are in a lot of trouble," Tilly sounded like he was about to give us a lecture. Even if Marla and I had nothing to do with Terry's bizarre plan, our connection to her would raise enough questions to destroy both of our careers. We could even end up in jail.

"We know about the land deal," I said, pulling out the only bargaining chip Marla and I had. "And these people are unarmed. Really. There's not a weapon on any of them," I continued blurting out whatever came to mind.

"By the way, Congressman," I emphasized his political position, "What were you doing at the Marlett Hotel without your secret service detail? Wasn't that the place you, yourself, referred to as a hot bed for high class prostitutes?"

"And, of course, there's this," Marla said, lifting her camera a bit. "Oh, and that," my sister said, pointing to my camera.

Marla and I both knew we hadn't shot a damn thing since we'd been invited into the house, but the look on Tilly's face showed he was convinced we had pictures of him in a state that no politician would want their constituents to see. The Congressman knew two things for sure; he had been naked and was high. Tilly's eyes darted back and forth between Marla's camera and mine.

Victim or not, Tilly began to realize that we had enough on him to destroy his political career. The Congressman was also smart enough to know that Marla and I had landed in a tangled mess that wasn't much better than the one he was in.

I wasn't sure if we were all either going to walk out of there as heroes or if we'd all be hanging our heads. The only thing I *was* sure about was the next move had to be Tilly's, and he'd better get it right or we were all screwed!

"Son of a bitch!" he said, a bit of spit popping out of his mouth. "Go tell them to call my security detail."

I let out the breath I had been holding, looked at Marla, and gave a slight smile.

"Terry, we won't be getting your story out there," Marla said to Terry, "but I think you've accomplished what you set out to do."

Terry nodded and then got up and left the room, leaving the door open behind her.

I did what the Congressman asked of me. I walked out to where Bison and his deputies were stationed and gave them the one demand made by the "MMO," to give Tilly's security detail access and for the rest of law enforcement to disappear.

Within an hour, local authorities had been replaced by the Congressman's Secret Service detail, and he had given his word that both Marla and I would get exclusive interviews about what "really" happened.

In return, Terry and her band of merry men were free to walk out of there and go back to their naked village unharmed. With an addendum, of course, that marijuana would not be cultivated on the property at Jake's Nest and that Tilly would cease to be interested in the massive acreage.

As the sun began to rise over the little white house, Tilly, who was surrounded by his entire Secret Service detail, watched as my sister delivered the news that he was safe; the story that would launch both our careers onto the national scene.

"Eight members of the MMO have been arrested and taken into federal custody," Marla spoke lies into a camera she'd always been honest with. The heavy equipment made my arms shaky but somehow I managed to keep her in focus.

"Congressman Ben Tilly, representative of the Ninth Congressional District, is safe thanks to the daring efforts of his Congressional Security detail. The motive behind what is now being referred to by federal investigators as the MMO Congressional Kidnapping, or MOCK for short, is still unclear.

High-level agents are busy questioning MMO members.

Channel 18 News, the only news station with exclusive access to this story, along with *News Sentinel* reporter Dancy Wilder, has been told that the identities of the MMO members will not be released due to issues of national security," Marla said, spinning the story so that no one who wasn't already there would attempt to learn anything other than what she was reporting.

Tilly limped toward the camera with two members of his security team holding onto him.

"Congressman Tilly, can you tell the American people about your ordeal?" Marla asked.

My sister's professional posture left her now more than a million viewers with no doubt that she had been anything less than genuine about Tilly's kidnapping.

The perpetual little sister in me wanted to shout at Marla, "Liar, liar, pants on fire."

I didn't say anything, of course, but my mischievous grin that had been lost sometime during the late seventies had found its way home.

CHAPTER NINETEEN

Healthy Outlook

"Dancy, your father is in the hospital."

Momma's voice sounded foreign to me. Not just what she said, but her accent when she said it. I hadn't spoken with anyone from back home in at least a month or even longer, except for Marla, and my sister had lost her accent even more than I had.

"In the hospital?" I repeated Momma's words, questioning their accuracy. My father had never been in a doctor's office so hearing that Everett Wilder was lying in a hospital bed was unimaginable.

"He went in for some tests and they found," I heard my mother swallow hard. She then cleared her throat, "a mass."

We both knew "a mass" was a euphemism for something more serious, but we didn't want to speak it into existence. We didn't want to be the ones to make it real.

"Where?" I asked, not really wanting to know.

"Stomach."

"Oh," I said, visualizing the tumor detaching itself from my father's stomach and disappearing. "What will -?"

"We need to call Marla," Momma interrupted. "Can you go to her office and the two of you call me from there? I tried to reach her a few minutes ago, and they said she was out."

"Yes, I'll go right now," I said, gathering my things the moment Momma asked.

"Try not to worry." Momma's words did little to comfort me. "I just want to talk to both of you at the same time."

The words "mass" connected with "don't worry" only made me worry more, but I knew my mother wasn't going to say any more when she changed the subject.

"What are you writing today?" Momma asked, trying to sound perky.

"Not writing, revising."

"Same thing?" Momma asked, and then laughed. "Chapter seven still giving you a fit?"

"No, that was last month. Now it's chapter eleven."

"Well, keep at it," Momma's voice was more pleasant as she talked about work. "It'll come together. Always does."

"Always does," I smiled as I repeated her words.

"Now, go on and get your sister," Momma spoke to me like I was a five year old. "It'll be all right."

"Love you, Momma."

"You too, Dancy."

I knew it would take anywhere from twenty to forty minutes to get from my house to Marla's office. The trek from Chantilly to D.C. was always unpredictable, depending on the time of day.

As I gathered up my purse and locked the back door, I found myself wishing Momma had gotten in touch with Marla first. Marla was so much better at dealing with unknowns. For my sister, every problem had a solution.

I, on the other hand, would make funeral arrangements in my head whenever someone complained about an unusual headache or a flu that lasted longer than a couple of days. I even once showed up in the emergency room because I had a weird-looking rash on my arm. The doctor smiled, trying not to actually laugh, when I said, "I think I have Lupus."

I'm sure my mother was worried that by the time I got to Marla I'd have Daddy paralyzed from the neck down, with only a week to live. That's probably why she tried to call my sister first. Again, I found myself wishing Marla had answered the phone.

"Hey, Dancy," Helen spoke to me even before I could get through the door. Her desk sat a good twenty-five feet from the revolving door, so her voice echoed my name off the wall-to-wall marble tile.

I threw my hand up to wave as Helen held up my last novel *Now and Again*. She then gave a thumbs up.

"Thanks, Helen," I said, smiling as I reached her desk. "Glad you like it."

"Here to see Marla?"

"Who else would I be here to see?"

"I'll ring her." Helen picked up the phone. "Marla's sister is here to see her."

I watched Helen's expressions, looking for any sign that Marla might not be there. Getting in to see my sister lately felt like trying to bust into the White House unannounced. Everyone had to be vetted, even those familiar to the receptionist, then buzzed in before reaching the elevators.

The National News Network always had threats from political extremists and, of course, the occasional stalker would become obsessed with the newest blonde to sit behind a news desk. But it wasn't until one of their reporters blew his brains out in the middle of the newsroom that they decided to lock the place up like Fort Knox. Marla had made me promise not to work the suicide into one of my novels, but I did it anyway.

It made no sense at all to ban guns because someone inside the network, an employee nonetheless, killed himself, but Marla said it was one of those executive decisions that made the corporate suits around the conference table feel better.

Now everyone coming and going at NNN was scanned for weapons via electronic wand by Tom, the bald, soft-spoken security guard. Marla's gun was already inside the building before the new security measures took hold. She kept it tucked safely inside the top drawer of her desk. Marla had another gun in her car and a shotgun in her apartment. For Marla, keeping a gun in her desk was no different than a golf enthusiast bringing his clubs to the office.

"Well, tell her Dancy's here," Helen continued the conversation with Marla's receptionist, Joni. "I'm sending her up."

"Thanks." As I walked away Helen waved at me and winked.

"Tom," I said to the man with the electronic wand and held my arms up so he could scan me.

"Dancy," he responded, waving the wand that looked like a light-saber over my torso and around my legs. "Have good day." He nodded toward the elevators, giving me permission to go.

"Christ," I said to no one in particular as I boarded the elevator and pushed the number 14. "I'm not a terrorist." None of the half a dozen people in the elevator had heard a word I had said until I said the word "terrorist." Then all eyes were on me.

Reporters. I knew them well. Their filters were always set to throw out every word except for those that, if followed up on, might lead to the next promotion or even a Pulitzer. Using the word "terrorist" in an elevator full of reporters was like whispering the word water in the middle of the Sahara.

"I'm just here to see my sister, Marla," I said, hoping they'd turn their attention back to ignoring me. Thankfully, it worked.

When I finally reached Joni's desk I had to roll my eyes. "Oh, thank God," I said. "Is this where I get strip searched?" I laughed.

"Yeah, I know," Joni said, laughing too. "I'm scared to death they might put me in charge of strip searches. I always get the jobs no one else wants."

I passed by the more than forty desks symmetrically placed in the cordoned-off newsroom. From the outer corridor it looked like a beehive, and the closer I got to the action the more the newsroom sounded like one.

"Jesus Christ, Marla," I said opening the office door, leaving the noise behind me. "How in the hell did you get all the way up here?"

"You ask me that every time you come," my sister said as she swirled her chair around to face me.

"That's because I still can't believe it," I said, picking up the brass-plated nameplate I had gotten her as a gift. "Marla Kaye, Senior Vice President," I read the inscription with some sarcasm as I ran my finger across the letters.

"Same as you, Dancy," she said, taking it from me and placing it back on the desk. "I have the Tilly career plan to thank."

"Yeah," I said, smiling. "Where is that piece of shit these days?"

"Congress," my sister said and then laughed. "Same place all the rest of the shit in this country goes to grow old and moldy."

Marla seemed more relaxed than usual. She had just returned from vacation. Since my sister's return from rest and relaxation, she had vowed take more time off. I hated to bring bad news but I knew she'd be pissed that I hadn't told her the minute I had walked in the door.

"I heard from Momma today," I said, not able to bear the burden alone any longer. "Daddy's sick. He's in the hospital."

Marla looked just as confused as I was when Momma told me. I could tell my sister was thinking exactly what I had thought when I first heard; that it just wasn't possible. Nothing could ever be wrong with Daddy. Only an hour earlier I, too, had thought of him as indestructible.

"What's wrong with him?"

"He has," I started speaking as my mind was saying cancer, but thankfully my mouth didn't say the words. "A tumor in his stomach. Momma wants us both to call her, together."

"How did-?" Marla was about to ask the same questions Momma had given me no answers for, so I held up my hand and interrupted her.

"That's all I know until we call her back," I said, handing my sister the paper where I had written the hospital's number.

"Wow," Marla said, looking down at the top of her desk. Scribbles and notes were etched over nearly the entire surface of the large calendar staring back at her. She gave a huge sigh. "You ready?"

I walked over and locked the office door while Marla picked up the phone, dialed the number, and then put the phone on speaker. Thousands of thoughts ran through my mind, and we stared at one another listening to the ringing phone now echoing in the room.

"Marla?" In just that one word, the sound of my sister's name coming from the other end of a telephone line, I heard a strength in my mother's voice that I didn't recognize.

"Yes. It's me and Dancy," Marla said.

"How is he?" I asked, letting Momma know I was there.

"Fine, of course," Momma laughed. "He already asked one of the nurses on duty if she was available for dinner."

Marla and I rolled our eyes at one another and smiled.

"He's on medication, but I'm not sure your father wouldn't have asked her on a date anyway, even if he wasn't high as a kite."

Momma laughed again. "I don't want you girls to worry, now. I'm taking care of him and I'm going to keep taking care of him when he gets out of here."

"What are they going to do? What is the treatment?" My sister began to ask questions I wasn't sure I wanted answered.

"They are doing surgery to take part of his stomach out and then chemotherapy after that." Again, my mother's voice sounded confident and unshaken. "It's all standard procedure. He'll be fine."

"We're coming down there," Marla said, nodding to me to get confirmation that I could go.

I nodded back.

"No need, girls," Momma said. "You've got your lives and your work," she paused. "I'll take care of this."

I wondered at what point since Marla and I had left home that Momma and Daddy had become a team instead of rivals. I had ignored the gradual shift taking place during mine and Marla's absence. The arguing could now be described as bickering, and our parents had somehow managed to keep the same set of ceramic dishes in the cabinets for at least half a decade. Momma and Daddy had either grown tired of fighting or losing their consistent audience of two had curbed their passion for violence.

"We'll be there tomorrow, Momma," I said, promising Marla's presence as well as my own. "Can we talk to him?"

"Sure, he's right here," Momma said. "High as a kite, but right here."

"What'd they give you, Daddy?" Marla yelled at the phone like she was talking to an eighty-year-old man.

"Xanax," he responded. "But just for nerves."

"You be careful with that, Daddy," I said, thinking of our family's history with prescription drugs.

"I know, I know," he said and then sighed. "Don't worry, you two. I'm fine. This is life. We're born. We live and then we, well, we get sick and then get better," he laughed. "Happens all the time."

"You get some rest, Daddy," Marla said, smiling at our father's attempt at parenting while intoxicated. "We'll be there tomorrow."

As my sister hung up the phone, she pulled the scribbled-on sheet from her large desk calendar, folded it up, and took it outside to Joni. I watched Marla from the window in her office as she spoke to the receptionist.

"Well, I guess we'd better get going," Marla said as she came back through the door.

CHAPTER TWENTY
No Apologies

Found these in the barn fridge," I handed Marla a cold can.

"PBR? Really?" Marla was still such a smartass.

"Yep, that's all that was in there, but there were two cases." I laughed as I plopped down next to my sister, both my knees making popping sounds in quick succession.

"You're falling apart, Dancy."

"I know. These old bones crack a little more every year." I mimicked an old lady's voice, making Marla smile.

"At least it's cold," I said, taking a sip from my can of PBR. As always the first drink gagged me, but after a few more gulps my taste buds conceded and accepted the old man's brew as quite tasty.

Old markings from the wooden bench that Daddy had built into the side of the barn stared up at me and Marla. The faded plank reminded me of how long ago it had been since the first nail had been driven into the soft oak. The initials DLW and MKW sat there between us like we'd invited those two little brats to join us. Even if we hadn't invited them, as usual those little bitches were always happy to crash a party.

Our feet looked foreign, propped up on that old log that Daddy had left there after the tornado of '82. Our father had said it looked like it belonged there in front of our little bench and he didn't know why he never thought of putting one there before. I was sure Marla's thoughts were mimicking mine while we both sat there staring at our feet.

Our tiny Chicklet-sized toenails were fresh with new pedicures and decorated with wine red polish. My over-priced sling backs looked unnatural lying there in the graveled dirt next to Marla's even more expensive charcoal pumps.

Out of the corner of my eye I could see my sister's ear and next to it a few wisps of grey hair moving slightly in the breeze. Only months before when I had asked Marla, she denied having any grey in her hair.

"You know, it's just the funniest thing," she had said. "Gina says she has gone through every inch of my head and can't find one grey hair—not one."

I had responded to my sister's lie by reminding her how much Gina got paid to report there were no grey hairs in the head of her most prominent D.C. client.

There was no need to bring up grey hair today though, even if just for the purpose of aggravating my sister. There were far too many reminders lately of the delicate and fleeting nature of human existence.

I finished my first can of PBR quickly, crushed it and threw it at the big oak tree, missing it by mere inches.

"Dammit, I almost hit that."

"You were a freakin' mile away," Marla said, and then fisted me in the shoulder. "And that'll be ten dollars in the cuss jar."

"What the hell?" I yelled at her.

"Now you're up to twenty," she said with a smirk.

"How did you know about the cuss jar?"

"Ken told me to keep track before we came down," Marla held her hand out waiting for payment. "I've been letting it slide because of, well, circumstances. But it starts today. Now pay up."

I folded Marla's hand and pushed it back at her. She crushed her empty beer can and then threw it at the tree, hitting it dead center, of course.

"Now that's how it's done, little Dancy Wilder," Marla said, turning to me with her usual smirk.

"Big bragging rights, Marla. You can hit a tree the size of a Volkswagen with a crushed PBR can," I said and then paused for comedic timing and effect. "I'm sure your friends at the club would love to put that in their monthly newsletter."

"You wouldn't dare, Dancy."

"Oh, but I would. I really would," I said in the voice of a Southern debutante, while I held my pinky out as I sipped from my new can of beer.

"Bitch!" Marla squinted her eyes and snarled.

"Slut!" I glared back at her.

"Now you're at thirty dollars," Marla said. "We may have to make a run to the bank."

I laughed and shook my head at her. Kenny had promised not to tell anyone about the cuss jar. I wondered who else besides Marla he had informed of my punishment. It was a fourteen-year old agreement I had made with a then young and handsome Kenny Watkins.

Jacob had just turned six and on the eve of Kenny's announcement to run for Congress, our son interrupted vice-presidential candidate Noah Shelley at one of the biggest

Republican on-air events in Virginian history with, "I'm hungry. Hurry the fuck up!"

The next morning, a clip of Jacob's little voice was on every major news network in the country, including Marla's. The money in the cuss jar had paid for Jacob's first car and an addition to our deck.

"I can't believe he told you about the jar," I said, still pissed at Marla. "How long?"

Marla interrupted me. "Oh God, Dancy, he told me right after Jacob's little Tourettes-like outburst at Shelley's big dinner."

"What about all those times you told me how proud you were that I wasn't such a potty mouth anymore?"

"I *was* proud," Marla said, acting shocked that I would think otherwise. "Just because you needed a little negative reinforcement to stop the profanity flying out of your mouth doesn't make me any less proud," my sister laughed. "But since we've been back home you've been slipping back into old habits."

"Well, who the hell wouldn't?" I yelled back at her as I grabbed yet another beer from the fridge.

"Now you're up to forty dollars," Marla yelled back.

"I *was* going to get you another beer, but you can forget it now," I said, grabbing Marla a beer even though I said I wouldn't.

I sighed and then handed Marla the can. "You're impossible," I said, sitting down next to her again.

"Cheers?" Marla held her can up for a toast.

"Cheers." I tapped my can to hers. The slight thud made us both laugh.

Marla and I were silent as we finished off the next cans of PBR. I could almost hear Daddy yelling, "You girls get in here, it's gettin' dark."

Back then, the run from the barn to the house left me panting for breath. It seemed a mile away. Looking at it now, ten long strides would get me there in less than thirty seconds.

"They say this is the driest summer on record in Rayes County," I said, looking up at the crispy leaves still barely hanging on the tree above us.

"Yeah, I heard that," Marla said, leaning her head back to see the dense branches. "Boy, if that tree could talk."

As the nearly dead leaves rustled together in the breeze, it sounded like a thousand tiny whispers were drifting off into the clouds.

"Listen," I said. "It *is* talking. It's telling all our secrets to the wind."

Marla paused for a few moments, pretending like she was trying to hear what this tree had to say.

"Dancy, you're still such a little weirdo."

"Well thanks for ruining my pensive moment, Marla."

"Somebody had to do it," Marla said, turning her face toward mine. "I can do without pensive for a while."

"Yeah. Sorry. Me too, I guess," I said, rolling my eyes but agreeing with my sister nonetheless.

"Anyway," Marla stood up in front of me stretching. "I'm sure I'll get to read about whispering leaves in one of your future novels."

"Eh, maybe," I said trying to look like it hadn't occurred to me already.

"I still can't believe Daddy is gone," Marla said as she sat down on the log in front of me.

"Well, you know he lived a good, long time. Fourteen years after his first diagnosis. Most people don't make it that long," I said sarcastically, parroting the sentence I had heard repeated all day.

"God, I know," Marla said with a sigh. "You don't know how many times today I wanted to smack the hell out of the next person who said that."

We were grateful my father had survived his first bout with cancer, but fourteen years wasn't a "good, long time" for our father. A good, long time would have been much more than a little over a decade. A good, long time would have been at least another thirty years or longer.

"I bet MKW would have smacked the hell out of someone today or at least shot at them," I laughed as I pointed to Marla's initials carved into the bench.

"You're probably right," Marla smiled as she looked down at the carvings. I could tell my sister's mind was traveling back in time.

"I bet DLW would have raised a little hell, too," Marla said, pointing a toe at my initials.

"Yeah, but those little bitches were crazy," I laughed, shoving my sister's foot away.

"No doubt about that," Marla said, and then came over to sit closer to me.

To fight the tears that had begun to fill both our eyes, my sister changed the subject. "It was good to see Chick today."

"Yeah, it sure was," I let out a breathy laugh as I remembered his grand entrance. Marla and I hadn't even seen the old biker come in. Chick had parked himself in the back of the room. All heads turned when the hum of his motorized wheelchair echoed around the church. When Chick reached Daddy's casket, he prayed for a moment and then turned to face the group. The paper Chick held in his hands shook as he read the words he had written about Everett Wilder.

"Good speech," I nodded to Marla.

"Sure was," my sister responded, smiling. I knew she was etching the memory of Chick delivering Daddy's eulogy in her memory just as I had.

"So, what do we do now?" I asked, looking around the old home place. I wanted to stay here, leave everything else behind, live in my past, do it all over again.

Marla didn't respond. I knew it wasn't because she didn't know the answer. Marla always knew the answer, and I knew it wasn't because she didn't hear me. Marla always heard me. My sister didn't want to say the words we both knew to be true, that we'd just go back to work and live our lives, wondering if we had said everything we needed to say, if we had done everything we needed to do.

Only a week before, I had looked into my father's grayed and sullen face and asked him if he was scared. "The only thing that scares me," he said, his voice cracking, "is that I'm going to leave you and your sister without being able to make up for the crazy life I gave you."

Until that moment I had assumed my father thought our lives had been perfectly normal, even though Marla and I had always suspected otherwise. It pained me to hear Daddy try to take back a life that had been lived so unapologetically.

"Daddy, if even the tiniest little thing, good or bad, had been different about the way I was raised, I wouldn't be the person I am today. And I like myself just the way I am," I had said patting my father's hand. "No apologies necessary."

Marla's thoughts, I was sure, had taken her back to her own final conversation with Daddy, now a memory, like mine, that would be forever burned into her consciousness.

"I'll get us another," I said, getting up to go to back to the barn fridge. When I returned I saw something I didn't expect.

"Where the hell did you get that," I asked, shocked at what Marla was holding.

"Terry gave it to me just before she left," Marla said, snickering a bit. "And now you're up to fifty dollars," my sister laughed, letting me know she was still counting the profanity shooting from my lips.

"Get the fuck outta here. Seriously?"

"Yeah, I swear," Marla defended. "Terry said, and I quote: 'This might come in handy for you girls tonight.'" Marla waved her hands around in the air and moved her head in a dreamy fashion as she quoted the Beatnik. "Terry said she grew it herself, 'pure and potent' is how she described it."

"So, what are we gonna do with that thing?" I asked with feigned innocence.

"I guess we're gonna smoke it," Marla said, pulling a hot pink Bic lighter from the pocket of her Marni trousers.

I bit my lips together to keep from laughing. "You know we don't smoke pot, Marla," I said flatly.

"Well, maybe today we do," my sister held the joint near her lips as she spoke.

I considered for a moment the ramifications of smoking a joint with my sister and could think of none. No one was out here, just Marla and me. I could think of no other time in my life when Marla had asked me to do anything wrong, illegal, or bad for me. So as she stood there, awkward as hell, holding a joint in one hand and a can of Pabst Blue Ribbon in the other, I finally responded with a question.

"Barn loft?"

"Yeah, let's go," Marla said, throwing yet another empty beer can at the tree, hitting it dead center again.

We both turned back toward the house to make sure Momma wasn't watching. The light from her study cast a yellow spot out onto the lawn.

"Unna's hard at it," I said, laughing.

"Wonder what this one is." Marla's eyes were drawn to the window like she was trying to read what Momma was writing.

"Maybe the fat lady is finally singing," I said, pulling at my sister's arm to get her to come with me. "Or dancing," I added, for comedic effect.

"Yeah, maybe she is," Marla finally pulled her eyes away from the house.

Once we were safely at the top of the ladder, we began gathering bits of straw to sit on. I watched as Marla sat Indian-style, wiggling back and forth on her straw as she tried to make a more comfortable seat for herself. I did the same.

The small flame erupted and danced around in the wind as she tried to shield it with her free hand. The paper burned quickly just before the fatty began to pop and spark.

Author

Melissa Newman is an award-winning journalist and writer.
Growing Up Wilder is her third novel.

Made in the USA
Charleston, SC
24 March 2013